THE
COLOR
OF FAMILY

OTHER TITLES BY JERRY McGILL

Dear Marcus: A Letter to the Man Who Shot Me

Bed Stuy: A Love Story

THE
COLOR
OF FAMILY

A NOVEL

JERRY
McGILL

Little
a

Published by Little A, New York

www.apub.com

Amazon, the Amazon logo, and Little A are trademarks of Amazon.com, Inc., or its affiliates.

ISBN-13: 9781542035637 (hardcover)
ISBN-10: 1542035635 (hardcover)

ISBN-13 9781542035651 (paperback)
ISBN-10: 1542035651 (paperback)

Cover design by Rex Bonomelli

Printed in the United States of America

First edition

Once again, to Doreen,
who started all of this family nonsense

Contents

BOOK ONE

THE EARLY PAYNES

THE '80S

Harold and Camille:
A Love Story

Harold Calvin Payne learned at a very young age that husbands could be uncontrollably cruel if and when the moment seized them.

He learned it consistently and he had the scars, both physical and mental, to prove it. A welt behind his left ear from a spatula. A caterpillar-shaped scar on his lower left back from a broken table leg. The cigarette burns fortunately had faded after a decade and were more like birthmarks. But they were not forgotten.

His mother, Josephine, had three different husbands during his childhood in Dearborn, Michigan, and as far as he could see, all the men had one primary thing in common—violence was their solution to most problems. Usually, his mother or one of his six brothers was the target, but every once in a while, he got caught up in the tempest. Such was the case on a cold February night in 1954. Harold was seven and returning home from buying his mother a turkey sandwich and a pack of cigarettes at the grocery store. While passing the back alley, he discovered his stepfather Nate gambling away the family's rent money on a dice game with a bunch of other fathers from the 'hood. Harold had witnessed his mother berate Nate for this activity on more than one occasion, and so when he got home, he told her about the scene right away. Regret set in when he saw his mother put on her heaviest coat and Sunday hat and march out the door of their fourth-floor apartment with a thick leather belt, buckle clanging ominously in her left hand.

He and three of his brothers tailed behind her discreetly and took in the scene in the alley. To the amusement of the gambling crew, his mother yelled at his stepfather at the top of her lungs. It was when she threatened him with the belt that things took a darker turn. Nate backhanded Harold's mother twice, sending her to the cold pavement. Harold ran to his mother and picked her up, which led Nate to then turn on him, striking him against the side of his head so hard the boy had to go to the emergency room with what turned out to be a ruptured eardrum. In the month it took to heal, Nate was out the door for good, soon to be replaced by Grady, an unrepentant alcoholic who was a foreman at Ford Motors. Grady was a man blessed with a huge frame. Many speculated he could have easily played on the offensive line of the Detroit Lions.

What Harold derived from his encounters with each of these men were a few lessons that he would hold close to his sense of value and self-worth: He was repulsed by what he considered to be these men's darker demons, and he resolved somewhere within himself that he would never be a heavy drinker. He would never be an unscrupulous gambler. He would never physically abuse his wife or his children. He would never be a womanizer.

He was able to achieve three out of four of these virtues.

What he *would* do was realize he had a terrible weakness for the female form.

It all started in junior high school. A popular center on the school basketball team, Harold courted Vanessa Coleman, Stacy Attlebury, and Jeannie Ann Todd, all at the same time, and wound up dating all three for a month until his duplicity was discovered and he lost all of them in a week. In high school, when his sweetheart Doris Culpepper, the daughter of the most popular baker in town, found out he had been seen making out with Leslie Matheson in the balcony of a movie theater, she baked him blueberry muffins laced with laxative. Fortunately for him, she was wracked with guilt and confessed after he ate the first two. He wound up with diarrhea and sour gums for two days straight. His oldest brother, Enos, warned him: "Someday you gonna wake up in bed with a knife in yo back you keep treating these womenfolk like they trading cards. Don't you know hell ain't got no fury like a female scorned?"

The combination of laxative burning in his intestines and his brother's words of wisdom *seemed* to have had a sobering effect on Harold. By the time he entered Morehouse College in Atlanta in 1963, he *seemed* to have matured and settled into a focused, more sensitive young man. Literature had always been his favorite subject in high school, and he realized early on that he had a genuine love for words. All his school essays had received strong praise and feedback from the teachers he admired, and he fancied himself a decent writer. He joined the team at the Morehouse newspaper, the *Maroon Tiger*, where he focused mainly on sports and dabbled in entertainment. On a cold afternoon in November, he was given an assignment to write about a popular glee club that his editor had discovered at Spelman College called the Nightingales. They were a group of five women, all with syrupy smooth voices, and after hearing them perform twice, he was convinced any one of them could go on to be the next Ella Fitzgerald. He interviewed them all individually over the course of a week and found himself instantly smitten with the shyest one in the group, a light-skinned natural beauty named Camille.

Camille Rosetta Preston figured out early in life that the role of the quiet observer fit her very well. She was born and raised in Athens, Georgia, one of two daughters. Her mother, Rose, was the head teacher at an all-girls elementary school. Her father, Elijah, was a Baptist preacher. She had a huge family of aunts, uncles, and cousins, and she often found herself seated at a large Sunday dinner, post–church outing, taking in the lively discussions at the table. Many of the most memorable ones were led by her favorite, Uncle Dwayne, a wiry man who was the only outspoken gay person anyone had ever known in their entire state.

Many a discussion he had with his siblings was an animated debate about whether homosexuals were entitled to equal rights, whether lying with another person of the same gender for the sake of pleasure was a sin, and whether homosexuality was simply a trait people came into the world with. Uncle Dwayne felt it was the latter, "Like being born with six fingers or one brown eye and one gray eye. It's simply a trait that set you apart from many of your peers, and not something you should be looked down upon for having. In fact, it should be celebrated!" Her father was not about to accept such a perspective, but he loved Uncle Dwayne nonetheless. So Camille was exposed to the concepts of "open discussion" and "difference of opinion" at an influential stage, which served the entire family well because, in their teenage years, her older sister, Melody, would come out as a lesbian and her cousin Franklin would become an outspoken supporter of the Communist Party and an open agitator of the government. Camille would develop an appreciation for rule breakers and misfits.

She had always been a naturally gifted musician, and she displayed an impressive soprano voice. Often, she led the choir in Sunday service. Her mother went to great lengths to nurture her voice, serving her warm tea with honey three times a day and practicing deep-breathing exercises with her on a regular basis. It was Rose Preston's determination that Camille become an opera singer (though Camille herself preferred playing the violin), and she sat her daughter down in front of a phonograph three to four times a week to listen to Maria Callas records. It was through music that Camille communicated best, though she was somewhat of a recluse, choosing musical instruments over the company of her peers.

It is possible that Camille would have gone on to attend some renowned opera school if her mother had stayed in charge of her schooling, but much of her life changed on a humid July day during a family outing at Lake Lanier.

It would always be unclear exactly what took place that particular afternoon, but everyone in attendance agreed that alcohol most likely played a role. As they did several times that day, Camille, Melody, and several of her cousins, aunts, and uncles dove off a small cliff into the cool waters of the lake to relieve themselves of the sweltering heat and humidity, and to escape the aggressive mosquitoes. They had gotten into the habit of racing one another to see who could jump off first, and sometime around 6:00 p.m., Camille, Cousin Prescott, and Rose all challenged each other to jump in. Prescott won, with Camille placing a close second. Camille and Prescott laughed as they came to the surface and looked around for Rose so they could make fun of her.

But Rose was nowhere to be found.

Some twenty minutes later, after a frantic family search, Rose was discovered floating facedown over by a fishing dock several yards away. Camille would never forget the deep penetrating wail of her father's cries as they pulled her mother's soaking, limp body ashore. Nothing would ever or could ever traumatize her more than that sight of her mother's back shining in the water, the rear of her scalp bobbing like a rotted head of cabbage. Camille would look back on that day often as the day she lost something more valuable than a beloved parent. She lost innocence. Lost faith. It was the day she was forced to reanalyze goals and plans for the future. In an instant, she moved from being an effervescent, optimistic child to being someone more questioning, more cautious. Neither she nor Melody could ever bring themselves to swim again.

Camille would also never forget how quickly her father would remarry, and to whom. Three months after Rose's funeral, Elijah Preston married Macey Aldermoore, the musical director of the church's choir. It didn't take a genius to realize the two had been having an affair for years, and a closer inspection would reveal Macey's four-year-old daughter (believed to be fathered by an oft-traveling train conductor from Memphis, but who looked so much like Elijah it was almost comical) was actually Elijah's flesh and blood. Camille would learn a lesson that would serve her well throughout the years: men were extremely capable and adept at keeping profound secrets. A strong part of her would lose trust in men. She never dated, never even kissed a boy throughout the early portion of her college years at Spelman. That all came to a blinding halt when one night after performing at a local speakeasy with her crew, the Nightingales, she sat across from a young college-age reporter with eyes so chestnut brown and clear she thought she could see into his soul. Later on, she would compare the moment she met Harold Payne to the moment Juliet first laid eyes on Romeo. Some emotions were simply out of your control. She had seen attractive men before, but they often came off as superficial to her. Harold, with his mild manner and genuine interest in her as a person, helped her realize what it felt like to yearn.

It took him a couple of weeks to build up the courage to ask her out, and he decided that to lessen the tension, instead of a date, he would ask her out to lunch first, under the auspices of doing a follow-up interview for the piece on the Nightingales. He would not make it to that lunch because, right before he was due to leave the house he shared with four other students, a huge news story broke and he needed to act on it immediately. Word spread throughout the campus that the president of the United States had been shot while riding through a Dallas neighborhood, and the status of his health seemed to be seriously in doubt. Camille thought she was being stood up and was angry and disappointed at first, but once she herself heard the news (by the time it reached her, he had been pronounced dead), she was so shocked that she forgot all about Harold. They would meet up again a few days later and share a first kiss over milkshakes at a local ice-cream parlor.

By the next summer, Camille was pregnant, and they would marry quickly, choosing to have a tiny ceremony for close family at a park in downtown Atlanta. Melody would be her maid of honor, and Harold's younger brother, James, would be best man. They had planned to name the child Rodney if it was a boy and Annie if it was a girl.

But there would be no child to name that year.

Camille miscarried in her third month. It was the first of two miscarriages before Roxanne came into the world in December of 1965. Camille would not finish her education at Spelman, choosing to be a full-time mother instead (she would return for a teaching degree a decade later). Harold would graduate from Morehouse with a degree in journalism and would get a job working as an editor and feature writer for a Black-owned newspaper in Chicago.

One of his first assignments—one that brought him much respect and acclaim—was an assignment that he did not genuinely want but that he could not help but be intrigued by. He wrote a feature on the mass murderer Richard Speck, a white man who tortured and murdered eight student nurses in their dormitory late one night in Chicago. Harold attended every day of Speck's trial, interviewed relatives of the victims, relatives of Speck, and retraced the last month of the killer's life leading up to his murders. Harold had considered writing a book on the murderer and was preparing a pitch for publishers when in the fall of that year he received his draft card in the mail. Life drastically changed when he went off to Vietnam.

He would spend a year in Vietnam, seeing major field battle twice. From a hospital in Cu Chi where he was being treated for a bullet to the hand, a victim of friendly fire, he wrote a two-page letter to Camille in which he stated, "I knew that mankind was cruel, but I had no idea of the depths of darkness that lay dormant in our hearts until I got here. I have never experienced such genuine fear, and if I make it out of this alive, I don't think I ever will again. Ali was right to not come here. I don't know anyone who has ever been more right about anything."

He returned home briefly, but then to his entire family's surprise, he volunteered to do a second tour, this time as a reporter on the war. His newspaper series Black Skin Killing Brown Skin (and Vice Versa) in a Foreign Land was printed in several newspapers and earned him numerous honors and distinctions. That success set the tone for his career. While he was away on his second tour, Margeaux was born. By the time Camille was pregnant with Kassandra in the summer of '69, Harold had initiated plans to launch his own monthly magazine focused on Black issues and with an all-Black writing staff, the first of its kind. He and Camille moved to Connecticut so that they could be closer to New York City, where the offices of his audacious venture would live. The first house they lived in was small, but it had a wide and impressive grassy lot in back. Camille had always dreamed of tending to her own garden.

The Charm of the Family Portrait

"Man, I don't think I've ever seen this many good-looking Negroes in one place in my life!" said Devon, the youngest sibling of the Payne family.

The oldest sibling, Roxanne, often said of her younger brother, "He has a real problem with not knowing it's often better to shut up rather than speak if you don't think about what is going to come out of your mouth first. His mouth is gonna cause him to learn some hard lessons in life." And she was partially right.

But on this sunny May afternoon, Devon was partially right too. Thirty-six members of the Paynes and their immediate family of cousins and uncles and aunts had gathered on a spacious lawn in Central Park to take part in that great tradition: the family portrait. The reason they had all come together on this afternoon was truly a momentous occasion. Roxanne had just graduated from Columbia University with honors and would that September be heading to the University of California, Berkeley, to start medical school. She was the first of Harold and Camille's six children to graduate from college, and truth be told, she was her father's favorite, but not her mother's.

The photographer, a wiry Ethiopian man, the fiancé of a cousin, struggled mightily to get the entire clan in the frame. He pleaded with everyone to move closer together. "Tighten it up, people, please!"

Onlookers and passersby glanced admiringly at the hugeness and the beauty of the family, and to the average jogger, dog walker, picnicker, or hot-dog vendor, the Paynes appeared to be the template of familial contentment. It was Kassandra who first spoke up about the contradictions. Looking back at this portrait while attending Harold's funeral many, many decades later, it was she who would articulate the deceptive charm of it all in a lengthy treatise on family that she had written for a revered magazine.

> The family portrait has the capacity to create an *illusion*. It has a dreamlike quality, and for many involved, it will be the preferred window to recall a place and time when everything seemed just perfect. The family portrait is as necessary as water, and as difficult to grasp. In some way, we all need this illusion, don't we? Who wants to believe their family could ever be broken? Personally, I blame television for fomenting this sham, knowing that it isn't really fair to do so. I mean, yeah, they gave us the Cleavers and the Bradys, but I knew somewhere deep inside that that was all artifice, meant to make us feel good and buy detergent. Cotton candy for the soul. Like the intelligent woman who chooses the handsome, gambling con artist over the stable, supportive tax accountant, I am to blame for my choices, and I chose to believe in family. And I don't regret it. But here now, reflecting on the death of my father, a great man in his own right, I do wonder about all the signs I missed. The cracks in the vase I ignored, and why I did so. The charm of the family portrait is

that it has a magnificent ability to convey perfection.
There is nothing quite like it.

In that portrait of the Paynes—although there were well over thirty family members in the frame—the positioning of the siblings tells a bit of its own story. In the center of the entire clan stand Roxanne and her proud father, each holding a side of her diploma. Off to the right, Camille is seen embracing James, while Margeaux rests a bored hand on her mother's shoulder. Kassandra is off in the back, barely noticeable while laughing it up with a female cousin. On the far left stand Devon and Dahlia, arms around each other, with Alexis and Michel kneeling in front of them. Everyone beams proudly. There doesn't appear to be a cloud in the sky, nor a bit of wind in the air.

Perhaps now is a good time to provide a brief description of all six of the Payne children, in chronological order (the two illegitimate siblings will be addressed later).

Roxanne was the first child, whom most everyone in her circle, friends and family alike, referred to as the "Blerd," the Black nerd. Roxanne was the high-school valedictorian and quoted Dorothy Parker in the yearbook (the club of which she was president): "If I should labor through daylight and dark . . ."

Many parents have memories of banging on their children's bedroom doors, asking them to turn down loud music, usually of the rock-and-roll, heavy-metal, or rap variety. Camille Payne fondly recalled knocking on her daughter's door to ask her to turn up the opera *Tristan und Isolde* so she could listen while she sewed in the next room.

Margeaux was perhaps the most unique member of the clan. She had a boldness some saw as arrogance, and she considered herself a true "artiste," which in her mind meant she was willing to die for the sake of art. As a teenager, she moved like a butterfly from music to painting to graffiti to breakdancing to performance to acting. She was the only one critical of what she deemed the family's obsession with "materialism" and being "bourgeois Blacks." Many who knew the Paynes well simply wrote Margeaux off as the rebel—the ironic black sheep of the family—and she seemed more than happy to take on that role. In fact, she wore it like armor.

It was Margeaux who provided the largest controversy the local high school had ever seen when the drama teacher, Andre Galasso, had been fired two days into the production of *Our Town* (in which Margeaux played Emily) because it was discovered that he and she, then fifteen, had been having a romantic affair, carried on mostly after rehearsals and on weekends. When an investigating detective asked Margeaux in front of her parents in the principal's office if she believed Mr. Galasso, a thirty-eight-year-old married father, had used any unseemly methods of intimidation or coercion to take advantage of her, she replied with her trademark grin: "Please, I don't get taken advantage of. That's not a role I would ever play."

Kassandra was the "sauciest" of the crew. She followed feminist icons religiously and in high school was secretly voted by her peers "Most Likely to Become a Stripper with a PhD in Sociology." She picked up where Roxanne left off, becoming president of the yearbook club and filling that year's book with quotes from Emily Dickinson to bell hooks to Flannery O'Connor to Audre Lorde to Madonna. She begrudgingly went to the senior prom, only choosing to do so once she realized she could use the event to make a statement. She went dressed as Angela Davis and proceeded to get thrown out by security for dancing too provocatively to a Prince song and making out on the dance floor with her date, the head cheerleader of a rival high school who, at Kassandra's insistence, wore a white satin see-through dress with pink panties and no bra.

Camille was horrified by many of Kassandra's exploits, but Harold endured every one of her capers with a wry smile and a wink. Though Roxanne may have been his favorite child, Kassandra's fiery passions reminded him most of himself. When she was arrested in downtown

New Haven for protesting gender inequality at Yale by walking through the streets topless, locked arm in arm with a group of female freshmen, it was Harold who came to the precinct immediately to bail them all out. When her and her friends' pictures appeared on the cover of the *Yale Daily News* the next morning with their breasts edited out, Kassandra shook her head and lamented. "Such a shame. The good people of New Haven deserved to see these fine Black titties."

Many of his siblings knew well that after having three daughters in a row, Harold was desperately longing for a son, and it became a topic of conversation and jest at many a family gathering. However, from the moment James was born, Harold held a slight resentment for him. At the time, he was a sports reporter for a Black-owned magazine, and he had a highly cherished press box seat to view the "fight of the century" between Muhammad Ali and Joe Frazier at Madison Square Garden. However, late that afternoon, Camille went into labor, and he wound up spending the next nine hours with her at Mount Sinai Beth Israel Hospital, hanging out in the waiting room with a man with a dislocated shoulder and the family of a woman who had been rushed in with appendicitis. He would have to follow the fight on a janitor's radio, and he would never truly get over it. James had to live with hearing the story any time Ali came up in the press.

James was born with only one true gift—his physicality. From an early age, since the time in second grade that he challenged teacher's pet Philmore Angstley to a race on the local high-school track and left the kid breathing heavily in his dust, he realized that he was given the ability to beat people in physical contests. He was a marked success at every sport he played, and when his mother enrolled him in a ballet class "to offset all of that testosterone," he even excelled at that. One teacher told Camille that if he stuck with it, he could very well become one of the first Black dancers to premiere in an American ballet production. But that wasn't what brought him genuine pride. Like a warrior on the battlefield, or a Roman gladiator from the ancient days of arena warfare,

James had a desire to pummel. He wanted to beat other men mentally and physically, humiliate them even. It was an aspect of his personality that nobody else in the family cared for. Margeaux and Roxanne both found it repugnant. Having been on an actual battlefield in Vietnam, Harold found it disheartening. Despite all of it, for reasons no one else could figure out, he was Camille's favorite child, and everyone knew it. Camille showered James with gifts and affection like she did none of the others. She attended just about all his events. His birthday was the most decorated in the house every year. "Number-One Son" they called him. Which was not particularly easy on son number two.

Much would be made of the hostile rivalry between James and his younger brother, Devon. It ultimately became such a destructive force that it would send tremors through the Payne family for well over a decade. Other siblings did their best to remain neutral, and almost all of them kept a healthy distance from the ugliness of their competition. But Devon was one of a set of twins, and as tumultuous as his relationship was with James, he had the exact opposite alliance—a supremely tender and loving relationship—with his sister Alexis, born twelve minutes earlier than he was. It was clear to anyone who watched the pair together that they had spent an overwhelming amount of time in one another's presence when it mattered most. All of that time swimming in the same womb had enabled them to master the rhythms of one another's heartbeat.

They took classes together. At six, it was finger painting at the YMCA. At eight, it was piano lessons with Jordan Holmgren, a local pianist who played at jazz bars and did weddings and special events. Over drinks with Harold one evening, Jordan told him, "They have an incredible innate talent, a thing you practically cannot teach. If they stick with it, they could have a real future. Compete, even. They would be unique in the youth piano competition world."

But the twins bounced around from hobby to hobby. At nine, they found youth basketball, spurred by James's success at the sport. Both played point guard. Both led their teams in statistics. One season, a coed competition sponsored by the local YMCA allowed them to play together on the same team against rival community centers. Together, they were a genuine force. Coaches marveled at their peculiarly similar skill sets, which led one to remark, "It was nearly impossible to differentiate between which Payne was in the game at any single moment. Both play suffocating defense and attack other teams' weaknesses on offense. You may as well call them Dexis."

In the summer of her junior year in high school, Roxanne got an internship at Lincoln Center. She started bringing the twins into Manhattan with her once a week, usually on Fridays, and it was always the highlight of their week. They started a tradition of going to the movies together. Roxanne took them to see *ET: The Extra-Terrestrial* when it debuted. They had to wait in a four-hour line outside a cinema in Times Square, and they loved every minute of the experience. The city was like an exotic foreign land to them. They would go back to see that movie four times that month and Margeaux and Kassandra joined them on a few of the trips. They all traveled to the city on Amtrak, and Harold or Camille was always there to meet them upon their return at the station in New Haven. Once, there was a minor scandal when they returned and it was clear to all that Kassandra was high on some substance (they always hung out in Washington Square Park before heading home, and at the time, Kassandra had a proclivity for mushrooms).

But that scandal was minor indeed compared to what occurred with the twins in the summer of 1984.

By that summer, Roxanne had already left home for her freshman year at Columbia and, always the model student, was heavily immersed in her workload. As a result, Margeaux inherited all the chaperoning duties, and was grateful for it as it gave her the opportunity to spend time with a guy she had recently met who lived in Brooklyn. The first few trips were fine. The twins quickly realized there were certain things they could get away with on Margeaux's beat, as she was nowhere near as strict and watchful as her older sister. Margeaux was keen to let them hang in the park all afternoon while she and her friend Oscar toured the Guggenheim or the American Museum of Natural History. It was an arrangement that seemed to benefit them all.

One afternoon, the twins were sitting on a bench, eating ice cream and watching a league of Broadway actors compete in a softball game, when they were approached by a suited, bespectacled, seemingly innocuous man who introduced himself as Graham Naylor. He sat beside them and engaged them in conversation about some of the theater actors involved in the game. He knew all their names and some histories of the shows they were involved in. Devon would recall later on that he did not think much of the man, found him anxious and overly chatty. But it was Alexis, always a fan of the theater, who appeared smitten with him and his strained British accent. Naylor wound up inviting them to his apartment two blocks away, claiming to have more ice cream and an extensive collection of Broadway albums. Devon didn't want to go, but with Alexis's prodding, he joined them.

At first, it was all just plain fun. Naylor had a very comfortable townhouse, and he also had a new contraption that the twins had heard of, but never actually seen before, called the video cassette recorder. On the first visit, they sat around and watched select movies he had recorded, mostly action, some animated, sometimes musicals to please Alexis.

It was somewhere around the third or fourth visit with him when Naylor approached them about a photography project that he was working on. He showed them photographs he had taken of various children and teenagers in suits and designer clothes, and he asked them if something like that might interest them. True to form, Devon was uninterested in the modeling gig, but Alexis was fascinated by it and leaped at the opportunity. Unbeknownst to Devon at the time, Naylor had also sweetened the offer for her by agreeing to pay her a healthy stipend on the side.

And so a process began, one that they were both asked to keep to themselves. Naylor would pick them up at the museum, taxi them over to his townhouse, and then proceed to send Devon out on an errand (usually shopping) that he would pay him for, while Alexis and Naylor conducted "business" in his studio/bedroom. The nature of that business Alexis would keep to herself for years, and when she was ready to reveal it, she did so only with Devon. In her mind, only her twin brother could possibly understand just what it was she had been through. He was the only one who knew Naylor, the only one who knew what charms the man was capable of. He was the only one who wouldn't judge her. Whatever occurred between her and Naylor during those sessions had a genuine effect on Alexis, but hers was a personality too indestructible to allow the experience to keep her from progressing at a rapid rate. Select moments with Naylor would stay with her forever, at times resurfacing in dreams or in scant circumstances that usually involved intimacy of some level. Male English accents became a great source of mistrust for her. A certain type of musky cologne particular to Naylor put her in a foul state of mind. Devon recalled one afternoon when they were watching a film in which a young woman was being prodded into giving oral sex to an older man and Alexis, seemingly in great discomfort, had to get up and excuse herself to go to the bathroom less than halfway into the scene.

At the end of that summer, the trips to New York stopped, never to be resumed again for the twins. Margeaux continued to go to see her guy—and a few other romantic interests—but the twins moved on to new hobbies and pursuits.

There is one more aspect to the twins that made them somewhat unique to the rest of their siblings.

When the two illegitimate children showed up out of the blue in the beginning of February in 1986, the weather was bitterly cold outside, but it paled in comparison to the frigid aura that took hold of the Payne household and floated through every corner of the three-story home. It was briefly explained to the entire family the night before that two children had been born in France as a result of Harold's long-going affair with a French woman and were now coming to live with them. Their mother, Harold's mistress, had died of a form of cancer that had spread much quicker than her doctors ever expected. Harold explained that he had never intended for it to come to this, that he had planned on supporting them from abroad forever. It was a grave lesson in the unpredictability of life.

The son, Michel, a couple years younger than the twins, and his sister, Dahlia, a year younger than he was, both arrived with glaringly light-brown skin, the pallor of raw cashews (a stark contrast to all the others), and to add even more complexity to the already complicated situation, they spoke only French. Any English they knew came from television and movies. Michel liked to quote popular situation comedies. Dahlia liked quoting action films. Both said "Who you gonna call? Ghostbusters!" way too often. Most of the family shunned them like they were the bearers of a deadly airborne disease, and their arrival birthed a period of deep, disturbing silence and outward hostility between Harold and Camille that would go on for years. Their relationship was never quite the same again.

However, for some distinct reason—perhaps owing to their similarity in ages—Devon and Alexis developed an almost instant affection for their French half siblings, and the feelings were reciprocated.

Alexis and Michel bonded over a love of music, particularly rap music, and their father bought them a drum set, which they shared. Many weekends, they could be found in the garage playing them, creating lyrics, and performing for local neighborhood kids. Devon and Dahlia bonded over sports, with Dahlia replacing Alexis in many of their athletic youth leagues. Dahlia, who was unusually gangly, excelled at volleyball and basketball. She and Devon shared a dream of someday earning athletic scholarships to attend the same university in Southern California, where they agreed they would spend half their time dominating on the court, half their time relaxing on the beach, as neither was a fan of schoolwork. Devon and Alexis were the main contributors to teaching the French kids English, and in return, they learned a good deal of French. On occasion, especially in the spring and summer, Harold would take the foursome out to dinner at a favored outdoor spot in Danbury. Camille never joined them on these excursions.

The Paynes would take numerous family portraits over the years, but this particular afternoon in the park, a day of celebration, was the last occasion in which all the children would be photographed together.

An Afternoon in the Alcove

Devon leaped out of his seat on the passenger side before his brother had even had a chance to bring the car to a full stop. He was anxious to be away from the overwhelming stench of dog piss that had grown ever more overpowering in the rising humidity of the August afternoon. Devon had never liked dogs, and he resented those who willingly brought them into his life.

"Damn, bro. Take it easy," James muttered as he briskly put the car in park and turned off the engine.

James emerged from the blue station wagon, wearing one of his many stylish and expensive sweat suits, this one a silvery gray. He slammed the door shut, bent over, and grabbed his ankles. This was part of his daily routine: long stretches sculpting a body he knew was as close to perfection as one could get. He wore promise and potential the way many savage animals wore danger.

Devon pulled a cigarette from his shirt pocket and watched his older brother going through the familiar moves. As he lit up, he smiled a wry and mischievous smile that cast an auburn glow over his handsome, smoke-streaked face. Anyone who ever saw Devon smile could tell that the young man was destined for a life of duplicity. He was too damned smooth. His uncle Blake had once referred to him as "a mug shot in the making."

James had a similar face and bone structure. He had sharp cheeks and a thick, full African-statue nose, just like their father. It was a point of contention for some in the family who felt such traits were an invitation to bad behavior. He glowed like an otter in the moonlight. At various points in his childhood, an unwise white kid on a playground or a field would dare refer to him as "charcoal" or "oil stain," insults that earned said white kid a black eye or a busted nose or lip.

Devon favored their mother. His was more of a burnt caramel pudding tone, and he had a softer, less intimidating aura. What the two had most in common was their physique. Both were toned and defined, paragons of grace and fluidity. It was obvious from the time they were in grade school that they were destined for athletic greatness of Olympic proportion. They had played side by side on the Roosevelt Middle School basketball team. James, older by two years and a natural commander on the floor, led the team in scoring, while Devon, the flashier one, led in assists and steals. Both also excelled in track and football. Both had won the coveted Player of the Year award in their class. James had shared it with his sister Kassandra, a gifted volleyball player, the year he won.

The Payne brothers brought an unprecedented glory and pride to Bantam, their provincial Connecticut town. The mayor once referred to them as the "Sports Kennedys." Their exploits often made the back pages of the *Bantam Post*. But it didn't take profound perception to notice a tension that was always present when the two shared a space. It was more than competition. There was genuine animosity.

"What did Roxy tell you 'bout smokin', boy?" James asked as he opened the back door of the car and pulled out a six-pack of bottled beer.

"Roxanne says a lot of things. It's hard to keep up."

Devon knelt and touched the soil. This spot overlooking Bantam Lake had been their chosen hangout for as long as they could recall. At this time of day, the lake was picture perfect in its simplicity. It was hard to imagine there was life under the surface. Normally, there was a swarm of loud kids swimming in the lake on a hot Sunday like today, but most of them were back home having dinner with their families. Two old white men, equal in their plainness, sat a distance away, fishing off the edge of the dock.

"You need to listen some. What professionals you know smoke a pack a day? You think Dwight Gooden smokes a pack a day? You think Michael Jordan smokes a pack a day? You think—"

"Yeah, yeah," Devon replied as he mashed his cigarette out on a wet branch. "I was hoping maybe I could be the first."

He rose to his feet and had to react quickly to the bottle of beer James hurled at him. He caught it in one hand and shook his head, grinning, a small victory. The brown bottle gleamed in the sun like a dark diamond. He pulled a small bottle of bourbon out of his pant pocket. It fit perfectly in the palm of his hand.

"You need to control that damned dog of yours, man," he said. "Car is all smelling like the bathroom at Kelly's and shit."

"Better get used to it. She's gonna be your responsibility soon."

"Like hell she is."

"Serious, man, I expect you to take care of her. You know she has bladder issues."

Devon laughed as he took a swig from the bottle of bourbon and chased it with a beer. He passed it to James.

"If you think I'm gonna be saddled with Ginger, you surely ain't thinking straight. You better talk to Dahlia about that shit. For real, that bitch is gonna wind up at the pound in New Haven if you leave her behind."

"Yeah? And you gonna be right behind her, nigga. For real, Dev. Don't let me come back from school Thanksgiving break and find her missing for some reason. That would be your ass for sure."

Devon watched James open his beer and take a sip and seethed at his brother's arrogance. He took note of the aggressive manner with which James flicked off the cap with one sharp jerk of the wrist. Although Devon was in many ways the superior athlete, he had learned the hard way not to ever push his brother too far. He had the scars to prove that James was the stronger, dirtier fighter.

"Nigga, why did you bring me here?"

He watched as James grinned and walked off in the direction of the lake, joyful as a mongoose with a mouse in his jaws. It annoyed him the way his brother always seemed to be holding secrets over him, teasing and baiting him. None of the Payne children had been raised in any religious manner, but once, in grade school, he had overheard a sermon about Cain and Abel on a television show and he got how one could hold that type of fury toward kin.

He heard the distant traces of a baseball game coming from the radio of the two old fishermen. He recognized them as regulars here at the lake. They were fans of the brothers and had been attending their games since they were in middle school. The more rotund of the two men looked over, and his eyes gleamed as he realized they were in the presence of greatness.

"James Payne," the man sang out as if they were old chums. "Headed off to represent us all at the University of Miami."

James went to the man just as he was getting to his feet, and the two shook hands as he pulled him up. In Devon's eyes, James had many faults, but on the plus side, he was always respectful and deferential to his elders. He watched his brother tower over the man as the two engaged in conversation. He noticed him place his left hand gently on the man's porky shoulder, a move he commonly employed that instantly endeared him to just about anyone he spoke with.

The two older men were well known in town. One was a veteran of World War II; the other, one of the most revered businessmen in all of Bantam, owner of a string of printing shops in the tri-state region. Devon heard them discussing campus life. He was not at all interested in hearing more bragging about James's future. He took a hard swig of bourbon and walked off toward the other end of the lake, where a small, open-air alcove sat in the middle of the grass like a mirage in the desert.

The alcove was a place where people could hang their towels, change clothing, and store their personal belongings. However, for Devon, the place would always have a more special meaning. It was where, just this past spring, he and Natasha Green had clumsily lost their virginity to one another, minutes before the school dance had finished.

They had each sworn to their parents that they would get home no later than midnight, and Devon's parents even went so far as to assign Kassandra the task of personal chauffeur. She had dropped them off at the school gym in the family's vintage silver Rolls-Royce at seven thirty and had been waiting for them outside at midnight on the dot. When the last song started playing at around eleven and all their friends had taken to the floor for that final shot at grabbing ass, Devon had seized Natasha by the hand, and the two of them made a hungry dash out the side door and ran all the way to the lake. Natasha had done so barefoot, ditching her painful high heels.

Devon recalled how he had been surprised at his general lack of perspective that evening. He had absolutely expected to be the one in control, the full-on aggressor. He had even anticipated a bit of a push-back from his feisty girlfriend of two months, and he was prepared to seduce. But it seemed Natasha had been waiting for this moment even longer than he had. From the moment they hit the entrance to the alcove, safely enveloped by the darkness and mosquitoes, she was on him like an owl on a field mouse. Her hands were all over the place, her fingers anxiously fumbling with buttons and zippers, clenching at his softest spaces with eagerness. She was the captain of the tennis team, but at that moment she could easily have doubled as captain of the wrestling team. In the end, it was Devon who had been vanquished, left spent in a heap on the cool, yet scorched, earth, a slight trembling in his thighs, a tear in the left knee of his rented tuxedo pants. As he dressed, he watched the silhouette of Natasha smoke coolly as she wondered aloud how many couples had been there before them.

James entered the alcove, carrying the remainder of the six-pack, and brought Devon back to the present. Devon lit another cigarette.

"Them fellas wanted me to give you a message," James said.

"Oh yeah, what's that?" Devon asked, taking a beer and popping the top.

"They said to tell you, 'You're next. Don't go blowing out your knee roller skating or some dumb shit.'"

Devon let out the slightest breath of a laugh. He had heard this sentiment expressed throughout his entire childhood. He would always be next when it came to James. He would always feel the chill that accompanied standing in the shadow of the chosen brother. He would always be fifteen. James would always be seventeen.

They were on six-pack number two as the sun began setting sharply, leaving a fluorescent orange streak across the open pool of the sky, giving the impression that the clouds were smoldering. The two old men were long gone by this time, and James and Devon sat on opposite sides of the alcove, facing each other. Several empty bottles littered the space between them along with a crumpled pack of cigarettes. The red-and-white cigarette box stood out like a candy cane on a Christmas tree atop the brown sand and beer bottles.

"I guess if you really need the sun, Miami is a good fit, but I'm telling you now, I would rather have a change of seasons. I think you should have chosen Iowa State."

There was a slight lisp in Devon's speech. A minor effort was being made on his part to pronounce certain consonants. Years and years would never diminish James's shame of not recognizing the signs in those moments.

"See, that's part of your problem right there, Dev. It's not just about the weather. You need to see the bigger picture."

Devon grinned at James in a not-at-all friendly way. His head tilted to the side, and his face conveyed both frustration and incredulity.

"This is great. *You're* gonna tell *me* my problem, huh? You, James Payne, the same guy who couldn't even take his own SAT."

Devon knew he shouldn't have said it before the words even left his mouth, but he couldn't hold back. The piercing intensity of James's gaze sent a shiver through him.

"I thought we agreed you would never bring that up."

"I'm sorry, man—"

"No, I'm serious, Dev. You think this is a fucking joke?"

"It just slipped."

"You don't let shit just slip, man! People's lives get fucked up with those kinds of slips!"

James lurched forward as if he intended to pounce. Devon bristled and prepared for the onslaught. He was relieved when James returned to his spot, pounding his back against the wall as he did. The sound of frogs belching filled the dusk air. Devon drew patterns mindlessly in the dirt with his fingers.

"You spoken to Gina lately?" James asked, his tone low, mock innocent.

The question baffled Devon, and he crossed out his design with his foot. He had drawn the letters *G* and *I*.

"What?"

"Gina. Have you spoken to her lately? I haven't seen her come around in a while."

It would occur to Devon many years later that had he been a somewhat more perceptive person, he might have noticed the minor shift in James's being in this moment. He might have seen the tell, James nibbling lightly on the left side of his lower lip. The way his left leg bobbed rapidly. He could have killed the bear in the trap right then and there. But whether it was the fifth beer, fourth shot of bourbon, or his naivete—quite possibly a combination of all three—he did not detect anything in the question. It would take him years before he would recognize the depth of this moment, when two brothers sat in the historic alcove, talking and not talking.

"I called her on Wednesday, tried to see if she wanted to go to the movies, catch the new Indiana Jones, but she sounded pretty sick. Thinks she may have the flu or something. So I'm giving her some space."

"That's mighty adult of you, bro."

Mighty adult of you. The tone of the statement frustrated Devon.

"Did you finish my paper?" James asked.

"Your paper?"

"*To Kill a Mockingbird*, nigga. Dad said I can't sit in first class if I don't get it to him by Wednesday."

Devon altered his voice and bowed his head low and took on an austere tone.

"'You'll see white men cheat Black men every day.'"

"What the fuck are you talking about, boy?"

Devon frowned as a harsh reality hit him. If they hadn't shared the same womb, they most likely would never have been friends.

James hurled an object at Devon, and the younger brother bobbed to his left to avoid being hit, thinking it might be another beer bottle. Curious, he reached over his right shoulder where he had heard jangling keys hit the dirt. After a little groping in the dark, he found them and picked them up.

"You get the honor, bro," James said, his eyes telling Devon he was doing him a favor.

"Serious?"

Devon looked from his brother to the keys and back to his brother.

"You and Alexis been bugging me to let you drive all summer, right? I let her drive me to the post office last week. Now you're up."

Devon's face turned from wonder to disappointment in less than a second.

"You let Alexis drive before me?"

"It was all about the timing, bro. Nothing personal."

Devon was not the least bit satisfied with this answer, but he had neither the time nor the inclination to argue. He didn't want to lose out on the opportunity. He had something to prove to this asshole who had managed to achieve just about everything before him. He rose a little too quickly and, in his haste, momentarily lost his footing. He stumbled backward and had to grab the alcove wall for support.

They walked out of the alcove and into destiny in an off-balanced fashion, exiting the shade and entering the cold orange of dusk, their silhouettes unsteady. The bullfrogs ceased their mating calls for just a moment, as if even they were aware of the fragility of it all.

The Marathon

Several years later, when he was fully ensconced in film school at the University of California, Los Angeles, Devon would find the appropriate language to adequately capture what the first three months of his hospital stay had been like. He would refer to the time as Felliniesque. In his essay, part of his application to enroll in the school, he would go into great detail about his accident and rehabilitation.

> It was all very much like a drug-induced dream seen through a dark and foggy lens. There were times when I would get these infections, and I wasn't sure my fever would ever break. On several occasions, I mentally prepared myself to die. I'm just grateful I survived. But there are many nights and days when an overwhelming wave of guilt comes over me like a cumulus cloud. I have been drenched in sadness for a long time. If given the chance, I would like to try to use film as a way of depicting all of the desolation and regrowth I have endured these last several years and expose audiences to an oft-overlooked population—the disabled.

In his entire young life as an athlete, Devon had never once broken a bone. When the car hit the tree, it flipped over, causing the roof to compress on the driver's side. The impact broke his fifth and sixth vertebra. Within a matter of seconds, he went from potential star athlete to limited-motion quadriplegic.

He would spend weeks in an induced coma. When he finally awoke to the sight of Alexis standing over his hospital bed, holding his hand, he started the long process of piecing together just what had happened to bring him there.

The alcove. The humidity. The beers. The sounds of birds. The shots of bourbon. James tossing him the keys. The road swerving before him in ways he had seen only in video games. The young blond woman heading toward him on a bike.

It didn't take long after awakening for him to realize that he wasn't alone in his loss.

The impact against the tree threw James from the car. Miraculously, he had only been badly bruised by his fall, a happenstance that was to Devon the ultimate irony. While James would spend just a night in the hospital for observation, an equally promising, yet unfortunate young woman on her new bike, a fellow student at their high school with a strong talent for math and chemistry, was the first thing the car struck.

Devon recalled, no matter how hard he willed himself not to, how her body flopped against the windshield and tumbled over the top of the car like the spinning brush in a car wash. He would eventually learn that Hannah Baldwin's parents had to make the horrible instantaneous decision about whether or not they wanted her organs to be harvested for a needy recipient. They chose to donate.

Devon spent his first several months at the hospital in a state of semi-shock. Everyone in the family came to see him as often as they could, but true to form, it was Alexis and Dahlia who spent the most time with him, and in all truth, he preferred them to any others. Whenever his parents came to see him, he perceived a look in their eyes and a gray pallor in their demeanor (especially in his father) that he took as a sign of their shame and disappointment with him. Though they reassured him they would do their best to get him all the best rehabilitation available, he could never shake the feeling that it was possible that what they wanted most was for him to just simply disappear.

Aside from the exorbitant hospital bills accrued, the Baldwin family sued the Paynes for millions in damages and grief. Devon never found out what the settlement number was, but he knew that whatever it was, it would never be enough. His father's attorney informed them that had it not been for his severe state of paralysis (his father referred to it as a silver lining), Devon himself would have likely served time in prison. As it was, he was on probation, and the term *vehicular homicide* would follow him on his permanent record wherever he went.

Along with the constant barrage of family members coming to see him in the hospital were visits from many of his fellow students and former coaches. He witnessed much head shaking and pity in their eyes as they spent time with him, prayed by his bedside, and left him cards and flowers. None of it was easy, but the most challenging visits came from Gina and James, who sometimes came separately, and sometimes together.

Devon had planned to go to a school dance and a bonfire with Gina, to celebrate the beginning of their sophomore year, and it took him some amount of time to come to the realization that these types of activities would not be a part of his life for a long time. Gina held his hand on visits and did her best to assure him that although he had a long road of healing ahead of him, eventually, with hard work and perseverance, things could get back to normal. But Devon had no idea what "normal" meant any longer.

He had been sexually active with three women in his life, but Gina was the only one who ever brought him genuine pleasure, and he was almost certain that he did the same for her. In the beginning, he wondered if they would ever have sex again. The notion they might not—that he would not be able to—scared him. This fear spurred him to look more closely into his condition. Though his arms were still too weak for him to sit up in bed by himself, he was able, with much effort, to push his sheets down below his waist.

It was then that he became painfully conscious of many uncomfortable realities.

It hadn't occurred to him that he had not had the sensation to urinate in some time, and there was good reason for that: he no longer had feeling in that area. A catheter tube snaked up into his shriveled penis. He was now—and had been for a month—peeing into a clear bag with measuring lines to mark the output of his urine. This realization, of course, inevitably led to him wondering just how he was defecating, as he had not encountered that daily urge in some time. The answer to that was even more daunting and saddening to him.

After this epiphany, Gina's visits dissolved into tiny pockets of depression for him. He had a feeling somewhere deep down in the pit of his soul that he could not continue with her in the way he always had, and he spent a good deal of time wondering how this subject would come up between them.

A decision rendered by his father saved him from the uncomfortableness of addressing that and many other issues.

Before the Thanksgiving holiday began, Devon was uprooted from the hospital in New Haven that had been his home for several months and transferred to a reputable rehabilitation facility in Southern California. The entire process was intimidating and frightening to him, but there were a few things about it all that brought him some comfort. His mother and Alexis would come out there with him and help him settle in for the first couple of weeks. Roxanne would be able to visit periodically, as she was enrolled in the medical school at Berkeley in Northern California.

On his last day at the New Haven hospital, the nursing staff threw him a going-away party in the dining hall, and many of his friends and most of his siblings attended. A light snow fell that morning, and Devon was somewhat relieved he would be moving to a place where the sun appeared to shine all the time, a place where he'd planned on going to college, albeit on an athletic scholarship.

His favorite nurse, an older Irish woman with deep-set blue eyes, who he found always conveyed care and love for him, had knitted him a beautiful red cashmere scarf. She acknowledged that although it was sunny there, these facilities usually cranked the air conditioning up high, and she knew how he hated the cold. When Millicent placed the scarf around his neck and posed for a picture with him, he couldn't help but look past the photographer, Margeaux, at a different picture being formed over by the ice-cream machine at the end of the room. James and Gina were engaged in what appeared to be a most intimate conversation, their faces close. As Devon continued to watch them, James reached out and sweetly touched her chin as if to say, "Buck up, kiddo, you'll be all right." Even then, he knew it was an image he'd never forget.

California had many things Devon needed in his life. The rehab facility, Silver Mountain, was well funded and well maintained. His development would thrive under the care of skilled therapists and doctors whose main goal was to make sure he left there with the tools to be fully independent. The place provided him anonymity, a supportive atmosphere, and, most importantly, young people in a similar situation as his. All of them shared a bond. They were creatures of misfortune. Life had rendered them unable to perform basic tasks on their own without assistance and guidance. They were like newborns, but not quite, and they were there to heal and develop. Many of them became each other's mentors. Devon formed two profound friendships that would mold his future self—both for better and for worse.

Shane Tollefson had already been at Silver Mountain nine days when Devon was wheeled in with his duffel bag in his lap and issued a bed next to him in a large ward the residents snidely called "Crip Corner." Devon and he hit it off right away. Shane was blond and blue eyed, with his long hair in a ponytail most of the time. He liked to quote popular TV shows and gangster movies, and Devon had the impression he had never read a book in his life. On his third day, Devon told Shane that the weekly afternoon group sessions they all had to attend reminded him of *One Flew Over the Cuckoo's Nest*.

"Whatever that means," Shane said.

Devon came from wealth, but Shane *really* came from wealth. His father was a successful music producer and handled a few B-list musicians and pop stars. His mother was an entertainment lawyer. They lived in a mansion in Brentwood where Shane had also gone to high school. He told Devon that he had majored in pussy, partying, and cocaine abuse. At the end of the summer, Shane dove into the shallow end of the family pool during a Labor Day weekend party his parents were not aware he was having. The impact of hitting the pool floor broke his neck, and he was fortunate he didn't drown, though in moments of drug-induced candor (they had a few of those at Silver Mountain), he told Devon it may have been better for everyone in his life if he had. Whenever Shane's parents visited, a thing they did on separate occasions, as they were in the process of divorcing, they brought three deluxe meal packs with them from local fast-food joints—one for Devon, one for Shane, and one for Juana, another resident they would come to grow close to.

Devon liked Shane's mother, a healthy-looking woman who always dressed in sharp business attire and referred to him as "Dev Baby." He did not care much for the father, a condescending, arrogant man who walked into the ward with a trade newspaper rolled under his arm, which he spent a lot of time reading from a corner chair by the window. The father also occupied himself by flirting with many of the young nurses and therapists, and Devon suspected that he was having an affair with a German nurse on the night shift who was seen getting into his Ferrari after her shift ended, well dressed, as if heading out for an evening on the town. Shane told him his father often had four girlfriends going at once, and Devon nodded, reflecting on his own father's history of promiscuity.

Devon's dislike for Shane's father was cemented one Sunday afternoon as they watched a football game together in the patient lounge. A news report stated that a popular running back had been suspended for an alleged cocaine-infused binge where he partied all night with three prostitutes in his hotel room and ran off when one of the women OD'd and died in the early morning hours.

"Well, what do you expect from these guys?" Shane's father said. "You take them out of the 'hood and throw shitloads of money at them, the likes of which they never imagined, and *of course* they're gonna make hideously stupid decisions. They need babysitting."

Roxanne came by every few weeks, sometimes staying for the weekend, other times just for the day. Devon always enjoyed her visits, as on the days she came by, he was allowed to go out on a day pass with her. They almost always went to the beach. Now and then, Shane joined them on these excursions, and Roxanne handled transferring them both in and out of her car and loading their wheelchairs in her trunk. When after her first visit she realized her trunk was too small to fit both chairs, she rented a small van that made it easier to transport them. Devon liked noting that whenever Shane was around his sister, he was very sedate, checking his often-foul language and doing his utmost to treat her with extreme reverence. He called her "Doc," which amused them.

Right before Christmas, Roxanne surprised Devon by bringing Alexis, Dahlia, Michel, and Kassandra. Devon and Alexis wrote each other often, and he had expected her to be coming soon, but the others were a genuine surprise and a delight. Margeaux was supposed to join them as well, but didn't, a mystery to all. Devon learned from Margeaux some years later that she was recovering from an abortion badly performed by a suspicious doctor in the Bronx, her pregnancy the result of an ongoing affair with the same fired teacher she had been seeing in high school.

His visiting siblings stayed at a Ritz hotel on the beach in Santa Monica, and on more than one occasion, they brought Devon back with them to the hotel, where they all hung out either on the beach or by the pool. Devon could not contain his happiness at spending this time with them, and he took great pride in showing off his progress. He was developing new muscles in his arms and was able to transfer himself in and out of a bed to his wheelchair with minimal assistance. The first time he tried to show off by transferring to Roxanne's hotel bed by himself, he miscalculated the distance and would have hit the floor had it not been for Alexis and Michel catching him. They all shared a good-natured laugh at his overzealousness, and they all agreed he needed to slow down some and stay on a steady track.

"Recovery is a marathon, not a sprint," Roxanne said. Devon took it to heart. Roxanne was the smartest person he knew.

Though he loved all his siblings, Devon looked most forward to spending time alone with Alexis and getting an update on all he had questions about back home. His first opportunity came late one afternoon as she suggested they go off and get some ice cream together. Dahlia, ever the eager and admiring little sister, joined them.

"How's your game?" he asked.

"Pretty good, Dev," Dahlia said. "You should have seen me against Jesuit. I scored fifteen points in the second half. I'm the second highest scorer after Janet Cleery."

"Cleery got lucky with that growth spurt she had last spring. Just wait until you grow a few more inches. You are gonna be a killer in the paint with those shoulders and the way you always plant your feet."

"Dad thinks I should focus more on tennis."

"Dad is off on that one. I don't get why he wants you to go there. Tennis is not gonna get you a free ride to UConn."

"That's what I thought."

"Dad isn't always right, kid. Remember that. Stick to your own opinions. You know what you do best."

"I wish you could be there to talk to him. He doesn't really listen to me."

Devon nodded and was overcome with an undefinable sadness. Alexis put a hand on his shoulder and kissed Dahlia.

"Hey, kid, why don't you go check out some of those performers we were looking at earlier? I want to get a little time in by myself with Dev."

"Okay. Can I go down by the basketball court?"

"Yes, but remember our rule, right?"

"It's okay to talk to people, but if an adult asks me to go somewhere, the answer is no and leave right away."

"Leave and go where?"

"Right back to you, no stopping. Jeez, Alexis, I'm not a baby."

"Shhh!" Alexis put a finger to her lips. "I don't want to hear any *merde* okay? You do it because I ask you to do it. It's that simple."

"Fine. Can I have some money?"

Alexis gave her a cold stare. Dahlia walked off, rolling her eyes, and headed in the direction of the beach. Alexis and Devon laughed.

"These fucking kids, man," Alexis said, planting herself in a chair facing him.

Devon smiled at her with soft, loving eyes. He shook his head.

"What?" She smiled back.

"You know, you go a little overboard with her."

"I do no such thing. She's young, French, and naive. A terrible combination."

"Still, I'm just saying, you can't protect her from every Graham Naylor out there."

"I don't need to protect her from *every* Graham Naylor. Just one will do."

They ate their ice cream in silence for a spell, taking in the beach and the surroundings.

"I saw a record store on the corner two blocks that way," Alexis said, pointing. "Wanna pop in there and see what they got?"

"Sure. I'm looking to get some new Prince shit. Hey, what's up with Dad spending so much time in Japan lately?"

"I don't really know. He said something about seeking out investors."

"Investors, huh?" He looked at her with arched eyebrows.

She recognized the body language and shot back a look that said, "Don't start, boy!"

"I'm just saying, I see some half-Black, half-Japanese kids in our future."

"Blackanese," she said, shaking her head. She pulled out cigarettes and lit up for each of them.

"How is Mom taking it all?"

"Like Mom. Deer in the headlights, all that stuff. Have you heard from her recently?"

"She called like a week ago. I was in hydrotherapy. I didn't get to call her back. The time difference is hard."

"The time difference. It's three hours, guy."

"I know it's three hours."

"I'm just saying, don't give me that time difference shit. I understand if you aren't that interested in talking to her. Or Dad. I bet you find time to call Gina, though."

At the mention of her name, his mood darkened, and it was clear right away to Alexis she'd overstepped. She reached out and touched his knee.

"It's okay. I actually haven't talked to her in a while. I want to give her time to process all of this. The things that we both wanted are going to be different now. I know she's very centered on her studies. She really wants to get into Brown."

"That's what she told me too. I saw her at the library a week ago."

"Yeah? How did she look?"

"She looked fine. Distracted. Awkward. She's not comfortable around me. You know she never has been."

"She envies you." Devon looked away and watched Dahlia cross the street. Sadness washed over him again. "I once thought I was going to be her protector, you know? I once thought I was going to keep her safe from all the ugliness that growing up a sports kid has to it. But I won't be that person now."

"Of course you will be. You haven't changed that much, Devon."

"If you say."

"It's not just if I say. You have to say it too. Have you heard from James at all?"

"We talked a couple of weeks ago. It was real quick. The coach isn't starting him, and that's pissing him off, but he just has to be patient. He really likes Miami. Says there are beautiful babes everywhere."

"What everybody wants in a college, right? I don't suppose he plans on visiting anytime soon?"

"No. And truth be told, I don't need him to. I don't miss him like I do some of you."

At that moment, a young teenaged white girl walked by them, strumming on a guitar and singing a popular song. Her voice was pleasant. Around her waist hung a small basket with a sign that said Tips Welcome. Will Take Requests. Alexis dug into her pocket and pulled out two wrinkly dollar bills that she tossed into the basket. The young girl nodded a thank-you and parked herself outside the ice-cream shop to finish her song. Devon was mesmerized by her.

"My God, she looks like . . ."

"I know."

They sat in silence and listened as the young girl sang the opening to "Tiny Dancer."

"I still see her face. Every day. I don't think it will ever stop."

"It will one day. It will."

"Maybe it shouldn't. Maybe I need constant reminding."

"You don't have to torture yourself."

"At least I'm still in a place where I can feel pain. She doesn't get to feel anything."

They watched the young girl finish her song in silence.

When they returned to Silver Mountain, Devon had to hear it from Shane and several other guys on the ward how fine looking both Alexis and Dahlia were. There were more than a few requests to join them on their next outing, all of which he graciously turned down. He appreciated every moment with his family, and on their last night together, he felt the inevitable postvisit depression coming on, as he had already begun to miss them. Roxanne, he knew, would be back soon enough, but he had no idea when he'd see the others again. Alexis assured him they'd be back in a few months at the longest. He gripped her hand tightly as they dropped him off at the entrance to Silver Mountain under a cool evening moon.

"Stay strong," Alexis whispered in his ear, her voice shuddering. "Remember what Roxy said about recovery being a marathon."

That night, Devon cried to himself in his bed for the first time since he had been at Silver Mountain. He did so discreetly, repressing any sobs, as not to alarm Shane. He visualized all his siblings getting on a plane the next morning and going back to the happy existences that fulfilled them. Everyone he cared about was moving forward with their lives and making clear plans for their futures, while he remained three thousand miles from home, stuck in purgatory.

New Year's Eve was a quiet affair at Silver Mountain. The residents watched the ball drop in Times Square on a huge television in the recreational lounge while toasting each other with sodas and ice-cream floats. Shane managed to get a couple of six-packs sneaked in by a high-school friend, and a few of them had a private party on a balcony around 1:00 a.m. When they went to group session the next morning, Devon, Shane, and several others were intrigued to find a new arrival to Silver Mountain, a pretty twenty-year-old woman with several tattoos on her neck and arms. When she spoke, she had the slight accent of a hardened street waif.

"Juanita Rabassa," she said, introducing herself. "But the people I ride with all just call me Juana."

Dear Diary

September 1986

Dear Diary,

I have to start out by stating I am pretty disappointed in Roosevelt as a whole. The students are pretty much just the same, if not worse, than they were at Taft. The same rich white kids, the same self-centered ghetto Black athletes, the same cliques, the same bullshit social politics. I really resent coming here. It feels like this is what Dad was trying to warn me about—that wherever I go, I'm still going to be me, and the world is still going to be the world. Disappointment will always be a part of my experiences. I guess at some point I will just have to accept this. Dad thinks I ask too much of things. That I set myself up for disappointment. I just think I deserve quality every now and then. I think I may need to accept that he could be right. I guess when I do accept that, I'll be mature enough to stop seeing Dr. Cather. I'll probably be mature enough to stop keeping this stupid journal. Hey, one can dream, can't they? Note to self: stop dreaming so much. It leads to heartache and disappointment.

Speaking of heartache, Mom and Dad seem to be having a harder and harder time of it. Last night at dinner, they barely said three words to each other. Shelly said she thinks she overheard Mom talking to a divorce lawyer on the phone the other day. We're both preparing ourselves. The hammer is about to drop. Who would I rather live with if they split? Shelly says she'd rather live with Dad, and I pretty much agree with her. Mom's mood swings have become really terrible lately, and I don't see how her medication is helping her at all. I mean, seriously, last week I saw her bawling in the car in the garage after she had gotten back from the grocery store. The woman has zero control over her emotions. "Unstable" doesn't begin to describe her. I will never understand what Dad saw in her, or what she saw in him for that matter. Shelly says, "When you are young, it is all about the hormones." I guess being horny will always outweigh being sensible.

Today, during the fire drill, Tyler Beatty came up to me in the parking lot and told me he heard I was going to be our next Olympic gold medalist in track. He has the worst braces. I swear to God, he should sue his dentist. Anyway, I told him I wasn't really that aware of my status, and he claims my latest time ranked third in the state, which I guess is possible. None of the other girls on the team show me any love. They are just jealous bitches. Coach Markham is always telling me to stay humble. Focused and humble. I'm taking it to heart. Tyler says nobody is surprised at how good I am. He says that having a Kenyan father gives me a direct advantage over the rest of us. He says Kenyans were born to run. I said,

"Kinda like Bruce Springsteen?" and he looked at me like I had two heads. Most of these kids are just morons. His response was, "You don't have to be so damned flippant about it." Whatever that means. I can't wait to get out of this place. Maybe when the parents split, Dad will move back to Kenya and take us with him. Is it wrong of me to want to be so far away from Mom? I mean, if Shelly and I both left, she'd have no one. I'd be scared for her. Even Aunt Tara doesn't want to be around her anymore. It must be hard to be the kind of person that pushes other people away.

More later,
Gina

October 1986

Dear Diary,

I've been struggling in Pendleton's class the last couple of weeks. It just feels phony and wrong. Pendleton sounds like a cheerleader for America when he teaches history, and I know it is more complex than what he's putting down. Okay, correct me if I'm wrong, but don't teachers have an obligation to teach us the full range of history and not just the part that shows us how genius and courageous white people (the settlers in particular) were? Dad says that this whole section we are learning on Lewis and Clark is hogwash (his word) and that it is deliberately avoiding the fact that the primary goal of their mission was to learn about the Native Americans, basically monitoring and spying on them, and make it clear to them

that their land was not actually theirs *and that eventually they needed to respect and give power over to their
US "fathers." Dad says colonialism is the dirtiest word in
the English language. Mom says Dad exaggerates everything when it comes to white people, and if he has such a
problem with them, then why did he choose her, the whit-
est, blondest bitch in Rhode Island, to procreate with?
Dad says he never had much choice, that there were only
three Black girls in all of Newport and two of them were
hideous walruses. I'm finding that Mom and Dad are
both kind of bitter, angry people and both are somewhat
lacking in sophistication. I wonder if they were always
this way and I'm just figuring it out now. Whatever the
case, I swear to you now, when and if I fall in love, it
will be the* opposite *of what Mom and Dad have. My
relationships will be based on mutual love and respect.
I will want the best for my husband, and I will know
that he wants the best for me. Am I just naive? Shelly
thinks so. She says that we all change over time. That
the things we once thought were important will change.
She says we all become jaded, more self-involved, and
ultimately will choose what is in our best interest over
anything else. That can't be true. Shelly has been staying
out late nights, making out with a Russian kid on her
chess team, and she is thinking of losing her virginity to
him, but she thinks Dad would disown her if he found
out. I'm just jealous. The only boy who even looks at me
is metal-mouthed Tyler, who has such bad acne he looks
like a leopard (leper?).*

    Yours,
    Gina

November 1986

Dear Diary,

Now I know. Now I understand all of it. The love songs, the movies, the paintings. Two weeks ago, I met Devon Payne at the newly opened Boys and Girls Club, and I swear he might be the closest thing to perfect I have ever imagined in a guy. He plays four sports, he is smart, funny, has the cutest set of dimples, and he can kiss! Friday night he asked me if I would go to Jonathan Wallace's birthday party with him, and while we were there, we sneaked off into Jonathan's brother's bedroom closet where we made out for like a half an hour. He tried to put his fingers down there, but I wouldn't let him put anything in. I'm really not ready for that just yet. I just started getting my period. But I kinda wanted it. I thought my head was gonna explode from the heat. When I told Shelly, she told me to be careful, that most guys are really only looking for one thing from us. She said she learned that the hard way with Andrew Janovsky. She says that two days after she gave it up to him, he basically cut her out of his life. Stopped passing her notes in math class, stopped returning her phone calls, stopped leaving Hershey's Kisses in her locker. Hell, he even quit chess club. She said she wishes she could take it all back, that in the end it wasn't worth it for three minutes of messy hip thrusting and his jizz on her stomach. I don't care. Part of me wants to try it, and I want Devon to be the one someday. He just feels right.
    Yours,
    Gina

December 1986

Dear Diary,

Dad moved out this week. Says he found a studio apartment in downtown New Haven and that once he is all settled in, Shelly and I can trade off spending weekends with him. It feels weird. The weirdest part is Mom couldn't care less. She already has a new guy. I heard them come in late last night, and I know he stayed over. I think he is the guy who makes the UPS deliveries in our neighborhood. Shelly says she saw him and Mom having a beer on the porch one afternoon in the middle of his shift. He looks like he could play linebacker for the Jets, a real meathead. Which will be just fine for Mom, I suppose. What she ever saw in an intellectual like Dad is beyond me. I think Dad deserved better.

I spent Christmas Eve with Devon's family at his house. They have a beautiful home out in Bantam. I swear, they did it the right way. They are what I feel we all aspire to be. His mother and father absolutely love and admire each other. You can see it in the way they interact. They have a large, loving family who all seem to look out for one another. I tell you, it should give us all hope. Roxanne, Devon's oldest sister, took us into the city to go ice skating and see a movie. The movie was really bad, but it was okay because it gave Devon and I the chance to hold hands in the dark the whole time, which was really, really sweet. Alexis makes fun of us a lot, but only in a good-natured way. I really like her. The only one I really wonder about is his brother, James. James seems to have some weird kind of problem with us. Devon says he has a "chip on his shoulder," which I don't even know what that means. Dad says it means he is angry about something. Anyway, he looks at us sometimes, and I get the sense that he is mad at us, or mad at Devon maybe. I don't know. I just know that sometimes it creeps me out, and I wish he'd go away. I guess maybe I was wrong about what I said earlier. Not every family is perfect. Maybe perfection is a little too much to ask. When I told Dad that I wished our family was like Devon's, he said, "Happy families are all alike. Unhappy families are all unhappy in their own way."

Whatever, Dad.

Yours,

Gina

February 1987

Dear Diary,

Dad told me something I'm having a very hard time wrapping my head around. Dad thinks that Mom is a drug addict and maybe worse. He wouldn't say what that worse part was yet because he wants to have more proof, but he thinks Shelly and I should live with him full time until he can figure it all out. He's looking at getting a bigger place. It's bizarre because I know I've seen Mom walking around the house looking like she's completely out of it, but I always assumed that was because she was having a hard day, or it was the side effects of her depression medication, or both. Now Dad is saying he thinks she's doing heroin or coke, which is just crazy. But maybe not so crazy. Ruth and Terri have been coming by a lot lately, and I know that they are both big potheads and that Ruth's son is a pot dealer at Lincoln (Devon told me that). So I guess it doesn't seem so crazy that Mom is going down a bad road. I wish I could talk to her, but I have no idea how to even start that conversation with her. We can barely talk about normal things anymore.

Shelly told me that she plans on moving in with Dad for the summer this June, before her freshman year of college starts. I kinda want to join her since I can't see myself being here alone with Mom. The other day, I came home from school early with a headache and caught her and Leon having sex in the kitchen. It was disgusting. I actually saw his pimply fat ass pumping away and Mom just screeching like a hyena. I might be traumatized. And I'm pretty sure she was only home because she called in sick. Dad told me that she is on probation at the post office for calling in sick too much and that if she does it again, she could be fired. Jesus Christ, how did Mom become such a fuckup? She didn't used to be this way. She used to bake chocolate-chip cookies.

Shelly and I went to McElroy's Fish and Chips on Saturday to celebrate my birthday, and something weird happened. I think it was weird anyway. I brought Devon with me, and Shelly brought Adam, and later Krystal, Stephon, and Jenny showed up. Anyway, we were having a good time, and then around ten o'clock, James and a bunch of his football buds showed up all sweaty and obnoxious straight from practice. We ignored them, and at one point, Devon and Adam went across the way to get us milkshakes from Eileen's. I went to use the bathroom, and when I come out, who is standing there? James. He has a magic marker in one hand and his football T-shirt in the other. It was weird, like he was waiting there for me. He asks me to autograph his T-shirt since he heard that my last race put me on pace to make the semifinals and he thinks someday I'm going to be an Olympic star. The thing is, he wasn't his normal brash, arrogant self. There was actually something sweet about the way he talked to me. He was almost a little shy. I got the sense that this was more who the real James Payne was. Like most of what we see of him the other times is kind of a macho act that he has to put on for his dumb jock friends. Later that night, he drove us all home. There were a few times when I could swear I saw him staring at me in the rearview mirror, even though Devon was right there. He would look away from me whenever I caught him, but I know *it was going on, and it was weird.*

And for some reason, I can't stop thinking about it.
Later,
Gina

May 1987

I haven't been able to write for a while for a lot of reasons. Mainly because of my very fucked-up life. I haven't wanted to write for a while. Still don't want to. But Dr. Cather thinks it would be healthy for me. So just to make her happy, I'll try to get back to writing regularly.

Where to begin?

They set Mom's trial date for late September. From what I understand and from what Dad told me, because this was her first offense and because the amount of weed they caught her selling was so little, she probably won't do "hard time." But she will have a record. It will be something that will make finding another job hard. Dad says the post office was never going to give her a positive referral anyway, and this will make matters worse for her. Dad says Burger King wouldn't hire her to make fries right now.

I say fuck it. Let her get what she has coming. This is the way life works. You break the rules, there's usually a price to pay. We have rules for a reason. Dad says he is worried about me. He says too often lately I sound "harsh and unforgiving." He says he worries for my soul. I told him he should worry about his own soul and the soul of that stripper he's been seeing.

He slapped me across my face. I spit at him.

He kicked me out of the house after that. I've just now come back after living with Aunt Gracie for two weeks. Aunt Gracie who constantly smells like weed and Thunderbird and her janitor boyfriend who stared at my ass every time I walked by. And now Dad is warning me either I address my anger issues and deal with them with Dr. Cather or he can't have me living under his roof. What a joke. I asked him what was he gonna do, abandon me? He couldn't come up with an answer. He just said he can't live with such a disrespectful daughter. In September, Shelly heads to BU. Maybe I can go live with her in her dorm. Though I really don't like Boston. Fucking parents.

I swear, if I am ever lucky (or unlucky) enough to be a parent, I am gonna shower my child with so much love they would drown in it.

Later,
Gina

July 1987

Dear Diary,

There was an article about Devon and James in the paper last week. It said that James was one of the most gifted and sought-after players in the nation and that colleges were tripping over themselves to sign him. It said that in two years, Devon could be in the same position. What an exciting time for them. When I went over to Devon's house for July 4 weekend, it was hard to get any private time with him. He has so many damn friends now. It was strange because I would've thought James would be the more popular one, but it's the opposite. James is kind of quiet and thoughtful. He surprises me. At one point, I was sitting alone by the pool while Devon played Frisbee on the lawn, and James asked me if I wanted to go up to his room and see old pictures of them. I went, and we had a really nice time. He was really sweet, and he showed me a whole album of pictures of him and his family. The Paynes are a very close bunch. I feel a little envious of them.

One strange thing happened that did throw me for a bit. When I was leaving his room, James asked me if I was in love with his brother. Weird, right? When I told him I wasn't really sure what love was, that I never really had a strong example of it in my house, he just nodded and said, "I was just curious. I just think you're real special, and if my brother can't see that, then he's a fool."

James Payne thinks I'm special.

Nobody ever says those things to me.

Later,

Gina

December 1987

Dear Diary,

This will be my last entry for a while and maybe, just maybe, forever. I stopped seeing Dr. Cather back in October. Dad lost his health insurance, and truth be told, I was sick of seeing her anyway. Psychologists are running such a scam. They sit there and they nod a lot, and they make you believe they sympathize with you, and they care about you, and they want to steer you in the right direction. They ask you a billion questions when really all the while what they truly want is that paycheck. That's why they keep you coming back. Who is that famous Hollywood director who says he has been in therapy for like forty years? He is the type of client they all really want. It's all such bullshit. A real scam.

My life has taken an unexpected turn, and I'm just going to put it down here so I have it documented somewhere just in case I ever need to look back on this time and reflect. I'm not really comfortable writing about this, but it's important to me that I record this somewhere.

I lost my virginity in September—but it wasn't to Devon.

I lost it to James. And it was wonderful.

I need to explain.

I started playing basketball at the Y. Just a fun thing to pass the time, and it was a chance to hang with Devon. I was on the same team as his sister Dahlia. We got along pretty well. She's a cool girl. James came in a few times too, and at first, I thought it was just because he wanted to warm up a little before his season started at Lincoln.

Later on, he would tell me that he could've played in the competitive games at the park downtown but that he really came to see me.

I want to be clear. Devon and I were having some problems. There was a rumor going around that he had slept with Natasha that summer while I was out of town visiting my mother in the hospital, and he said they may have gotten drunk and fooled around a bit but that he didn't sleep with her. I still don't know if he was being fully honest with me, but regardless, there had been a distance growing between us for some time. Devon thinks that I'm depressed all the time and not a lot of fun. He thinks I should have more therapy, not less. He leads a really charmed life, that Devon.

Anyway, one day during a game with the guys, I got elbowed hard in the face by Ronnie Lustig, that douchebag transfer kid from Croatia or Slovenia or wherever the fuck he's from. It wasn't intentional, but he's such a damn klutz. The kid has no grace. I don't know why Coach wasted his time bringing him over. My left cheek hurt like a motherfucker, and James was worried my cheekbone might have been broken, so he and Dahlia drove me to the ER. Devon was away in New Jersey, playing in a basketball tournament, and my dad was away on a camping trip with his new girlfriend. I had the apartment all to myself. I left the ER with no broken bones, just a deep bruise, and was told to take ibuprofen for at least forty-eight hours. James and Dahlia dropped me off at my place and then hung around watching TV with me for about an hour. My face was still in a lot of pain, and I didn't really feel like I could eat much. James told me he would drop Dahlia off and bring me back some soft food for dinner. He came back an hour later with garlic mashed potatoes, cream corn, and chocolate pudding. Totally sweet and totally thoughtful. I was touched.

We hung out a good part of the night, watching TV on the couch. It was kind of what I needed. Companionship, knowing someone cared about me, human touch. I felt like he was so generous with his time. When it started getting late, he said he could sleep on the couch just to make sure I was okay throughout the night. He said he'd just be there if I needed anything. It was a really thoughtful idea, and again, I was touched. I went to bed that night feeling genuinely cared for and feeling a little bad for James because our couch is not the most comfortable to sleep on. But he was cool with it.

When I woke up in the morning, the side of my face felt better, and after using the bathroom, I went to check on James. And here's the thing—the sunlight was hitting the couch in such a way that it gave James this beautiful glow (which he didn't really need 'cause the guy is already pretty damned gorgeous). It was like a picture. He was lying there asleep, his too-long-for-the-couch legs dangling over the side. He wasn't wearing a shirt, and his muscles really shined in the light.

I couldn't help myself. I knelt beside him and just watched him for a while, not wanting to disturb his sleep. He must have felt my eyes on him, because he woke up right away. When our eyes met, there was something so undeniable there. He touched my cheek and asked me how it felt. Something in the warmth of his hand just shook me. I had never wanted anyone more. We spent the next two hours in my bedroom, and then he went across the street to get us breakfast bagels at Ellis's. We ate on the couch, and then went right back to the bedroom. He was beautiful with me. It was such an unexpected, unplanned moment, and yet it felt so natural and so right.

And I have no idea now what I'm going to do.

James and I have been doing this thing secretly for months now, and I'm supposed to go over to their house for Christmas Eve this week. James says that we should keep it all on the down low to protect all our feelings. And I agree. Shelly thinks we are kidding ourselves and that it is just a matter of time until something slips and it all blows up in our faces. I think Shelly is being overly dramatic, and maybe just a little jealous. I just know that I have something that fills me with so much pleasure, and I want to hold on to it. All the books say love like this doesn't come along every day. We need to savor these things. I'm Juliet. I'm Elizabeth Bennett. I'm Cinderella if Cinderella were fucking the captain of the football team.

Anyway, you get the picture. I'm gonna go hide this somewhere under lock and key. Maybe someday if I'm smart, I'll burn this.

Later, or maybe never again,
Gina

Sex, Drugs, and
Rebirth in Los Angeles

What Devon noticed and respected about Juana instantly was she was not like the rest of the residents at Silver Mountain in nearly any regard. Where many of them came from some form of financial comfort, she came from no such world. Many had a healthy smattering of visitors from time to time. She had none. At least not at first. Not until she made friends with some locals, but that took time. Many of the residents held back from going into too much detail on their stories, unwilling to open up to strangers so soon in the game of healing. Juana had no such filters, and she told them all everything they might have wanted to know about her (and maybe a little they didn't) in that first group session. She was a ray of sunlight to Devon, and he knew that if he could learn anything substantial from anyone at Silver Mountain, it would most likely be from Juana.

She introduced herself as "Mexirican" and told everyone any family she had that was still alive was back in a small Mexican town somewhere and she hadn't seen them since she, her brother, and an uncle ran away and crossed the border at age six. She lost the brother and the uncle two years later somewhere in Phoenix and hadn't looked back for them since. For reasons "too complicated and shady to go into," she found herself living with a crew in Salt Lake City, Utah. She was a naturally gifted dancer and had dreams of moving to New York someday and dancing in rap music videos. She had also taken a strong interest in DJing and had been apprenticing with a professional club DJ for several months before being given the chance to do a solo gig at a Halloween party in the Arcadia Heights area. She knew the host well, as did everyone in her community. He was a reputed drug dealer and did a lot of gang recruiting in the area. She knew that any event with his name attached held a certain level of danger, but she was a self-confessed "danger addict," and not much intimidated her.

During her second set, shortly before midnight, an argument broke out in the middle of the dance floor, and several shots were fired. Crowds of partygoers scurried for the exits, but her DJ booth was in a section that left her greatly exposed. A bullet ricocheted off a wall and cut through her lower spine. She spent two months in a hospital in downtown Salt Lake before a religious group raised enough money to get her to Silver Mountain.

At the end of the session, many of the residents came up to introduce themselves to her, Shane included. Devon, however, held back. He didn't want to be part of the crowd. He wanted his own time with her.

He would get that time three days later, when they were scheduled to be side by side on the tilt tables the clinic used to bring the wheelchair-bound residents to a progressively upright position. A physical therapist strapped Devon and Juana in for their hour-long session and gradually tilted them upward every fifteen minutes. Rosemary, a cherubic redhead and the most beloved therapist there, left the television on for them to watch while she went to work with others. Juana requested she leave a telenovela on and asked Devon if he minded.

"Not at all. You just gotta help me with the plot."

"It's easy, trust me. This bitch started out as the family maid. Now she's doing the husband and the brother. Blackmailing them both."

"I see. Nothing too complicated."

During commercial breaks, they got to know each other. Devon was surprised at how easy it was to talk to her. He liked that she cursed a lot and that no topic appeared to be out of her comfort zone. He also couldn't help but notice she was quite lovely to look at. She had large brown eyes that sat placidly on a lighter-brown face. She had full lips and a sculpted physique that shone through her worn gray sweats. He had a feeling she had been a major head turner once, and most likely would be again very soon. She cackled when he shared the story of his disability with her.

"I tell you, you rich boys are the worst."

"I don't know if I'd call myself a rich boy."

"Oh, you a rich boy all right. Trust me, I have a nose for money. It's cool, *hermano*. Trust me, I'd rather see *morenos* getting that money than the *blanquitos* any day of the week. At least we earn that shit the hard way. We didn't steal it from people who were here before us, you know what I'm saying. *Blancos* are some duplicitous fuckers. But hey, I'm not racist, don't get me wrong. *Blancos* got me here today."

After the tilt-table session, they went out on the second-floor balcony, where they ate leftover pizza and sneaked a cigarette. To Devon's awe, Juana stealthily went over to the corner and lit up a joint after making sure they were out of sight. She offered him a hit, and he felt a euphoric rush as he accepted it.

"How did you get that in here?" he asked, unable to contain a grin.

"*Hermano*," she said, placing a warm hand on his shoulder, "there's one thing I know for a fact: if you know the right people, you can get *anything* into *anywhere*. Doesn't matter if it's a prison cell or the White House. It just takes connections. It's why whenever you go somewhere new, you always gotta look around and ask yourself, 'Who are gonna be my people that I can ride with? Who is gonna be my family?'" She handed him another hit, and he nodded, seduced by her confidence. "Trust me, *hermano*, we deserve to enjoy this brief time together. We get to make that choice."

Eventually Shane found them hanging there and joined in, grateful for company. The late-afternoon joint smoke hour became a regular event for the trio, and over time, newer, more potent substances were introduced to the scene. Devon received an education in many things his high school never provided. He learned skills he would carry with him throughout much of his young-adult life and that he would refer to and rely on much more than he ever would geometry, "Intro to Computer Science," or *The Great Gatsby*.

On Roxanne's next visit, she took the newly formed trio out for lunch at a popular sandwich spot in Westwood. Devon was so taken with the city and the energy of the nearby campus that it planted a seed in his head. He saw students meeting over books in coffee shops and student athletes in matching UCLA tracksuits, running down a busy sidewalk. He saw businesses all over with signs up offering student discounts and restaurants offering special nights where "students eat all you can!" Everyone seemed healthy and productive—even the homeless looked a lot less dirty than any he'd seen in New York. He thought he might be able to fit in at such a place. He just needed to figure out what he wanted to do with his life when he grew up.

At one point during lunch, Juana excused herself. Devon watched her as she went outside and addressed a couple of older guys on motorcycles who looked like they could be members of a punk band. He could tell they didn't know her from Eve, yet he marveled at how easily she conversed and laughed with them. After a few minutes, one of them took out a piece of paper, wrote on it, and handed it to her. She shook hands with them both and then rolled a few feet away to smoke a cigarette. Devon went out to join her.

"Old friends?" he asked, nodding at the guys who were now revving up and taking off.

"Better," she replied with a wink. "New friends. Gotta have assets."

"Assets?"

"I'll explain later on."

Next, they journeyed a couple of blocks up the street to an ice-cream shop, and they all had sundaes and shakes. At around four, Roxanne went to fetch the van, and she left them to wait for her outside of a movie theater. None of them recognized the title of the movie.

"What's this shit about?" Shane asked.

"I saw the commercial. It's, like, a Black comedy about a bunch of fucked-up high-school kids," Devon responded.

"Black comedy as in it has Black people in it?" Juana smirked.

"I bet I could make a movie. I'm a pretty good storyteller," Devon said.

"What makes you think you have to be a good storyteller to make a movie? You ever see the horseshit comes out of this town?" she replied.

"I guess what I mean is I bet I could make a good movie. Maybe about people like us. You never see people like us in the movies," Devon said.

"That's 'cause nobody wants to see a bunch of crips in a movie, bro. We are society's dirty little secret," Shane piped in.

"Besides," Juana added, "when is the last time you saw Snow White or Prince Charming rolling around in a wheelchair?"

"It doesn't all have to be Snow White and Prince Charming," Devon replied.

"No, it does. I guess you're not familiar with the term *escapism*. People go to the movies to forget people like us exist," Shane said.

He nodded, although he didn't actually agree with either of them.

"They're supposed to have a respected film school here. What do you guys think? Are either of you gonna go to school?" Devon asked.

"Nah. I barely finished elementary school, much less some fucking college," Juana said. "That's for you rich kids."

"I ain't going," Shane chimed in. "There's nothing there for me. Everything I ever dreamed of doing won't be possible anymore."

"I don't know if I agree with that," Juana replied. "I mean, we all have it within us to create new dreams, right?"

"Nah, there's no replacing what I lost," Shane said.

Devon just nodded and made a note to himself to call UCLA and request a catalog. On the ride back, all three of them smoked out the window, and Roxanne couldn't help herself.

"You know, you guys, I hate to be that person, but I am in the medical profession, and all of this smoking? I don't want to discriminate, but it is actually worse on you guys' health than it is on normal, able-bodied folks."

"Oh yeah? Why is that?" Devon asked.

"Well, I've done a little research since my last visit when I noticed how many of you smoke in that place. Here's the thing—smoking exacerbates so many spinal-cord injury conditions. Like, I don't know if any of you experience regular pain, but nicotine has been seen to widely increase levels of musculoskeletal pain. Then there's the increased heart rate many SCI persons already have. Smoking just increases your risk of heart disease. I'm talking by a substantial amount. It's nothing to play with. Not to mention that your lung capacity—"

"Maybe we don't want to live forever," Juana interjected. She flashed a slight grin.

"Nobody is saying live forever. I am saying—"

"Maybe we really don't want to live that long, period," Shane added. The three of them shared a wink, a gesture not wasted on Roxanne.

"Okay, I get it," she said with a sigh. "That's your prerogative. I guess I'm selfish and want you guys around for as long as possible."

"We could all die from a nuclear bomb blast tomorrow," Devon said.

"Yeah, it's either gonna be we do it to the Russians or they do it to us," Juana added.

"Fine, fine."

"I think what we're all trying to say, sis, is that nothing in life is certain. We just want to live in the moment."

"Fine, live in the moment," Roxanne replied. "But I've seen emphysema patients and lung-cancer sufferers up close. Mark my words, it isn't a pretty picture."

"Life isn't a pretty picture, Roxanne," Juana said.

When they got back to Silver Mountain, Roxanne helped Devon do his laundry in the basement. Devon couldn't stop reflecting on campus life over folding clothes.

"Hey, do you think tomorrow we can go check out the campus again? Just the two of us?"

"Yeah, we could do that. If you're serious about this, though, you should figure some things out. Like, what is your status right now? You're going to need to repeat this year for sure. And what's your GPA like?"

"My GPA? I haven't thought about that in ages."

"Your GPA, kid. It's important for college entry. You and James never took that shit seriously. That's the problem with you high-school athletes. The system tells you it is okay to be dumb."

"Hey! I'm not dumb."

"I know you're not. And I'm sorry, that came out wrong. I just think the whole school sports scene is kind of fucked up."

"I wonder what Alexis's GPA is."

"It's three point nine. She's most likely going to UConn."

"UConn? Wait, I thought she wanted to go to, like, University of Hawaii."

"She did at first. But she thought about it more and changed her mind. Honestly, I think she wants to be closer to you."

Devon was stunned. The notion his sister would give up her long-dreamed-of school in a tropical setting all because she believed it best she be nearby him for support was more than his mind could handle. He burst into tears.

At their next tilt-table session, Devon read a letter from Alexis when Juana leaned over to him during a commercial break in the telenovela.

"Hey, I need to ask you a favor."

"A favor? Sure, what's up?"

She checked to make sure no one would overhear, a move that piqued Devon's curiosity.

"Tonight, I'm gonna need to sneak out around eleven thirty. I'm meeting some people in the parking lot across the street from 7-Eleven."

"Okay. You need me to cover for you on bed check?"

"No. Shane can do that. I need you to wait by the door for me to come back. Last time I left it wedged open with a book, and it triggered an alarm. I found out that happens if the door is open longer than two minutes."

"Oh okay. How long will you be?"

She took a deep breath before telling him everything. He was impressed with her directness and how comfortable she was relaying the entire scheme to him. How confident she was in implementing her well-thought-out plan. It was amazing to him how business savvy she was for someone who had admittedly never taken a finance class in her life. To hear her tell it, it was all quite simple. She saw a demand at Silver Mountain. A demand she knew she could fulfill. Juana Rabassa was a capitalist with a capital *C*.

Many people, including several staff members, were mired in the drudgery of everyday life at the facility, visible in the blankness of their stares, in their demeanor. Some were physically never going to get any better and were, in essence, wiling away at Silver Mountain until they were forced to move on to "real life." Some, who were there as hired help to assist in the growth and development of the residents, left the facility at the end of their shifts and went home to abusive partners, unfulfilling lovers and relationships, and moribund family structures. For so many of them, a flame had gone out in their souls, and it was only natural they would turn to one another for some level of fulfillment.

Devon and Juana watched with amusement as many staff and residents developed "inappropriate" relationships with one another. They determined their favorite out of the numerous dalliances was that of Keith Ballard, a Black cook in the kitchen from South Central, and Cassidy Forsythe, a white quadriplegic from San Diego who had become paralyzed while sky diving with her then fiancé, a golf pro. Juana often joked Keith was "as 'hood rat as you could get," a former gang member and pot dealer currently on parole. He wore tattoos of his former gang affiliation on his neck and arms, and every ounce of him was solid muscle, a result of much well-spent time in the prison gym.

Cassidy, on the other hand, was "bougie as hell" in the eyes of most residents. She had studied abroad in Italy for a year during college and at times took to cursing people out in Italian just for effect. Her nickname, given to her by her younger brother, Ryan, who stopped by often, was "Cotillion Cass." People enjoyed calling her that, though most there had no idea what a cotillion was.

Their obvious differences didn't stop Keith and Cass from getting it on regularly after hours on the occupational therapy mat in the rehab room or in the hydro pool. Devon once came out to the balcony late one night to have a smoke when all the others in his ward were asleep, and he was amused to find Cassidy in the dark corner, giving a standing Keith, still wearing his cook shirt and cap, a blow job in the moonlight. Their appetite for one another appeared insatiable, and Devon chided Cassidy that he would someday tell their story in film, the working title, *The Debutante Crip and the Hood Crip*.

Shane too was in on the lusty action, taking up with a volunteer massage therapist named Sunny, who came by once a week to provide a "service" to the residents there. Unlike others who found secret rendezvous spots at the facility, Shane preferred dashing out to a local

Best Western for a couple of hours to have his intimacy time with the blond, ebullient Sunny, who looked like a woman still trapped in the Woodstock of the sixties and who bragged she once had sex with a well-known rock star when she was twelve. Juana got in on the action as well, having sex with Cassidy's brother, Ryan, with cocaine-fueled trysts in the janitor's closet and making good use of the back of his Jeep in the parking lot.

So many at Silver Mountain desperately desired an escape, one they'd previously found in cheap liquor and weed.

That all changed dramatically when Juana came along.

She knew where to look outside their community to find people who could help her bring a stronger mind-bending experience to her compatriots. She had gotten a good lead from the two motorcyclists she had met outside the sandwich shop that afternoon, and now she had a connection who delivered to her on a weekly basis high-quality weed, heroin, and a small quantity of cocaine, all for a fifteen-percent cut of the business. The demand for cocaine at Silver Mountain would prove to be so high that Juana would deal mainly in the sale of that substance for the first month. Her first big launch was Super Bowl Sunday. Most of the people in attendance for the party in the residents' lounge were high on Juana's product. Those who weren't were either soon to be or kept their silence out of loyalty.

Devon was most surprised when he spotted Sunday-church-attendee Rosemary dip into the ward in a jittery state early one afternoon and take a walk down the block with Juana. When Juana returned alone, he saw her deposit a wad of cash in an envelope she always kept well hidden.

"What's up with you and Rosemary?"

"Girl needed some H. She's going to her sister's wedding this weekend in San Fran, and she can't stand the bitch."

"Rosemary is on H?"

"Rosemary is on a lot of shit. You sound shocked, *hermano*."

"I'm not so much shocked as—well, I thought Rosemary had her shit together."

"You think drugs are only for people who don't have their shit together? That's some narrow thinking, *hermano*."

Her statement both baffled and embarrassed him, and he made a conscious choice to try to check his judgments. Later, from the 7-Eleven phone booth, he called Alexis and shared everything with her.

"Sounds like quite an enterprising lady, your friend does."

"She's asked me if I want to help her out and she'll cut me in on some of the profit. Do you think I should?"

There was a long pause on the other end of the phone. The family dog barked in the background.

"That's a decision you'll need to make on your own, buddy."

"Would you think less of me if I did?"

"Listen, as far as I see all of this, your friend is simply providing a service. She sees a demand for a product, and she's filling that demand. In that sense, she's no different from a doctor, a lawyer, or a stockbroker with Morgan Stanley. In fact, some of those professions have much shadier characters than your friend, I'm sure. You do what you feel you need to do, but remember, that line of business is full of potholes. If TV crime drama has taught me anything, it is no one stays on top forever in that business. The risks are huge."

He knew she was right, but he also could not resist the pull to work alongside Juana. Soon enough, he was going over to the 7-Eleven to make payments and re-up on new supply. Things were going well until he was told by one of Juana's connections, a Mexican named Ernesto, that the 7-Eleven location was "too hot," and although he wasn't certain what exactly the phrase meant, Devon knew enough to know it was troublesome. They moved the re-up meetups to a Dunkin' Donuts about a mile away. At first, the change annoyed Devon, as he had to take a bus to get there, but two things changed his attitude right away. Juana raised his salary considerably, which made complaining about the bus trip petty. Second, and most important, he had developed a bit of a crush on Mirabel, the half-Black, half-Armenian girl who worked the Dunkin' Donuts counter.

He and Mirabel often joked with each other, mostly about basketball. She was a die-hard Lakers fan, while Devon preferred the Knicks. They had a natural chemistry, and she always seemed to brighten up whenever he rolled in Wednesday evenings right before closing. One night, he accompanied her to her bus stop, and she shared with him that she was an aspiring singer and songwriter. After some prodding, she promised she would bring her guitar with her next time and share some of her work.

Juana heard about their flirtation through Ernesto and a couple of the other dealers who worked with him, and she and Shane prodded and teased him about his intentions. He remained steadfast that they were just innocent friends and no more. And besides, he told them, he had a girlfriend waiting for him back home. This was news to Juana and Shane, who never so much as heard a peep from this other woman or saw any evidence of her in his life.

"Man, stop fronting and ask the bitch out," Shane said.

"Dude, it's not so easy. She lives in Glendale."

"Last I saw, you didn't need a passport to get into Glendale," Shane retorted. "Have you even gotten your dick wet since your accident?"

The question caught Devon off guard, and his lack of a response made it apparent this was an area he had not explored. The very idea of physical intimacy scared Devon. He was concerned that he would not be able to perform sexually anywhere near the level he once had.

"You can still get it up, right?" Juana asked him, somewhat gently.

"Well, yeah, of course . . . but I just don't know, like, for how long and stuff."

"Hey," Shane interjected. "Your injury is less severe than mine, and I can get it up. You don't believe me, ask Sunny. I fill her shit up like you wouldn't believe. So trust me, you will be fine in that area. You just need practice."

"And even if you're not, hey, take my word for it. I don't know another woman who doesn't love a good brother who has skills at going downtown. Trust me—we love it. *Love it!* But you gotta know what you doing."

"She's telling the truth. I make Sunny sing when I'm licking it up between those thighs."

He watched as Shane and Juana high-fived each other. The conversation made him uncomfortable, but he was relieved to have friends to share it with. Later that night, he went to the 7-Eleven, purchased a long-distance calling card, and dialed a number he hadn't called in nearly half a year. A part of him hoped she wouldn't pick up, and he felt a tiny earthquake in his chest when on the fourth ring he heard her familiar voice.

"Gina, hi."

"Devon?" Her tone relayed surprise. Her voice cracked. "Devon, oh my God, I've been thinking about you."

"Hey. Hopefully good things."

"Yes. Yes, of course good things. Mainly just . . . I've been meaning to write you."

"Yeah, same here. There's so much going on all the time."

"Yeah, yeah."

Devon looked around him, in need of a distraction. He saw an older Mexican couple standing outside their car, studying a map on the hood. "How is life there? How's your mom?"

"My mom is okay. She's okay. In fact, I've gotta go pick her up from AA in about ten minutes."

"AA, huh?"

"Yeah, she's really trying. Struggling, but trying."

"Good, good."

Devon felt the phone trembling by his ear. "How about you? How's therapy and stuff?"

"Therapy is therapy. It's tough some days, you know? Definitely takes patience." Devon sighed, slightly annoyed at the awkward silence between them.

"I saw Alexis the other day at Verratti's. She said you were thinking about going to film school out there."

"Yeah, it's just something in the back of my mind. You know me, I've always loved movies."

"I know. Ever since *Rocky*."

"Yeah. And *Casablanca*."

"Of course, *Casablanca*."

He wished he hadn't brought up the film. It conjured a memory he cherished, of him and her on a couch at her house, watching the movie on a small TV. He was introducing her to the film, and she was finding it boring. They were holding hands. He knew he would never hold her hand again.

"What about you? How's the whole college picture looking?"

"It looks good, yeah."

"Still looking at Brown?"

"Brown? No, actually Brown was a while ago. I've had a change of heart. I was thinking something more like FSU."

"FSU?"

"Yeah, you know, Florida State."

The word *Florida* struck an odd chord within him.

"Oh. What made you decide there?"

"I don't know. They have a pretty good law program."

"Law? You wanna be a lawyer now?"

"Yeah, why not? You know, seeing my mother be pushed around by the system. It's been interesting. It made me think."

"Huh. That's great for you. Perfect, really. Goodness knows you love you some beach."

"Yeah, you know me."

"Hell, you might even bump into James out there."

There was an awkward, stillborn pause for a few seconds.

"Well, it's a big state."

"Yeah, true. But still." He looked back over to the couple. They appeared to be arguing over the map now, and Devon felt a discomforting surge in his bowels. "Have you talked to James lately?"

There was another pause on the other end, and in the vacuum of silence, he heard his heart beating.

"Have I talked to James lately?" she responded. "He's at school, you know."

"Yeah, I know. But surely he comes home every now and then."

"Yeah, that's true." Devon sensed her holding something back again, and he grabbed at his stomach.

"Dev, I've gotta go pick up my mother. She can't drive now."

"Oh, okay then. You go ahead."

"Can I call you at the rehab center sometime?"

"We don't have our own phones."

"Okay. I'm sorry, it's—"

"I just wanted to touch base and see how you were doing."

"No. Thanks. I appreciate that. I'm sorry I haven't done better at staying in touch."

"Hey, we're both busy, right?"

"Right. Keep healing, Dev. We all love you back here."

"Right, I will. Take care, Gina. I hope your mom keeps doing well."

"Yeah, she will. Bye, Dev."

"Bye, Gina."

He took his time hanging up the phone. His bowels felt ready to erupt, and he wondered if he should try to make it back to Silver Mountain or use the bathroom here. Then he heard a loud slap and a scream and turned to see the woman fall to the ground, the man standing over her ready to strike her a second time. The map had fallen to the ground, and the woman was holding the man's fist to stop the next blow. The man pulled his fist away and kicked her in the back. She screamed again, and Devon debated whether he should intervene. Before he could make a move, the man kicked her in the back once more, and he stormed off down the street. Devon watched the woman just lie there on the warm ground, alive, but motionless.

He didn't make it to the bathroom in time.

Over the course of a month, Juana sent so much business Devon's way that he could no longer keep his money in the manila envelope underneath the clothing in his dresser. He had at least twenty-five hundred dollars in cash, and Juana assured him that more was on the way. Many at Silver Mountain had referred her to other friends and family members who came by as "visitors" to pick up their packages. Across the street from Dunkin' Donuts was a Citibank. One morning, Devon went there with his ID and opened a savings account. He rolled away from the bank the proud owner of a shiny new blue bank card, and he tested it out at the ATM, withdrawing a hundred dollars. He went straight over to Dunkin' Donuts, where he sat at a table. As per their routine, Mirabel brought him a chocolate-glazed donut and a cup of coffee with one sugar and cream.

"You are too kind," he said, nodding.

"I *am* too kind." She had a smile that, every time he experienced it, reminded him there was still so much natural beauty in the world.

Mirabel wasn't only beautiful. The young woman had talent. One afternoon, after she had gotten off work early, the two traveled a few blocks east to a quiet park where children played and locals walked their dogs. Mirabel had brought her guitar as promised, and Devon listened as they sat under the shade of a large oak tree. Her voice was soft, untrained, and vulnerable. Her guitar playing was simple but effective. Most of her songs seemed to be about loneliness. His favorite was about the father she never knew too well. The chorus was hauntingly sweet.

Thank you for the brown eyes, thank you for the brown skin
Thank you for the joy you bring me from deep within
I'll always wish I knew you, not just the shadow of a memory
Thank you for the warm hands, thank you for the strong bones
Thank you for the clear voice and the autumn tones
I'll always wish I knew you, not just the shadow of a memory

Each time he heard a new version of the song, he noticed it filled her eyes with tears before she finished. Once, she sang it to him at her bus stop alone on a Wednesday night, and he pulled her in close. She placed her guitar down, sat on his lap, and the two of them just swayed there in each other's arms for a while as traffic drove by. Devon sensed they both felt something. There was an air of expectation in the moment. It was the perfect time to say something, or even better, do something. The idea worried Devon because he recognized the symptoms. This was love all over again. He felt a strong urge to take the lead as he felt her warm breath on his neck. He stroked her cheek, and her pleasant face looked up at him, eager.

A part of him had adjusted to the notion that Gina would most likely no longer be a part of his life. She would probably go to Florida State, meet some other student or some dude on the beach, and forget all about Devon. He had to come to terms with the thing he told himself before he left for California.

Let her go, for your good, but mostly for hers. She will be better off in the long run without you.

But a part of him was stubborn, and he fantasized about returning home to Connecticut a fully healed man, showing up at Gina's place, declaring his never-ending love for her, and having her tell him the same. He played the scene over and over in his head some nights like the happy ending of a romantic comedy.

"I knew you'd come back to me," Gina would say. "I fought it, but I just couldn't get over you. I knew someday you'd come back to me, and we could start all over again!"

It was this scene replayed over and over in his mind that left him unable to fully allow Mirabel into his heart.

Devon had other things on his mind. Juana had recently informed him and Shane that her rehabilitation was progressing so well that her social worker would probably release her sometime next month. The problem was she didn't have anywhere to go. But she was determined she needed to be in one place. She told them she had to return to Salt Lake City. Her stay would be brief, but it was a thing she had to do.

"I have unfinished business there. Somebody—and my friends there know exactly who—did me very wrong back there. That person needs to be held accountable. That person needs to understand that karma is a fucking bitch."

"Will you stay in touch with us? How will we know how to reach you?" Devon asked.

"Of course I'll stay in touch. You guys are my family now."

Devon and Shane shared a concerned look. Neither wanted to imagine a life without their charismatic friend.

One gray afternoon threatened the first rain of the year. Devon sat at Dunkin' Donuts, reading a magazine on motorcycles. He had made his pickup about an hour ago and now waited impatiently for Mirabel to have a free moment, but she was incredibly busy. Two coworkers had called in sick, and she couldn't remove herself from the register at the counter, as the lunchtime crowd was hectic. Devon looked around, frustration setting in, until he saw Keith and Cassidy heading his way, having just entered. He made eye contact with them, and they came to his table. They exchanged greetings, and Keith excused himself to go wait in the long line of customers. Devon and Cassidy sat across from each other. He watched with amusement as she stared at Keith's ass when he walked away from them.

"Damn, girl, let it go for a second."

"I don't know what you are talking about."

"So, tell me, is it true what they say about Keith?"

"That depends. What do they say about him?"

"That he has a dick the size of a boa constrictor?"

"Oooh, that's crass. I tell you, you gossipers. Besides, I wouldn't know. When we hang out together, we just read."

"Just read, huh?"

"That's it."

"What you reading today?"

"I think we are about halfway through *Wuthering Heights*. Heathcliff and Catherine, what a crazy couple!"

Devon did his best to stare her down, and the two dissolved in laughter. Cassidy picked at his donut.

"Hey, look," she said. "I need to ask you something."

"I don't do threesomes."

"Sucks for you. No, seriously. I have a few girlfriends coming by this weekend. They want to take me to the coast for a day. I want to place an order but, like, a big order."

"A big order, huh?"

"Yeah. And I want in on this thing too. I think I'd be good at what you guys do."

Devon folded his hands in front of him and took on a faux professional tone. "We're not hiring at this time."

Cassidy rolled her eyes. "Come on, just think about it. I've got a really strong potential client base. I can bring in three times what Gabriel brings in."

"Gabriel? Who says Gabriel brings in anything?"

"What?"

"Why did you bring up Gabriel?"

Cassidy shifted in her chair. "Gabriel has been bragging that you guys are about to bring him on as the fourth man."

"He's what?" Devon said, eyes wide. "Gabriel is full of shit. Shane can't stand his Texas ass."

"He says he's been hooking up some of the janitors on the fourth floor for you guys. And he says he's been fucking that new OT, Debra, and giving her some hot dope."

"If he's doing any of that, he's doing that shit independently. We don't want nothing to do with that Cowboys-loving motherfucker."

"So wait, you guys aren't bringing him on?"

"What did I just say?"

"Then why would he tell me that?"

"It's a good question. I'm gonna find out, I tell you that much."

When Devon talked to Juana about it that night, she sounded less surprised than he was, much to his disappointment.

"I gave him a little extra weed two weeks ago, just to see if he could move it. He's telling me he's hit up some janitors and a few construction workers across the street."

"You cut Gabe Spatifore in?"

"I know you guys can't stand him, but the kid is pretty smart. He's got just enough charisma, and he's got a lot of contacts back in San Antonio."

"We ain't in San Antonio, *novia*."

"Hey, listen to me. You never know when you're gonna wind up somewhere else. You should make friends wherever you can. You hear me?"

Devon shook his head. "Fucking Gabe Spatifore. You know he's, like, the most-hated guy here, right? I'm talking by everybody."

"You don't have to love everybody you work with. But you should love the results."

Devon shared the news with Shane later that night, and he was livid.

"This shit ain't gonna fly," he said on the balcony, sipping beer from a thermos. "That fucking Spatifore kid is bad luck. Fucking snake eyes. This is a bad idea."

"Bombing Hiroshima and Nagasaki was a bad idea," Juana shot back, smoking a cigarette. "If Spatifore doesn't work, it can always be fixed. Worst-case scenario, we can his ass."

Devon had exaggerated a little when he said Gabriel Spatifore was the most-hated person at Silver Mountain, but he was most definitely not well liked by the majority. Gabriel was a rich kid from a large, conservative, Italian family who all hailed from an enclave in San Antonio, Texas. He held views with which many in the facility clashed, such as a woman's right to choose (he was against it), affirmative action (he was against it), and gay rights (he was against them), and he and his family had been huge supporters of Ronald Reagan. Prominently displayed on his bedside dresser was a framed picture of himself as a young teen shaking hands with the former president at a political rally.

Gabriel had been at Silver Mountain for nearly three months after an ATV accident out in the desert during his eighteenth birthday celebration left him paralyzed. He had a whiny, nasally voice, and his face was dotted with dark acne. He overtreated this condition with various facial creams that seemed to do no more than exacerbate the problem. Most days he exhibited a pus-filled exterior that smelled of medicated onion extract and rotted flesh. Behind his back, many called him "Leperface." He was a huge fan of rap music, and he wore sweatsuits, chains, and sneakers that emulated many of the rap celebrities of the time. He constantly blasted rap music from his boom box radio, irritating everyone in the ward, even those who were fans of the music. The volume reached a point where he often had to have his boom box removed by staff at night for violating quiet-time rules. On a few occasions, he returned from a therapy session to find it missing, but it always turned up again eventually.

For Devon, his annoyance with Gabriel was compounded by the fact that Gabriel believed early on that the two of them held something in common and that it was okay for him to refer to Devon as "my nigga." They first met in the recreation lounge one Sunday while Devon watched the Giants game. Gabriel entered and, without asking, picked up the remote control and searched for the Cowboys game. Devon approached him.

"Listen, my nigga," Gabriel had told him, holding the remote up and away from Devon's reach. "Your game is almost over. The Giants are crushing the Eagles. Let me watch my boys."

"First thing, I'm not your nigga. Get that straight. Give me that remote."

"Come on now, let's talk about this in a civilized manner."

"I'm not gonna tell you again. Give me that remote."

Devon reached for the remote, and the two locked arms. Gabriel swung his arm, striking Devon in the shoulder, and in the ensuing tussle, they knocked over a lamp. Two staff members came over to break up the scene, and when it was over, Devon and Gabriel were banished from the lounge for days.

Devon confronted Gabriel in the ward later that night, and the two had to be separated by staff again before things got physical. Neither were in any shape to have a true fight that could hurt the other, but their animosity was genuine and cast a cloud over anyone in their vicinity. The head nurse warned them that if their threatening behavior kept up, they would each be sent to a private room on the fourth floor, a section all the residents referred to as "solitary confinement" due to the extremely poor conditions and the hideously oppressive nature of the rooms. This section was where people with severe mental health challenges were at times sequestered, and it was seen as punishment to be housed there. From that moment, Devon and Gabriel decided it best they stay as far apart from each other as possible, a workable arrangement—until Juana arrived on the scene. Gabriel was instantly intrigued by her, and he slowly wormed his way into their crew to get in good with her.

Both Devon and Shane made it clear to Juana that they would not have anything to do with working with Gabriel, and she respected their feelings on the matter. She took it on herself to delegate tasks to him, giving him light assignments, dealing mostly pot and sometimes light amounts of heroin. Gabriel made a few attempts to get back on Devon's good side, but Devon would not budge.

"Keep your redneck ass on the other side of the ward like we always done, and we'll be just fine," Devon said.

Things went smoothly the first month, with Gabriel turning a decent profit for the group and hoping to expand his outreach, a move Devon and Shane vehemently opposed.

"Don't trust that motherfucker with anything more than MJ," Shane told Juana as the three ate takeout Chinese food on the balcony.

"Serious," Devon chimed in. "You know he's using too, right?"

The three of them had an agreement since the operation began. They would be allowed to smoke weed whenever they pleased, no problem there, but the heavier drugs they would lay off, as they deemed it bad for business and a bad look to get high off your own supply.

"I guess we forgot to send him the memo," Juana joked.

"Ha, ha, funny. Shane is right, this dude is not to be trusted with more responsibility."

"You know, the two of you could really benefit from stepping back and being more open minded."

"Fuck open minded," Shane said. With that, his eggroll fell on the floor. "Shit! See, just talking about that fucking leper is bad luck!"

The three of them did their best to avoid the true elephant in the room. Juana had been given a release date of March 30. She had already purchased her train ticket back to Salt Lake City. There was a genuine concern about just how things would operate once she was no longer there to lead them. None of them wanted to have the uncomfortable conversation, nor face the reality the band might be breaking up.

As it turned out, they wouldn't have to.

On the morning of March 18, Devon woke early. Roxanne had planned to come by and take him out to breakfast at his favorite spot in Westwood. As he was making coffee in the cafeteria, he saw out of the window an ambulance and fire truck pulling up in front of the lobby. It wasn't all that rare to see an ambulance at Silver Mountain, as every now and then, a resident injured themselves or someone was arriving to begin their stay. But the speed and seriousness with which these EMTs moved intrigued him, so he left his coffee behind him and went to the elevator. When he got out on his floor, he saw what looked to be every resident in the facility, crowding the hallway, gathered outside the door that led to the women's ward. He reached out to the person nearest to him, a quadriplegic named Leslie.

"Do you know what's going on?"

She turned to him with tears in her eyes. "It's Cassidy. She didn't wake up."

"What do you mean she didn't wake up?"

"She was just stiff, pale and cold. She's dead, I'm sure of it."

Devon's stomach fell into his knees. Cassidy dead? He had just been hanging with her two nights ago in the parking lot, celebrating Keith earning his GED. They had smoked weed and drunk Olde English. Cassidy had looked great in a revealing blouse and colorful mini skirt. There was talk she might be heading home soon and jokes that she and Keith would have to elope before she left. He looked around for

Juana or Shane, but neither were there. He waited around, hoping to get a report. Eventually, the door opened, and two nurses emerged. They dabbed their eyes with handkerchiefs. Marlene, the head nurse, followed soon after and was immediately hit with questions from the crowd. Marlene simply shook her head, too overwhelmed with grief to articulate much more.

"She's gone," she muttered. "She's gone."

An hour later, EMTs rolled Cassidy's body out on a gurney covered by a sheet. A collective gasp and a shrill roiled through the crowd like a wave. Devon had been searching for Juana and Shane, but they were nowhere in sight. Gabriel was, though, drinking a Pepsi and looking on, pained and anxious. Against his better judgment, Devon went to him.

"You have any idea where Juana and Shane are?"

"They went to some St. Patty's Day party in Venice Beach last night. They were supposed to get back by midnight. Never made it."

Devon knew of the party. He was supposed to go with them but chose instead to go to a coffee shop in La Cañada where Mirabel was performing at an open-mic night.

"I can't believe this shit," Devon said. "She was healthy as fuck."

"Yo, man, I saw her last night. She was hitting the H hard, man. She was all worried about going home and what life would be like when she left here."

Devon felt the skin on his neck warm and bristle. "Wait, what? She was doing H last night?"

"Some of us were trying to tell her to slow down."

Devon looked down at the floor and breathed short and shallow. He grabbed on to the arms of his wheelchair to hold himself up. He felt light-headed. Then, to his great relief, he saw Roxanne walking toward him through the crowd.

"Hey, what's with all the excitement?" she asked him.

He grabbed her arm. "Please, get me out of here."

In the parking lot, he explained what had happened to Cassidy. He thought it best he leave out anything else about her death other than to say he thought it was possible that she had a weak heart. At their lunch spot, he was barely able to eat his California omelet.

"I talked to your doctor this week."

"You did?"

"Yeah, he was anxious to update me on your progress. He thinks you're doing really well. Your upper-body strength has increased considerably. You ought to be very proud of yourself. He thinks at this rate maybe you can go home first week of May."

"First week of May?"

"Yeah, isn't that great? So now I'm wondering, have you spoken to Mom and Dad at all about what your return home will look like? 'Cause our house is not wheelchair accessible at all. Have you . . ."

He looked up at her with sad eyes. He'd barely had any communication with their parents since he arrived at Silver Mountain months ago. Roxanne sipped at her coffee and stared at her plate.

"In a way, I kind of wish I could just stay here."

"Kid, this place is nice and all, but there's a real world out there waiting for you. You still have school and friends and family."

"I was thinking maybe I could finish out high school here. Maybe I could stay with you?"

They remained silent for a minute. The hum of the busy restaurant filled the space around them. After asking for a refill on her coffee, Roxanne spoke.

"Can I be honest with you about something?"

Devon nodded.

"I think you're scared. I think you're scared to go home and face the music. And I understand that. Trust me, I really do. But it's something you're gonna have to do eventually, Dev. It's something your soul has to do. You need closure on some of this. Do you agree with that?"

He tapped on his plate with his fork and looked down at his cold omelet. He recalled Cassidy's laugh and Hannah's smile, simultaneously.

"I don't know, Roxy, that I'll ever have closure to this."

"Well, that's where I think therapy might be able to help. I mean, mental health therapy."

"You want me to see a shrink?"

"You say that as if there is some stigma attached to that."

"I'm not crazy, Roxy. I'm not suicidal."

"You, my friend, have the wrong idea of just what therapy is about. *I* see a therapist."

"You? What the hell you need a therapist for? You're the most together person out of all of us."

"Oh, kid. You're so damned young."

Devon returned to a grieving Silver Mountain. The minute he rolled in the door, he could feel the staleness of spirit, as if the building itself were in mourning. When he got off the elevator and entered the recreational lounge, he saw Juana, Shane, and Gabriel talking in the corner. He made eye contact, and they approached him. He felt the other residents' eyes pressing on him and his crew as they all went for a stroll down to the park. Juana, as usual, did most of the talking.

"I liked that girl as much as the rest of you, but she had a real self-control problem. This is not on us. But it could come back to bite us, hard."

"How you mean?" Gabriel asked.

She looked at him as if he were a dunce. "People are gonna have questions. It's no secret that Cassidy was using."

"They're probably gonna look to Keith," Shane said.

"Maybe. Then what's Keith gonna say? Her father is, like, a politician or something. Like, a congressman or councilman or some shit," Juana said.

"Where is Keith?" Devon asked.

"Who knows. Are we even sure he knows what happened?" Shane asked.

"He's due to be on tomorrow morning," Devon said.

"Who has his number?" Juana asked.

"I got it," Devon said. "I was their main source. But he also had a guy in Carson. He said the guy was only good for weed."

"Call him," Juana said, a little forcefully. "If he doesn't know, he should hear it from a friend."

Devon went back to his room, pulled out his phone book, and went to use the 7-Eleven pay phone. He stopped as he passed by the cafeteria. Through the window of the door, he saw all the staff gathered in a circle and talking to a large man in a suit. Next to that man stood Reginald Van Atter, the chief operating officer of Silver Mountain. Van Atter had a strained look on his face as he listened to the man address the staff. Devon realized the suited gentleman must have been some type of investigator because of the way he took notes as staff members spoke. To Devon's shock, Keith was among the staff gathered, holding his head low and occasionally rubbing his eyes. Devon watched for a few minutes and then went back to the park. When he told the crew what he had observed, they shook their heads collectively.

"This situation is fucked," Juana said.

"I still can't believe . . . we'll never see her again," Devon stated, his voice unsteady.

A shadow descended over the crew, and they stared downward. An ice-cream vendor pulled up and asked them if they wanted anything from his cart. Juana waved him off.

"Still, though, I mean, what's the worst that could happen?" Gabriel asked.

That answer came within a matter of days.

Cassidy's father was a state representative from San Diego County named Milton Forsythe. He had a reputation for cruelty and was rumored to be on a list of top choices to run for lieutenant governor on the Republican ticket. When he learned his only daughter had died of a heroin overdose, he demanded a complete investigation of the culture at Silver Mountain. Van Atter, shocked and embarrassed such a thing could occur there (in addition to fearing legal action), acquiesced and spearheaded the effort to get to the bottom of Cassidy's death.

It did not take long to get certain residents to speak out on the pervasive drug use at the facility and to point fingers at the primary offenders. Several staff members were interviewed, regardless of tenure, and many, including Keith and Rosemary, were immediately fired. Juana, Shane, and Devon were interviewed personally by Van Atter, and each admitted to using, but none admitted to selling or dealing. Their stories all supported one another perfectly—with one exception.

Gabriel.

Gabriel turned on all of them to make a special deal with Van Atter. In exchange for giving Van Atter the full story of their operation, Gabriel was sentenced to probation and had numerous perks and amenities taken away from him for the remainder of his stay. Van Atter, awed and sickened by all Gabriel relayed to him, acted swiftly and expelled Devon, Juana, and Shane from Silver Mountain, effective immediately.

Luckily for all of them, Shane's family was able to come through for them amid the chaos. Devon and Juana were able to stay on in guest rooms at the Tollefson house until they could arrange to get back home. Juana's last night was the final day of March. That evening, Shane's mother and new boyfriend threw a going-away party for her. There were about fifteen people in attendance, including a few from Silver Mountain. When the time came around for a toast, Juana was compelled by the crowd to give a speech. She wasn't truthful with any of them, except Devon, with whom she had already shared her intentions for returning to Salt Lake City. She told everyone there that she had distant family in Utah who planned to help see her through the remainder of her rehabilitation. She vowed to return to Los Angeles for a visit once she was fully healed and felt strong enough to travel on her own.

The next morning, they all hugged goodbye in the driveway as a taxi waited to take her to the train station. To Devon's surprise, tears flooded his eyes as he pulled her close to him and smelled her all-too-familiar strawberry-scented shampoo.

"Stay strong out here," she told him. "I promise you, I'll find you. You're my *hermano*. We'll see each other again. Even if I have to go to fucking Connecticut to do it."

Devon smiled. He had no doubt that she would keep her word.

He spent the rest of the week in a mild funk. He had no idea what life was going to look like for him once he returned home. What he did know was that his parents had been given a full account of his expulsion by Van Atter and they were most unhappy with him. But it wasn't their disappointment that bothered him most. Truth was, he couldn't care less about their assessment of his character. What bothered him most was Roxanne's utter revulsion at his behavior. His parents had given her the full story (much to his chagrin), and she went to see him at the Tollefson house to get his side of the story and confront him. As they sat in the foyer, with the sunlight drenching them, Devon could see the disappointment in her face.

"I just don't understand how you could even consider getting involved in something like that. How could you think that would have been a good idea?" she said.

"I never forced anybody to take anything, Roxy. I was just a middleman."

"Don't give me that. You were complicit in a completely immoral practice, Devon. Don't you see that?"

Devon thought back to an earlier conversation he had with Juana, and he regurgitated to the best of his ability what she had told him.

"I was simply filling a need, Roxy. There was a high demand for a product, and I was able to provide that product at a cheaper cost and convenience. It's capitalism, plain and simple. It's what makes America great."

He had never wanted to hurt Roxanne. She was someone he had come to depend on and appreciate more than any other family member, and their relationship had strengthened considerably in recent months. But he saw in the lines on her face, in the paleness of her gaze—this was a turning point for them. Their relationship would never be quite the same again. Roxanne had empathy, but she also had a value system he found to be conservative and judgmental. He personally hadn't killed anyone, but he could tell that in her mind she believed he may as well have strangled Cassidy himself. When they said their goodbyes, he did his best to apologize to her for letting her down, but he tripped over his own tongue.

"I know I fucked up. I'll try to be better."

He watched her pull out of the driveway, and he stared at her car until it was out of sight.

It was his last meaningful contact with her for many years.

In all his concerns and anxieties about what lay in store for him back home, Devon did have one experience in the Tollefson household that would have a profound effect on his future.

One night, while Shane was out on a date with Sunny, Devon sat in the living room, watching a rented videotape of an old Sidney Poitier movie, when Shane's mother entered, carrying her high-heeled shoes in her hand, smelling of liquor and cigarettes. She still wore one of her many stylish suits, so Devon assumed she was returning from one of her work happy hours. She plopped down on the seat next to him and watched the television for a moment.

"Oh!" she said. "I love this movie. Sidney Poitier has such a presence. And the theme song!" She began to sing: "To Sir, with Love . . ." She walked over to the counter and poured herself a glass of bourbon. "You want anything?"

"I'll take a glass, thank you."

After adding ice cubes to both of their glasses, she walked back over to him and handed him his drink.

"Say, what's this Shane tells me about you wanting to attend UCLA film school?"

"Well, it's just kind of a silly pipe dream, really."

"No, no, no, don't think that way. Anything is possible. Do you want to go there or not?"

"You kidding me? It would be like a dream come true."

"Is that so? Do you have any idea how many people I've worked with at that institution? How many people I've helped to the point where several of them owe me favors? This is one of the beauties of my profession."

Devon blinked and took a sip, intrigued.

"You let me know when you are ready to submit an application. You write a heartfelt letter about yourself and why you want to be a filmmaker, and then you give all of that shit to me, you hear me?"

Devon nodded. "Really, Mrs. Tollefson, I don't want to impose or—"

"Fuck that. It's no imposition. Things like this need to happen more. I'd rather go to bat for you than for some fucking trust-fund Partridge family prick from Encino Hills who never worked a day in his life for anything. Trust me, this is the way to do this 'cause, in this town, it isn't enough to just have talent. In this town, you have to know people who know people who then might know people."

They toasted, glasses clinking so hard it knocked his drink out of his hand and onto the floor. They laughed.

It would take him almost a year to get his application in, but Mrs. Tollefson stayed true to her word. Devon was accepted to UCLA film school in the fall of 1990. Film school truly had become his second dream after painfully letting go of athletics. Devon believed in himself, believed that he had what it took to tell a compelling story.

But first, he had to return home and face the music.

The Hartford Hammer

August 1990

Bantam Bolt Touches Down Hard in Miami

By Pierce Halloway

To many college-football fans, James Payne is a relatively new phenomenon—a running back and wide receiver who, in his freshman year, came off the bench halfway through the season and nearly shattered several rushing records held by previous full-time starters.

Some of you are only now coming to recognize his greatness. But for so many of us Connecticans who care about sports, the name James Payne, a.k.a. Bantam Bolt, has been with us since he was in middle school, where he and his younger brother, Devon, dominated the stats pages for nearly six years before the tragic car accident that would remove Devon completely from the sports world and have serious emotional effects on James.

I sat down with James at a local coffee shop in New Haven to talk about his sports life, his family, that horrific car crash, and what he expects his future to look like both at the University of Miami and, eventually, in the NFL. Below is an edited version of our conversation.

PH: First, let me say congratulations on a stellar sophomore season at the University of Miami. You produced numbers there that anyone will have a hard time surpassing. How did that feel?

JP: Thank you, thank you very much. Honestly, it felt great, you know. I always knew I was capable of it. It just took Coach believing in me, really. But I always knew, given my chance, I would shine.

PH: Let's talk about that for a minute, because although he recruited you pretty heavily, you had to earn back Coach Whittier's respect after the whole Sigma House scandal. What can you share with us about all that?

JP: Honestly, Pierce, there isn't much to share there. I know I'm a man and all, but sometimes that little kid is still inside of me, you know? And when that little kid has a chance to come out and celebrate? Look out! So that's what happened to me. I let my inner kid come out, and I let my teammates down in the process. What more can I say?

PH: I just want to be clear with our readers who may not be all that familiar with just what went down. You and your teammate Lindell Braddock were at a party at Sigma House over the holiday weekend, and several members of that house reported the next day that several of their rooms had been raided and burglarized and that the two of you had been seen loading several boxes into a parked car just hours earlier. Some items reported stolen were later found in Braddock's dorm suite, and the team released him following a brief investigation. You were given a penalty of a one-game suspension.

JP: Yeah, that's pretty much the extent of it, and I would really just like to put this ugly, immature chapter of my life behind me.

PH: Understandable. Can you maybe say in one sentence what you learned from the entire experience?

JP: One sentence, huh? We all have the power to learn from our mistakes and become better people in the process.

PH: Fair enough. Well then, let's move on to some good news I just learned recently: you are going to be a father!

JP: That I am, sir. That I am.

PH: You and your high-school girlfriend are going to tie the knot next month in an outdoor ceremony on the coast. First off, congratulations. How does that all feel?

JP: Thank you, man. I really appreciate that. It's a mix of feelings, you know? It's beautiful, but I won't lie, there's also a level of fear. It's a little overwhelming. It's exciting, yet scary. None of this was planned. In fact, my girl, Gina, was in school herself studying for a degree in hotel and restaurant management when we found out that she was three months along. We had to really stop and ask ourselves—are we truly ready for this type of responsibility at this point in our lives? The short answer was yes. We are so strong together that we are ready for anything and everything. We always knew it would be something we would eventually do anyway, so why not now? Both of us have bright futures, and we hope this is the first of many kids.

PH: Let's get into that future. Word on the street is this may be your last season as a Hurricane before turning pro. Care to share if there is any validity to that rumor?

JP: You know, Pierce, I'm not sure just where you heard that particular rumor. I can tell you, having been around this game a while now, you always hear crazy things that may or may not have any basis in reality. You remember back when I was in high school, there were all those rumors that I was considering jumping ship early and declaring for the NBA draft, which was just a crazy thought.

PH: I believe that was more wishful thinking among many members of our city's sports community, to be quite honest with you. But you wouldn't be the first to make such a transition after your junior season. Has the thought ever crossed your mind?

JP: Lots of thoughts have crossed my mind, man.

PH: Playing it coy?

JP: I ain't trying to be coy. I'm just saying, give a brother space to weigh his options.

PH: Want to know what Coach Whittier said when I asked him about it?

JP: Can't wait to hear.

PH: I quote: "That young man is filled with so much talent and God-given ability, one would almost have to question his sanity if he wasn't considering it."

JP: Coach is a very supportive guy.

PH: And here is what Offensive Coach Welsh had to say: "Given the nature of this game and the richness of this landscape, I'd bet my house and my daughter's college savings that this year will be the kid's swan song here."

JP: Not sure I even know what a swan song is.

PH: Bottom line—he's saying he'd bet it all that you're going pro sooner than later. Your response?

JP: I don't believe betting one's child's college savings is a wise move.

PH: Clearly, you aren't going to give up much here. Let's move on. On the personal front, it was nearly two years ago to this date that you and your brother, Devon, also a highly recruited athlete at the time, got into that horrible car accident that left a young girl dead and your brother *paralyzed for life. Any thoughts or reflections on this somber anniversary?*

JP: First, my thoughts and prayers are always with the family of Hannah Baldwin. Nothing will ever be able to replace what was taken from them that day. Devon and I—Devon in particular—have done our best to grapple with all that took place that day and the repercussions. There will always be a certain level of guilt and shame there. I know Devon feels it deeply, processes it all the time.

PH: Do you two ever talk about that night?

JP: Honestly, not that often. I mean, in the beginning, maybe a little bit more, but we both went through therapy to try and process and manage a lot of that trauma that we experienced, and I believe we both came to the conclusion that we can't dwell on things. We can't keep rehashing it and wishing we had done things differently or what have you, you know? We had to move on and accept that fate dealt many of us a terrible blow that day. But you can't wallow in sorrow. You have to keep moving forward. Like I said earlier, make mistakes and learn from them.

PH: Would you say you've both been successful at that? I mean, you certainly have made a great deal of strides forward. If I may ask, where is Devon's life at this moment? He didn't want to speak to me for this piece, and I got the sense there was some anger there.

JP: One of the best things I learned from my time in therapy *was that we all process pain in different ways. And there is no one way that is better than any other. It's just different. We are all such complicated people. Since the time me and Devon were kids, we always had different ways of seeing the world, and it often caused a certain tension between us. As you can imagine, the accident heightened some of that tension and, in some ways, made our relationship more difficult than it ever was. I got to go on and continue to live this dream, and in many ways, he had to start life all over again. But I love my brother, and I root for him every day. That will never change. And he has done a great job of readjusting. You know he's getting ready to leave for the West Coast? He's going to be a film major at UCLA. Dude's gonna be the next Orson Welles or something.*

PH: It must make your parents so proud. I know your dad has told me that he hopes someday someone makes a documentary about your family. He thinks you are all special in your own ways.

JP: I heard that documentary idea. We used to joke we could call it The Pain of Being Raised Payne. *But that's just a joke. We all doing all right, I suppose. We just a family like many other families, you know? Ups and downs, victories and defeats.*

PH: That may be, but having known all of you throughout the years, I would say the victories have greatly outweighed the defeats. Starting with your parents, I would say exceptional *is a word that comes to mind when you think about the Payne family.*

JP: You are being generous.

PH: Okay, so back to sports then. Let's just say that this could be your last season as a student athlete. Is there any one team you look at in the pros and think, "Yeah, they would be a good fit for me?"

JP: Are there teams I always dreamed of growing up that I would love to play for? Yeah, there's a couple of those teams. But also, if I'm lucky enough to ever get selected to play for a professional team, then I'm just going to embrace that opportunity and ride that good fortune.

PH: Coy about not answering the question again?

JP: I suppose you could see it that way. But since we don't get to choose our fates, I don't see what good answering that question would do me or anyone reading this.

PH: How about we close out on a question you can't dodge around and equivocate?

JP: I wasn't aware that's what I was doing.

PH: What did you have for lunch this afternoon?

JP: I believe it could have been a roast-beef sandwich. Could have been a slice of pizza. Could have been a chicken burrito. I'd rather not go too much into detail on it.

PH: It sounds to me like whenever your athletic career is eventually over, and I hope that's not for a long time now, but it sounds to me like you are ripe for a second career in politics.

JP: Senator Payne, that could have a nice ring to it.

PH: Maybe go alongside a few championship rings?

JP: I like your thinking, sir.

The Olive Branch

You are constantly amazed at how much time you spend wondering where things went wrong. And it seems to you like a lot of things went wrong. This is not a recent development. It seems like things have been consistently going wrong for as long as you can remember.

But really, are things going all that wrong?

You have just gotten off a cross-country flight where, as usual, you flew first class (yes, you had to sit next to an obsequious and arrogant philosophy professor, but anything is better than coach). You are waiting for your daughter to pick you up outside the airport and take you to your five-star hotel in Beverly Hills. Many observers would say things can't possibly be that bad. But you feel you deserve better. You have always felt you deserve better. Deep down inside, you know you are a snob. You are part of a Black elite class that is proud of the fact that when you were younger, you could sometimes pass for white. You've tasted privilege. You won't look back.

When your daughter gets to the terminal, she looks tired. You aren't too concerned, because you know her to be one of the hardest working people you've ever met, and from what you've heard and read, medical school is a bitch and a half. When she pulls you in close for a tender embrace, you have a hard time returning the sentiment. You have been this way a long time, and most all your children are accustomed to it. And for whatever reason, you never really warmed to Roxanne. Or

Kassandra. Or Margeaux. Truth be told, you never truly found love for a child until James came along.

Dearest James. Just his name is enough to fill your chest with thorns. James. He is what has brought you here to California, a state you have never had any appreciation for. It is James who has you reaching out to the child you liked least of all. You hate to admit that about Devon, but it is the plain truth. And the worst part is, both you and Devon know it. He told you he knew it the last time the two of you spoke on the phone. He tried to dissuade you from making this trip. He told you, "Stay put, Ma. Your number-one son needs you a lot more than I do. And I'm not changing my mind." You wanted to respond that you don't have a number-one son. But you didn't. You couldn't deny it then, and you can't deny it now. You were never a good liar. Your husband has always been a good liar, but you? Not so much. You envy and resent your husband for this, but that is another story. Old water under the bridge.

As you drive through the dense, constipated traffic of a city that seems eternally dry and filthy, you try to pay attention to what your first child is telling you. She is droning on about the difficulties of medical school, the endless sleepless nights, the heartache of residencies. You don't actually care that much. She mentions that she has been dating a chiropractor, and that piques your interest just a bit. She says he is Jewish, and that sends any curiosity you may have had out the window, smashing against the hot freeway like the cigarette you just discarded. It's not that you dislike Jews, you just don't love them. You blame it on Ira Schulmann, the boss you had that summer in high school when you worked at the makeup counter at Woolworth's. He treated you like dirt. He once sent you home early because he said he could smell you menstruating. He thought it was funny to call you "Lena Horny." Once, after he helped you with a customer (help you didn't particularly need or ask for), an older Wasp woman, who looked a little like the Wicked

Witch of the West, turned to you when he finally walked away from the counter and said, "Your boss seems like a real asshole."

"Ma'am, you don't know the half."

"Yeah, no, trust me, I get it. Hitler may have gotten just a little carried away."

The two of you laughed. You laughed because you wanted people to like you. You laughed because it was polite to laugh at an older person's jokes. You laughed because challenging others has never really been your thing.

You didn't realize at the time that this was how the poison got baked into the cake.

Your hotel room is just as you like it. It smells fresh, has a decent view of the California hills. It has fancy soaps and amenities. You can never imagine going back to being poor. You would rather die. Once when you were kids, you and your sister stayed with your aunt in a rundown motel outside of Memphis. You saw cockroaches and rats every day. It stayed with you. You take your firstborn child to dinner at a luxurious restaurant, and over dessert you discuss the topic you have been avoiding all day—how to approach the last-born child. How do you get him to see reason?

"He's angry, Mom."

"Everybody is angry, Roxy."

"Yeah, well, that may be, but I really think it would behoove us all to understand just *why* Devon is so angry. It's important."

"More important than his brother's life?"

Just saying those words causes your eyes to fill with smoky tears. You put your hand to your chest to steady yourself.

"Anger clouds judgment, Mom. He feels deceived, betrayed. You need to approach him with contrition."

"I raised him, Roxy. Poured my soul into him for twenty years. I don't owe anyone an apology for anything. He needs to understand there is a lot more at stake here than his hurt feelings."

"I think that attitude is a mistake, Mom."

"I appreciate your opinion."

You are lying. Some small part of you believes that this daughter of yours, the smartest of all your children, is correct. But you have stubborn pride. You will not consider pandering to your youngest. He has disappointed you on so many levels, and you genuinely believe he owes you this one. Owes the entire family. You will not pander, and you will not plead. He must listen to reason. You were in labor with him for six hours.

When your daughter hugs you goodbye in the hotel lobby, you place a hand on her shoulder. You lock eyes with her. She looks much more like her father than she ever did you. You realize now you've resented that. She pleads with you to reconsider what she has said. She reminds you that three thousand miles is a long way to go to fall short of your goal, and you nod and say you will seriously consider it. At the hotel bar, you have two cognacs, and when a well-dressed male, close to you in age, asks you what brings you to town, you lie and tell him you are thinking of purchasing a home in the area and are looking at several places over the next two days. The man, Gordon Summerlin, gives you his card and tells you he'd love to buy you dinner some night if you are up for it. Gordon Summerlin is a high-level executive at a powerful media company based in Atlanta. Gordon Summerlin has kind gray eyes that complement his head of silver hair quite nicely. Not too shabby for a white guy. You shake his hand and thank him.

In your room, you fall asleep to an old film on cable that starred Diana Ross and Billy Dee Williams. You joked with your husband in the early days that the only man you would ever leave him for was Billy Dee Williams. That was long before you realized he had fathered two kids in France. Perhaps another in Japan. Perhaps another in Germany. You would never leave your husband, but the idea you would be faithful to him is funny. And sad.

In the morning, you cry in the shower. You cannot stop thinking about James. The last time you saw him, he looked thin and haggard. Your husband didn't seem to think it was that serious an issue, but that was eight months ago, before kidney failure began to set in. You each had a family member who suffered from type 2 diabetes. You never suspected it could happen to one of your own children. You thought only excessively fat people got diabetes, and the only obese person in your immediate family was your uncle Gus, who did eventually die from his condition. But Uncle Gus and James could not have been more physically disparate. How could this happen? And why did it have to happen to your favorite child? You would never ask God such questions. You stopped believing in that nonsense shortly after your mother failed to rise from the bottom of the lake in a timely manner. And even before that, you had your doubts. And yet lately, you found yourself thinking in quiet moments of desperation, *Please, Lord, if you exist, save my son. Help James heal.*

Devon has asked that you meet him at a coffee shop near his school, which has frustrated you because you were hoping he would come to you. He has learned to drive. You know this because your husband paid for his specially equipped car, fitted with hand controls and an easy-to-rotate steering wheel. You didn't want to rent a car, because you hate driving in big cities, so you hop into a taxi and hit the freeway. His insistence on doing this all his way (despite the fact that you flew three thousand miles to get here) fills you with a sense of dread. Nothing has ever been easy with this child.

You are wearing a freshly purchased light-blue pantsuit and chic designer sunglasses. You think you look like an actress, the name of whom escapes you. She was a bigger deal in the '60s, maybe the first Black actress to star in her own TV show. You wish you had a better memory. You try to remember the last time you had real affection for this son. You recall a time when he was in junior high school, and he was singing in the chorus for the annual Christmas pageant. For about thirty seconds, he had a solo, and you remember distinctly the way the spotlight shone down on him and framed his face, a picture of angelic bliss. He was always handsome. Always charming. One of the few things both sons shared.

But the twins were unexpected. Unwanted, really. They came at a time when you were very much over the magic of parenting. It wasn't their fault, but it wasn't yours either. They were your husband's last dash at manhood. Or so you thought at the time.

The taxi driver, a man with a heavy Eastern European accent, calls you madam, which always makes you feel good. On the freeway, most drive at speeds that you are uncomfortable with, and you are relieved when he finally exits and you are on side streets. You struggle with just how people choose to live in a place like this—so charmless, so plastic, so shallow. Westwood, the neighborhood where UCLA is located, feels so much better, more like a real city. At least Devon made a good choice there. When you exit the taxi, the driver hands you his card and tells you to call him if you need a return trip.

You spend a few moments outside the coffee shop, looking in at your youngest son. He sits in the center at a small table. There is hustle and bustle all around him, but he seems oblivious to it. He is slumped over, and at first, you think he is asleep, until you realize he is deeply focused on reading something. Still, he looks uncomfortable. He has always looked uncomfortable since the night you showed up at the emergency room and sat by his hospital bed for hours. Numerous tubes protruded from his body, and you were not sure he would ever wake up and speak again. You remember being intensely concerned, but also profoundly relieved because you had just learned your first son would be just fine. Once, long ago, you had asked a favorite cousin if she preferred one of her children over another, and she said every mother does. It's one of those realities we just don't talk about.

You realize as you open the door to the coffee shop it is very possible you have been a terrible mother.

You go to hug Devon, and he extends his hand to shake it. It's an awkward moment, but you move past it. He invites you to sit down and offers to buy you a drink. He saunters up to the counter to get your espresso, and it is apparent that the staff there know and like him. You look around at several students, some studying, some simply socializing. One young woman sits with two adults, who appear to be her parents. In the nearly two years he has been a student, you have never visited Devon here. You have checked in periodically by phone and sent money whenever he asked for it. You depended on Roxanne for updates on him, but she has had very little contact with Devon since his expulsion from the rehabilitation center. What exactly happened, you don't know, as you never wanted all the sordid details, which Roxanne told you were quite shameful. You know he was involved in selling drugs and that a woman died. That would mark the second time Devon was closely linked to the death of a woman. It is a good thing you don't believe in hell.

While he is away, you take a glance at his reading material. There are several pages sprawled out, all typed. Some of it appears to be dialogue and some of it appears to be stage directions and camera angles. In the upper-left corner of every page are the words *The Olive Branch*. You must remember to ask him about it.

When he comes back and places the cup of espresso before you, you aren't quite sure why, but you feel slightly overcome with emotion. It's something about the way he carries himself. His moves are deft, almost elegant, and you are impressed to see that he has grown so much since those early months of home rehabilitation when he could not even get out of bed on his own, and home-care attendants had to bathe and dress him daily. He is not that same scared teenager who depended on everyone for nearly everything. He is far from that. His muscles are more toned, his skin clearer. He sports a mustache, a new feature. His father had the same mustache at his age. Genes are an uncanny thing.

You want to tell him you are proud of him, but instead you ask him how film school is going. You ask him if he is going to be the next Francis Ford Coppola.

"Don't get me started," he responds. "I'm about to flunk out."

At first you think he is joking. He goes on to tell you a story, a story that clearly has him frustrated and resentful. You don't really understand much of it, but you listen, though truly uninterested, and hope he cannot tell. Sometimes while he is talking, your mind wanders to James, and you are instantly reminded that you don't have much time. Here is as much as you can decipher of the story:

Apparently, he has been hard at work on his thesis film. He and a crew of fellow students have been shooting a short film on thirty-five millimeter. He has been filming all over the city and even spent two days in the desert at one point. The film is an existential study on depression, sadness, longing, and ultimately forgiveness. The main character is played by himself, and they were just about finished with the shooting portion when something horrible happened. One of his assistant directors—the person tasked with transporting the film to and from the lab—made a ridiculously amateur mistake. This person was known to abuse cocaine on the set, and Devon is sure this had something to do with it. The AD stopped off at a local shopping market and left several canisters of film, the majority of them containing what they had shot over the last few weeks, in the back seat of his car while he went in the market to get a meatball sub and a six-pack. It was an incredibly hot day, and he left his back windows open. When he returned, he found his entire car had been ransacked. Every canister of film had been opened and dumped on the pavement several feet away.

This was the part that caught you up a bit. You found it confusing, but from what you can gather, it is extremely detrimental to film to be exposed to sunlight for a certain period of time. It appears what this

AD did was ruin several weeks' worth of filming, and there was no way to go back and get all that material again with their limited resources. Imagine, Devon tells you, if an author had finished 180 pages of a 200-page novel, and then 150 of those pages were destroyed in a fire and there was no backup copy to it *and* the publisher was demanding the entire finished novel in a week.

"So basically, we're all fucked," he said. You don't recall him ever using harsh language with you in the past. "This idiot AD, who I was once close friends with, has put all of us in jeopardy of failing this entire semester all because he was too stupid to roll up his window. We're all heartbroken. And frankly, I don't know if I want to continue on. Filmmaking is a brutal process, and the odds that someone like me actually makes it to the next level is pretty damned rare. I have no idea what I'm supposed to do with my life now."

"Surely there is some way to go back and fix this, Devon. Maybe there is a method to restore film that has had this happen to it?"

The way he looks at you makes it clear you have no idea what you are talking about. You feel sheepish and stupid, and you make a fumbling attempt to change the subject.

"Are you dating anyone?"

You get another look from him, this one more condemning than the previous one. You get flustered. You realize you are just dancing around the real topic.

"Yeah, right," he says snidely. "There's a whole line of women going around the block just waiting to date someone like me."

There is a little bit of pain in this last statement, and your heart compresses some of it at the realization that this comment is really about something else. This comment is about Gina, and the heartbreak that came for him as a result of numerous tiny betrayals that much of the family was complicit in. You let out a hushed exhale, as you already know your trip here was a waste of time. Still, you want to—need to—address it with him. You came this far, and so much is on the line. You take a last gulp of espresso and are relieved when he speaks up first.

"Listen, Mom . . . I've already had two conversations with Roxy about this in the last two weeks. You know I adore Roxy—"

"And she adores you, son."

"Well, I think the shine has come off me in the last couple of years, but whatever."

"Devon, you can't be glib about this."

"Who's being glib?"

"I mean, you can't just wave this off as whatever. It's not whatever. Your brother's life is on the line here."

"That is out of my control."

"Devon, all we are asking is that you just get tested. Just drive down to the medical labs at the hospital here—what is it, two blocks away—and get tested. We've all been tested already, and the reality is female-to-male kidney donation is very rarely successful and not considered a healthy choice for the recipient."

"Wow, listen to you. Still watching *General Hospital*, I see. You're up on the lingo."

You resist an all-too-familiar urge to slap him across the face.

"What about Michel?" he asks, knowing the emotion it will evoke in you.

The name causes you to recoil. You will never recognize the light-skinned boy with the hideous accent or his sister. They are as real to you as the Easter Bunny or the tooth fairy.

"He isn't a match. And your father is too old. You are the closest realistic candidate, Devon. You are James's best hope."

You study his face to see just how those words land. You believed they were powerful. His face does not reflect that. You feel the tears rushing to the shore of your eyes as fresh images of James in the hospital bed emerge. He looked so much thinner.

"How ironic, that I would be James's best hope."

"Devon, please."

"I know, Mom . . . I know James is the apple of your eye. I know that you worship him above any of the rest of us—"

"That isn't true, Devon. You need to get that no—"

"Please, spare me, Ma. Please. I've talked about this with Alexis, with Dahlia. Hell, Kass even alluded to it once. It's always been so obvious. And that's okay. I really don't care about any of that. I've done a lot of growing up here in this city. I've had the chance to reflect. I've had *a lot* of time to reflect. You know *why* I've had so much time to reflect? Because I've been alone, Mom. I've been a-*lone*! Do you know what that has been like? Do you have any idea?"

You stare into your empty espresso cup. You've heard this story one too many times, and it sickens you to have to sit through it again.

"And the funny thing is, it didn't start out here. I've been alone since I got back home from Silver Mountain. You know what happened when I got back home from Silver Mountain? I learned that most of my family was conspiring to keep me in the dark about the fact that my brother, while I was recovering in a hospital bed, pursued, impregnated, and married the girl who was supposed to be the love of my life. How do you think that felt, huh? To learn of their lovely little private wedding ceremony on the coast in Newport, the one you and Dad both attended, by the way, while I was in the hospital for the third time that year with a urinary-tract infection. Any idea how that kind of revelation can settle into the soul and harden the heart, Mom? Any at all?"

You look into his eyes the whole time he is talking, and you are painfully aware that there is a blackness there in the space that once held some hope and optimism. When he was a child, his eyes were light brown, like melted caramel. Life has changed him, as you know it does all of us. But the worst part? You know in some way you have contributed to the blackening within. You have played a role in the filling of that dark place. Now his eyes remind you of the bottom of a lake, which makes you shudder.

You know now it wasn't right. So little of it was fair to him. But you also know that much of it, all of it, was simply out of your control. You didn't make Devon get into a car in an inebriated state and take the wheel. You didn't make James fall in love with Gina. You didn't make Gina fall in love with James. It was not your decision that it was best nobody told Devon about their relationship until he was in a "better space to handle it." That was all your husband's idea. When one person wins, it means another must lose. In this scenario, Devon clearly saw himself as the loser. It was a sad thing for you to acknowledge. You were happy for James and Gina the whole time, but you were not fully aware that their happiness came at a real cost. It saddens you how much damage has been done. How much you looked away from. How much your husband looked away from. You begin to wonder why you seemed to bear the brunt of the hostility. Weren't you just following Harold's lead?

"I'm sorry," you say. You know it's too late. Fate will play its hand again. There is nothing you can say or do now. The son that you loved the least will not be swayed. He has no love in his heart for the son you cherish. Nothing will change this. The two of you sit in silence for a bit while life goes on around you. Somewhere, a machine is grinding coffee beans with no regard for the agony the sound is causing everyone around it. You have another espresso, but you are not able to taste it. Your tongue is heavy with the weight of shame.

When the two of you agree to part ways, he walks you (rolls you, really) to your awaiting taxi. You don't bother with the awkward hug goodbye this time. You shake hands as if you just closed a business transaction. You can't think of anything better to say so you say, "Good luck with *The Olive Branch*."

You watch him strain to smile. You can't remember the last time he smiled at you with sincerity. It's okay. You don't deserve it.

"The olive branch has rotted," he says. "Maybe I'll transfer to UConn, get an advertising degree. I've always been good at selling things."

You can't tell if he's joking or not. It doesn't really matter. You know this is the last time you will ever make a true effort to have a conversation with this son. There is damage words have no ability to repair. You ask the taxi driver to wait before he pulls away, and you watch as your least-favorite son struggles to push his wheelchair across the street amid a throng of students. He seems alone in the crowd. Nobody else looks like him. It hits you that the isolation he feels often must be deafening.

When you return to your hotel room, the first thing you do is call Roxanne and let her know how it went. Roxanne does not sound surprised. She also sounds emotionally spent. She attempts to make arrangements to come by for dinner tonight, but you wave her off, telling her you really need to be alone. Instead, you make plans for brunch tomorrow before she takes you to the airport. You hop in the shower, stand in the hot water for nearly twenty minutes, and when you get out, you rub shea butter all over yourself. You stare at your body in the full-length mirror. You have held up well over the years. Your breasts are still impressive to you. You are afraid to be alone tonight. You put on a sexy skirt and blouse.

You call Gordon Summerlin to see if he wants to have drinks, and he is at the lobby bar in forty-five minutes. Over dry martinis, he asks you if you had any luck finding a place, and only then do you remember the original fabrication. You tell him that you looked at three beach houses but will need to return at a later date to look at more. He tells you when you return, he would love to take you out for a night on the town. He is so earnest when he puts his hand on your knee that you place your palm atop his, and your fingers entwine. He has soft, thick fingers like sausages. After the third round of martinis, he tells you he bets the sunset would look gorgeous from your balcony. You discover that he is right, but you don't see the entire sun go down because he is kneeling on the balcony, face up your skirt, going down on you, and when he is done, you take his hand and lead him to the bed. You straddle him and make him say your name with every thrust of your hips. If he doesn't say it loud enough, you slap him across the face. You can tell he likes this. He likes it a lot. He pleads, but you don't allow him to spend the night, telling him you have an early flight.

At the terminal, before you start to board, Roxanne holds you close and seeks to remind you that there are other ways things can turn out. James has been on a kidney-donor waiting list for several months now, and that may produce something positive. You nod and hear yourself say mechanically, "It will turn out the way it turns out, sweetheart. It is out of our hands now."

The next time you are in the same room with Roxanne and Devon, it will be in late November, in a small church, after James has succumbed to end-stage renal failure. Your favorite son will be suited, lying in a casket, looking more peaceful than you can ever recall him looking in the past six months. During the ceremony, listening to the pastor's empty words, you will turn to see your only living son's face. He is sitting next to Alexis and looking down at the floor. He is not crying. You doubt he has ever shed a tear about this entire situation and wonder what he is thinking. Is it possible for him to feel any guilt in this moment? You stare at him for a good two minutes or so, willing him to look back at you, wanting to see if the blackness still resides in his eyes, or if it has been replaced. But he doesn't look back at you, and you take that as a sign.

You look around at the rest of your children. You even acknowledge the French ones. Every one of them appears to be in their own world, none of them returning your gaze. You turn to Gina, the daughter-in-law you grew to appreciate but could never truly respect. She never deserved James, did she? She holds the hand of your two-year-old granddaughter, who, to your delight, does bear a strong resemblance to her father. It fills you with a purple desolation, like a slow-healing bruise, to realize that should any of these remaining children of yours drop dead tomorrow, you would not feel anything close to the utter melancholy you feel in this moment now. None of them will ever matter to you as much as your precious James mattered. These are the facts. You are not ashamed of it any longer.

BOOK TWO

THE LATER PAYNES

A NEW MILLENNIUM

A Reunion in Berlin

I absolutely should have known better. I'm not a public transportation kind of guy. Hell, I grew up in a tiny provincial town in Northern Connecticut. I learned how to drive when I was thirteen. My sister, Colleen, swears she knew how to drive by the time she was seven. If I had to guess, I'd say I've been on a subway maybe three times in my life. And two out of three of those times, I was with a friend who knew New York well. The one time I was alone, I managed to get on the wrong train (or was it that I got off at the wrong stop?) and wound up in the Bronx, near Yankee Stadium, when I should have been in Queens, at Shea Stadium. Why I ever thought I could manage the train system in a foreign country, by my lonesome, is a mystery to me. Well, not that much of a mystery when I really think about it. I had a strong incentive to challenge myself. I wanted to impress her—woman on whom I'd had a crush since we were in high school and whom I hadn't seen or heard from in close to a dozen years but had always wondered about.

So there I stood, looking like the major tourist that I was, staring absentmindedly at the public train map in the Warschauer Strasse station, trying to figure out just where in the hell I was. It's one thing to be lost in New York City, where most of the people around you speak your native tongue and, worse comes to worst, you can hop in a cab and get to your ultimate destination. But no, I was in Berlin. When I looked around me, all I saw were Europeans as far as the eye could see, with the occasional Turk or African thrown into the mix to add color to the blank slate.

"Jesus Christ, I'm screwed," I mumbled.

I'm also dreadful at reading maps. Always have been, so that wasn't gonna work. It had been raining steadily all day. In fact, for the entire three days I had been in Berlin, either it was raining, it was on the *verge* of raining, or it had just *finished* raining. Were it not for my assignment, I might never have left my hotel room. But there I was, with water dripping from my fedora, trying to decipher at which of these stops I was meant to be. Senefelderplatz sounded familiar, but then so did Spittelmarkt. So did Stadtmitte. Why didn't I do a better job of writing these things down? You would think that, as a journalist, I would have that as part of my skill set. But no. I was clever enough to get a master's degree, but when it really mattered, I was not that smart. College doesn't teach you everything. People who we label "survivors" are called such because they possess an organic strength. If I were Robinson Crusoe, I would have hung myself from the nearest tree posthaste.

It was an overly concerned, gregarious police officer who proved to be my savior. A slightly chubby fellow with a face straight out of a barbershop quartet and a head of curly brown hair, he, and his colleague, approached me as I gawked at the map. In that unmistakable World War II SS guard accent, he asked me if I needed any help. When my eyes met his, he knew right away. His partner, a gruff-looking woman who had probably once worked as a physical-fitness trainer before landing this gig, laughed me off and continued down the platform and engaged some teenagers who looked to be members of a punk-rock band.

Luckily for me, not only could I recall the name of the restaurant where she had said we were going to meet up, but I also remembered the name of the town. It reminded me of an old fraternity brother, a German kid who was the star of our soccer team. I recited it to the officer the best I could, and he knew exactly where it was. In broken

English, he laughed and told me he could understand how I could become confused.

"All those *s*'s," he snickered before pulling out his map and going over a few details with me. Apparently, I had gotten off too soon and was four stops off the mark. Didn't surprise me. I've always been an early finisher, and I've paid the price for it. I needed to be at the Nollendorfplatz station. The kind officer walked to the ticket machine, issued me a new ticket, and saw me on to the next train that pulled in. I prayed it was going in the direction the officer had told me to go. When I heard the conductor say "Nollendorfplatz!" I heaved a sigh of relief.

Nollendorfplatz was one of those outdoor stations in the middle of a bustling city, the kind where anxiety-ridden people like myself get out at and immediately begin to hyperventilate due to the sheer mass of people and places. I took a deep breath and followed the crowd. I just knew I was going to wander down some back road and get mugged by a street-smart gang of soccer hooligans. I could already see the newspaper headline, written in English for some peculiar reason:

American Sportswriter Found Dead in Berlin Alley, Clutching Copy of *Sports Illustrated* and Drinking What He Thought Was a Latte but Was Actually Coca-Cola with Warm Milk

I wondered what my funeral back home would look like, when I saw her standing there—like every writer has ever attempted to write poetically about the North Star—waiting for me with that same Margeaux Payne smile I recalled so well.

At first, I was concerned she might not remember me at all. We had taken several classes together at Lincoln High. Once in Miss McPherson's English lit class, we were paired up to act out a scene from *A Doll's House*. I remember how fortunate I felt to draw her name. All the guys in class had wanted to be paired with Margeaux every time one of those assignments came up, but it was I who hit the lottery that time.

I don't even know what the scene was about. Didn't understand it then, still don't now, but I can be certain she was stellar in it. She was great at just about everything she did. And me? Well, I was most unremarkable. At that age, I just kind of floated through school, joining the chess club, the school newspaper club, the yearbook club, the overweight-Dungeons-and-Dragons-playing-dork's club. I worked four days a week in the cafeteria, but I bet you'd be hard pressed to find a student that could tell you an amusing story about me. I was that guy who never left an impression anywhere I went. That odd ability to not affect anyone has stayed with me even today.

I would never be one of those people who stood out. I realized it early on and resigned myself to it. I was content to sit back and watch people like Margeaux shine. And shine she did. She was a phenomenal dancer, a melodic singer, even played a little hoops (though her brothers were the real stars in that area). And to top it all off, in our senior year, she won the prestigious Ms. Bantam Award for outstanding community service. She got to go to the governor's mansion and everything. There were rumors around that she was romantically involved with a well-respected drama teacher at school, but I never believed them (though, oddly, he did get fired a few months later).

What I do know for a fact is she was the first woman I was ever in love with. That she was browner than deer fur and I was whiter than mayonnaise never once occurred to me.

And so, last week when I was back in Bantam, giving a lecture at the community college, I was elated to run into her mother, Camille. I placed her in her midsixties, but through some rare gift of genes and magic, she still looked as regal and energetic as she did way back when. She had approached me to congratulate me on my book and to let me know that, since I was going to be in Berlin, I had to call her daughter and get together. As you can imagine, once I heard that daughter was Margeaux, I nearly fell off my seat with euphoria.

"Margeaux is in Berlin, eh? What took her there?" I asked, doing my best to mask my excitement.

"Oh, you know Marge. She's doing something she believes is artsy and creative, anything to keep from doing real work. I think, last I heard, she was a part of some puppet theater troupe of all things."

She said *puppet theater* the way some conservatives say *liberal*, and I laughed, already somewhat envious and very curious. Margeaux Payne had not taken the easy way out. Of all the Payne children, she was easily the most compelling. And that is coming from someone who wrote a cover piece for our local newspaper on her brother James while still in college.

Margeaux had dared to be special. I tried to imagine what she would be like today. If her mother was any indication, she would look the same, her features frozen by that beneficent Payne gene. I had seen James just before he died, the poor fellow. He had taken a very bad turn, and it was clear to all around him that it was just a matter of time.

I could hardly contain my excitement at the thought of seeing Margeaux again. Standing there outside that train station, watching her walk toward me, it was like we were back in English lit class, only I was somewhat thicker, somewhat more serious. She was still her same old lighthearted, cheerful, lovely-to-lay-eyes-on self. My blood turned to warm syrup. Margeaux Payne had found me at an obscure Berlin train station. I was going to be all right. Immediately, she took my hand in hers.

"Look at you, Pierce. You haven't changed a bit, have you?" she said, embracing me with her free arm.

She was a few inches taller than I was, and I smelled her lotion as we hugged. It had coconut in it. Her hair was moist from either the rain or the shower. I did not know. Did not care. I was just supremely grateful to be there with her in this place where we were both strangers.

"And you are still a great actor," I replied.

She hadn't let go of my hand yet, and I was happy to realize she had no intention of doing so as we began walking down the street. I felt like a teenager on my first date. But this was no trip to the town mall to see a Sylvester Stallone action flick with Millicent Bucknell, mouth full of braces.

On the way to the restaurant, she filled me in on all that had gone on to bring her to this point. She had been living in San Francisco the past two years, performing in a few different dance companies, not ever really earning a living but surviving off a generous "Payne grant" before she hooked up with some German puppeteers at a street festival in Berkeley. One thing led to another, and she began a "passionate affair" (was there any other kind of affair with these dramatic types?) with the company's director. He invited her to come back to Berlin with them to work on shows they wanted to bring back to the States that next summer. She shacked up with the director for a few months, and once they split up, she stayed on in the house with his sister and helped with her three children.

"I'm a glorified au pair, a Black Mary Poppins, I tell you!" she exclaimed as she clenched my arm even tighter.

I hung on her every word and am ashamed to admit I was secretly delighted to hear she was no longer living with the director. Why I was happy about it, I am not proud to acknowledge. I am, after all, a somewhat happily married man with two kids myself. Aside from an unremarkable drunken kiss with a coworker at a Christmas party several years ago, I have never been unfaithful to my wife. But something about Margeaux Payne made me forget myself. Something about her took me back to another time, a time when I felt things on a deeper level. As horribly trite and clichéd as it sounds, seeing Margeaux in a foreign country pulsing with culture and energy—well, it reminded me that I was alive.

We got to the restaurant, and I removed her coat before mine. As I hung them on the rack by the front door, I noticed that her coat, a very pretty lime-green wool piece with white furry cuffs, gave off an intoxicating lavender scent. Everything about Margeaux always seemed so alluring. I watched her hug and kiss the hostess, a dainty Asian woman around our age, who wore a lovely purple sari and a matching ribbon in her hair. She and Margeaux chatted briefly in German, which I found impressive. When she introduced me, she went back to English. We were seated by a window, and I looked around the place as Margeaux ordered drinks. It was quaint, the kind of place a team created to look and feel like a room in their own house.

The hostess in purple placed a full glass of iced tea before Margeaux, and the two shared a lingering, somewhat intense look as she walked away from us. It made me think the two of them might prefer to be alone.

"So, do you notice anything special about this place?" she asked, a sly grin on her face, sipping her iced tea through a straw.

I looked around again. It was a small place, ten tables, tops, and we were one of maybe six people there.

"Should I?" I asked. "I'm really terrible at these things."

"Everyone in here is gay. This is the gay district. Lanya, the hostess, owns this place with her brother, Stefan. He and his lover, Antonio, bought this place after Stefan hit the lottery two years ago. Lanya has a lover too, Nicole. She's a teacher in Heidelberg. They only see each other about once a month, so Lanya has a lot of time to flirt. Isn't she just incandescent?"

"I would say *incandescent* is a very good word, yes. Do you know the girlfriend, Nicole?"

"I do, and quite frankly, I don't get it. She's kind of one of these short, butchy things you see riding a motorcycle with blue jeans and a leather jacket, white wifebeater underneath, trying to emulate some *Easy Rider* bullshit. I tell you now, if I was a lesbian, I'd want a lover much more like Lanya. I think I would crave that type of femininity, wouldn't you? Well, it's probably hard for you to say."

Lanya came back with my iced tea, and I attempted to say "thank you" in German. She smiled at me, a condescending "nice-try-Caucasian-American-boy" kind of smile and, after winking at Margeaux, walked away again.

I sipped on my iced tea and thought about the awkwardness of what she'd just said. Had she really asked me to put myself in the place of a lesbian? No one had ever asked me to do that before, and I must have grinned, because she stared at me, a huge smile forming on her still-youthful face.

"Whaaaaaaat?" she asked, reaching across the table and pushing my hand.

"Nothing, nothing. I just—I never had anybody ask me that type of question before, that's all."

"Why, Pierce Halloway, I do believe you are blushing."

She was right. I must have been about as red as a sun-ripened tomato. I looked away to clear my head for a few moments, and when I looked back at her, she was still staring at me. Her mouth was twisted to the side a little, and I could tell she was poised to say something.

"I want to ask you a question," she said, leaning in slightly. Our table rocked a little. "And I want you to do your best to answer me honestly."

"Okay . . . I think I can manage that."

"This is serious stuff, Pierce."

I watched her closely, the way she fingered her glass, the way she collected herself before speaking. The couple next to us, two men who appeared to be close to us in age, were speaking French. Their tone implied they were disagreeing about something.

"My mother. I know you saw her at your book signing. She told me the whole story. But—and this is going to sound odd, I know—did she ask you to check up on me at all?"

I blinked quickly, three times, maybe four. I was thrown by the question. I knew of the recent family history, the troubles the Paynes had endured during James's illness. I knew it better than most, as I had helped write his obituary for the local newspaper. There had been a great deal of unpleasantness at the end. I noted at the funeral many of the family members chose not to sit with Devon. Clearly, familial lines had been drawn. It was all so very sad.

"Well, first, I wasn't doing a book signing. I was giving a lecture."

"A lecture? What do you teach?"

"I don't teach. Not really, anyway. I was speaking to a bunch of journalism students. But to answer your question, no, she didn't ask me any such thing. Why would you think that?"

She scanned my face, my eyes, for a few good seconds. I got the feeling I was being sized up for honesty. She must have concluded that I was up front with her because her brown eyes softened a bit, and her fingers eased their grip on her glass.

"It's just—it's all very strained with so many in my family still, after all this time. I don't suppose you've spoken with any of them since the funeral."

"I saw Michel once briefly in Seattle. It was after one of his shows. He invited me to an after show at a local club, but that really isn't my thing."

"Ah yes, the ever-popular Michel."

"Your mom is the first Payne I've really spoken to in a while. I looked for you there—"

"No, you wouldn't have found me," she said abruptly. I began to sense a shift in the air. The Margeaux who had received me at the train station just twenty minutes ago was now retreating to a darker, less comfortable place. I was both thrown off and fascinated by the transition.

"There's a consensus among my family that after James died, I kind of lost it. That I ostensibly became a basket case, you know? I find it pretty insulting. Especially after receiving my diagnosis."

The waitress came over to take our order, and Margeaux snatched up her menu. She asked the waitress a few quick questions in German and turned back to me.

"I hope you're not a vegan or something horrible like that," she said.

"No, I definitely like my red meat."

"Good. Have you had genuine German bratwurst yet?"

"You know, I actually haven't. I've been sticking to fast-food pizza and burgers since I've been here. I'm not a very adventurous eater."

"Then allow me. You're in for a treat, Pierce."

"So . . . you were saying something about your diagnosis?"

"Bah, mainly psychobabble. But there is a belief held by some that I may be manic depressive. Possibly even bipolar."

She said a few more things to the waitress while I processed what she said. I was quickly distracted by the couple next to us. Their conversation was growing heated. The one sitting on my side, clearly African, had just slammed down his fork. After the waitress walked away, I turned back to her.

"Bipolar? Really? I—"

"Bah, quite frankly I wonder if it isn't just a catch-all diagnosis for women who won't conform. Who society views as difficult. Nina Simone, Virginia Woolf, Sylvia Plath, all were suspected of it."

Then suddenly, she turned to the couple and lashed out, saying something very serious sounding in German. She turned back to me and smiled.

"It's pretty impressive, your grasp of German. How long did it—"

"So basically, the family has divided themselves down the middle. Either you sympathize with James or you sympathize with Devon. There is no seeing it both ways, I'm sorry to say. And in all honesty, I found myself quite repulsed by Devon's behavior, you know? But at the same time, I could see where he was coming from. His hurt was real."

I could see something starting. The sheen of her clear brown eyes grew brighter, more intense. She turned to the left and looked out the window. Outside on the street, a group gathered. It was hard to tell if it was a bunch of friends getting together or the beginning of a rally of some kind. One thing I did know was that Margeaux was not seeing them. She was somewhere else.

"About two weeks ago, I was driving down the freeway with a friend. We were going to Frankfurt for a seminar of some kind. I wasn't sure what it was for. She had been the one to insist that we go, and I honestly had nothing better to do, so I went. Anyway, we're on the freeway, and as normally happens in Germany, we get stuck in a traffic jam. Well, my friend starts bitching, just cursing at the top of her voice. Fucking-German-drivers this and fucking-Austrian-drivers that. I just kept silent. She's a bit over the top, my friend. We eventually pull up to the scene of what's causing the jam, and we see there are two ambulances on the side of the autobahn, and about eight or nine police officers. Two cars had been involved in a horrible wreck, and on the ground, a body was covered with a plastic tarp. The tarp blew up as we passed, and I saw a young woman. Couldn't have been any older than you or I. Her hair was matted with blood, and the entire left side of her face was . . ."

She stopped herself. After a deep breath, she returned her gaze to me. I wanted to reach out and take her hand in mine, but something told me it wouldn't be appropriate.

"Every time we're in a traffic jam, we complain, don't we? My friend Genevieve sat there, slapping at the wheel, cursing the Fates as if life had done her such a horrible wrong, and yet somewhere out there . . . somewhere out there, someone was receiving a phone call, being told their wife or girlfriend or sister or daughter was never coming home again. That the last time they saw her and patted her head goodbye or kissed her on the cheek before she raced out the door, that really and truly was *the last time*. They were never going to hear her silly jokes again or watch her bake a birthday cake for her father. They were never again going to watch her as she combed her hair in front of the mirror before her big date. None of it. It was all gone. Her laughter was a memory. Forever."

It was at this time I noticed she had left me. I had come all the way to this obscure restaurant on this unfamiliar continent to see someone whom I had admired forever and that person was still back in our hometown of Connecticut. And I knew exactly where she was because I had been there too once. I remembered exactly where I was when I had heard the news of her brothers' crash on Concord Lane. I had raced to the hospital, thinking I would comfort Margeaux, only to realize once I had gotten to the ER that I absolutely did not belong there. Still, I wanted to be near her.

I felt an extreme sadness envelop me, and in that moment, for some strange reason, I thought about my wife. I wondered why I ever bothered to get married in the first place. It was because I had been a coward. We both had. I had settled because I didn't believe I could do any better. She had never been passionate about me, thus that whole business with the physical therapist in Danbury. But that was the past, as our couples counselor had repeatedly reminded us.

"I'm sorry," she said, closing her eyes and resting her forehead in the palm of her hand. "It's peculiar, me behaving this way. I guess I haven't really had anyone to talk to about all this outside of family. And you, you know our history so well. Maybe I just needed an objective soundboard. Maybe."

I took her right hand and clenched it firmly in my own. She held on tight and looked up at me with puddles in her eyes.

"I called Devon late one night, something like midnight my time. My mom had begged all of us to call him, to reach out and make an appeal to him. I basically begged him to get tested. And do you know what he said? He said that he refused to get tested because, even if it turned out he was one-hundred-and-fifty percent a positive match, he wouldn't move a finger to save James. He said he wanted James to know what it was like to lose everything. He said he wanted James to know just what it was like to die before your funeral, as he had done. To live every day wishing that you had died. I had underestimated my brother's anger. We all did. We had all lacked the necessary empathy for him. And I can't speak for the others, but I feel like now, knowing what I know, I'll never be whole again."

And then it all went to hell. The tenor of the couple next to us reached a high pitch. Margeaux snapped at them again, this time issuing a stinging verbal assault in French, and after nearly getting into a physical altercation with them, the African man rose from the table and stormed out. The other one looked at Margeaux as if he might strike her, and for a moment, I was concerned. But it became abundantly clear that he was no match for her—that he was actually fearful of her. He slowly rose, tossed a few euros on the table, and walked out. Margeaux said something nasty in French under her breath and then returned her gaze to me.

"It's always this way with these two drama queens. August, he is Nigerian, always jealous, always suspicious. And Pascal, the Algerian, he is unable to stand up for himself, unable to articulate, which just makes it worse. I tell you, nobody truly understands the subtle violence of men. How the danger is always there, just beneath the skin. Like a disease."

Margeaux rose, apologizing profusely all the time, and excused herself to go to the bathroom. I watched her disappear behind a multicolored beaded curtain, and then I turned and looked out the window. It was still raining, and I wondered what the weather was like back home in New Haven. I knew that Margeaux was crying her eyes out in that bathroom, and it occurred to me rather suddenly: some houses should not be returned to after a fire. Some houses simply need to be demolished and rebuilt from scratch.

Hey, Paula

No one will ever be able to say for sure just what was going through Harold's mind on that early evening in November, shortly before the Thanksgiving holiday break, when he entered the elevator on the forty-fifth floor of the Midtown Manhattan office building he had called his workplace for the last thirty-eight years of his life and all at once bawled like a child who had their favorite lollipop stolen from them by a bully.

When questioned by building security later the next day, Molly Cremins, one of three other people in the elevator, a receptionist from an architecture firm on the fifty-sixth floor, remembered one distinct thing about him. It struck her as "so peculiar, that look on his face when he walked in the elevator and heard the song playing over the speaker; it was that 'Hey, hey, Paula, I want to marry you' song. It seemed to really affect him in some way."

No one in his family, not even his wife of forty-three years, Camille, thought that moment meant anything. But Harold Payne had kept a major secret from all of them for nearly two decades, and to this day, there are still parts of his life that are completely closed to all of them.

Shortly after Harold walked out of that elevator, he suffered a stroke while on the PATH train, heading to his New Jersey apartment. He had managed, with very limited speech, to give the head EMT in the ambulance Kassandra's phone number, and it was she who arrived first at the hospital.

She couldn't understand it. She had cried all the way over in the cab, trying to figure out how such a thing could happen. Her father, despite being in his early sixties, was still a vibrant, forceful man. He looked svelte in his tailored flannel suits. Women and men tilted their heads his way in public places, still found him attractive. He walked to work every day from the train station, a good mile each way, and he worked out at a local gym two to three nights a week. Kassandra held his hand tightly by his bedside and tried to assure him that all would be fine. She had never seen her father so frail, so vulnerable. He was wearing an ill-fitting powder-blue hospital gown, and his brown eyes were flush with fear. She wondered what was going on behind them. He just kept staring at her, drooling out of the right side of his mouth.

Harold was in a hospital bed in Hoboken, that much was a fact. But his mind, his memories, were somewhere distant. It would take Kassandra years to discover that her father was thinking of Paris.

When he was twenty-seven years old, a blazing ray of fortune had shined down on Harold Payne. For the previous year, he had been the assistant editor for an immensely popular magazine, one of the first of its kind, geared toward a primarily Black audience. A bold decision had been made to launch a French edition. He was approached by the magazine's board of directors to head up the Paris office and get it on its feet for the first year or two. It was a difficult request, as his wife had just given birth to twins the year before, giving them a total of six kids, making it impossible to uproot the entire flock. But the offer was a rare opportunity that anyone, much less an ambitious Black male like Harold Payne, would be foolish to pass up.

Harold and Camille spent many a distressing night deliberating over this new situation, and though each hated the idea of being apart, they also knew that to turn down the offer would undoubtedly be a mistake that would leave them with the pungent, unresolved stink of regret. Harold worked it out with the editorial staff so that he could rotate between the continents. He would spend three months in Paris, three in Connecticut, three in Paris, three in Connecticut, and would do this for as long as all parties involved found it was reasonable and effective.

Harold had minored in French while at college, thinking that someday he might teach it at the high school or college level. He had always had an affection for French writers like Voltaire, Hugo, and Camus. The one time he had met his hero, James Baldwin, it had been at a luncheon thrown by his boss, Richard Leon, to celebrate the release of Baldwin's latest novel. At that event, Baldwin had spoken highly of France, telling him and Richard, while they munched on cucumber sandwiches in the corner, "Don't get me wrong, France is not perfect. They think every American Negro going over there plays the trumpet. But there is a beauty to Paris and a respect for artists that I just find enchanting."

Richard Leon was one of the most powerful Black men in New York at the time (his father, Marcus Leon, had been one of the first Black men in the South to start his own record label), and it was Richard who, over martinis at the Empire Hotel one evening, drove home the importance of Harold's accepting the offer.

"Payne, you are a natural fit for this role, and it is truly the opportunity of a lifetime for you and your loved ones. If you don't get your Black ass over to Paris this instant, I can assure you, you will regret it for the rest of your sorry days. You owe this to yourself, but you also owe it to all Negroes, past, present, and future, who will benefit from knowing that an opportunity like this was there and, when it presented itself, a Black man looked it in the eyes and seized it by the throat. Nigga, this is history making."

Harold left the United States that August of 1974 feeling extremely confident that he could handle the task before him. Camille had given the rotating schedule her blessing, so the guilt he initially felt was somewhat alleviated. He brought eight-year-old Roxanne with him those first two weeks of his trip, and the two had a grand time going to local stores, picking out furniture, and shopping for groceries for his apartment. He had found a cozy one bedroom in the sixth arrondissement, the trendy Saint-Germain-des-Prés section of the city. They visited all the touristy spots and ate at the finest restaurants. Roxanne was impressed with her father's fluency in French, watching intently as he conversed with waiters, bus drivers, store clerks, and dog walkers. She swore to him that she would master the language herself someday.

For the first three days, they played a game in which Harold would only address her in French from sunrise to sunset. He wasn't allowed to speak any other language. By the fourth day, however, she had grown completely disillusioned with the game. Her frustration manifested in an outburst of much foot stomping and tears while trying to pick out a cookie in a café off the Champs-Élysées. It was decided that they would return to speaking English full time and revert to French only when the mood seized them. Both would recall those two weeks as the best time they ever had together, and it played a part in Roxanne getting the "favored-child" label that stuck—until Kassandra broke it decades later.

When he returned to Connecticut that first autumn, six-year-old Margeaux made him promise to take her there next. He told her that he would, and in that moment, he honestly meant it—but he never did take any of his other children back with him. On his third trip to Paris that next August, Harold Payne became somewhat "preoccupied."

It had been a particularly brutal summer, and Paris, as he noticed was the case in many a European city, didn't seem to embrace the concept of air conditioning that had grown so popular on the East Coast during the summer months. Harold's apartment was unbearably humid during those days, and he chose to work from his office most of the time. One Sunday evening, he found himself feeling somewhat lazy and unwilling to deal with the swamp of mass transit and chose to work from home. After realizing that the large yet underwhelming fan he had gotten from a shop in the Latin Quarter was not going to get the job done, he went downstairs to a newly opened Japanese restaurant across the street from his building, having heard great things about it from neighbors.

He brought several work-related documents with him in his brown leather briefcase and pulled up to a table by the window. As he started to spread his files around him, he noticed that the table next to his, though empty at the moment, was occupied by someone. He assumed the missing person was a woman, as a precious light-green cashmere sweater was draped over the back of the empty chair and various fashion magazines were scattered around half a plate of yakisoba noodles. On the upper corner sat a smoldering cigarette with a seal of fresh red lipstick on the tip, and beside it a nearly empty glass of chardonnay stained at the rim with the same lipstick.

He didn't give much thought to his mystery companion as he ordered himself a Japanese beer and several pieces of sushi and dug into his paperwork. Five minutes in, while going over an annoyingly poorly written article by a recent hire about the popular Black actor of a hit police drama, the song "Hey Paula" began to play softly over the speakers of the restaurant.

Harold smiled. He'd always been a fan of the song, and he began to hum it. He soon heard the clack-clicking of fast-moving heels coming from behind him over his left shoulder. He took a swig of his beer and instinctively turned to face the source of the sound. Harold Payne would remember this moment for the rest of his life. Patrice Delphine would too, though her life was destined to be shorter than his.

She was not necessarily a beauty in the classic sense, but she was in possession of a character that caused men and women to take notice when she entered a room. She was a small woman, not petite, but just outside the norm. She had a penchant for tight, hip-hugging skirts and bright, cleavage-revealing blouses. Her hair was a shiny black and cut short in an almost boyish manner.

He took her in as she strode by without noticing him and picked up her cigarette. She took a drag and was disappointed to see that it had died out. Before she could reach for her purse, Harold was already offering her a flame from his stylish, silver lighter. She did the quickest of double takes—his skin appeared so warm and smooth in the orange glow of the flame—and all at once, she self-consciously, albeit gladly, accepted him into her space.

A tall man at six foot five, Harold had looked crisp and confident in gray slacks and a velvety white button-down. He had large almond ovals for eyes that every one of the Payne children had inherited. He watched her mouth as she puffed away, igniting both her cigarette and his desire. As the smoke dissipated, their eyes met. She offered him her pack, and though he wasn't particularly fond of cigarettes, he knew that if he didn't take one, he would regret it for the rest of his days. He lit up and coughed. It was the telling sign of an amateur, but it did the trick. They spoke mostly in French.

"Thank you very much, sir."

"It was my pleasure, madam. Truly."

"It is so hot, you know?"

"Yes. I think we should both take our work to the beach. Though it looks like yours is much more interesting than mine."

"Oh, this? Pffffft! I am bored with it all."

"Are you a designer?"

"I am a purchaser for Maelle, it is a beauty shop. Are you familiar?"

"No. I am not from these parts."

"Ah. We have two boutiques. One here in Marais, one in Cannes. Where are you from, may I ask?"

"You may ask whatever you like. I am from America, home of the hot dog."

"Ah, but the hot dog is German, no? Frankfurter?"

"The Germans may have invented it, but we perfected it."

They appeared to enjoy one another's company, and she was particularly impressed with his command of her language.

"Oh my, but your accent is too good to be American."

"Why, thank you, madam. I studied for many years at university."

"You were a very good student, I think. What brings you to Paris, may I ask?"

"I am here working on a magazine. It's very popular in the States, and we are starting a French version. We plan to go to press in four months."

"Oh? What magazine?"

"I don't imagine you've heard of it. *Bessie* magazine."

"Oh yes, *Bessie*, I am familiar with it. We are hoping to carry advertisements with you. My colleague has spoken with one of your colleagues about this."

"Really? My, this may be your lucky day! You must allow me to put in a good word for you. Your name is?"

"Patrice. Patrice Delphine."

"My honor, Madam Delphine. I am Payne. Harold Payne."

"A true pleasure, Mr. Payne."

When they shook hands, he took note that both their palms were a bit sweaty. Her hand trembled ever so slightly.

"I would be honored to buy you another glass of wine. Or perhaps something cooler, with ice maybe?"

"Oh no, thank you. I am enjoying my chardonnay. But I do not want to disturb you, sir."

"Oh please, on the contrary, you are the loveliest disturbance I have had in ages."

Patrice blushed and looked down at her feet. It took every bit of effort not to smile too brightly, but in the end, she lost the battle, and a soft glow overcame her. Harold felt a shudder in his chest, which seemed to be on fire, and he took in a deep breath. It felt to him in the moment as if a thousand orange butterflies had been released from his heart.

"Perhaps it is better for you if I speak English?"

"I would not want you to put yourself through any struggle."

"Oh, it is no struggle for me. I have spent two years in America at Northwestern University in Illinois. I speak well enough."

"Ah, you're a Northwestern girl? You must think you're pretty smart then."

They went on into the night, utterly ignoring their work and talking until two in the morning, alternating between French and English at a whim. They talked about the few things they had in common—being raised by poor parents, coming from large families, having been made fun of and treated with cruelty in public school for wearing ratty clothing, for smelling badly often, for looking desperate whenever food was around. They talked about a shared fondness for Puccini, and for Godard films. Both had protested the Vietnam War (though he declined to mention he had fought in it). She had once studied to be a classical violinist but had suffered a nervous breakdown at the age of fifteen and never went back to the instrument after being briefly institutionalized. She then thought she might become an actor, having been wooed by a film director she met at a museum who told her she had *une présence captivante*. He paid for her to take a few acting lessons while they dated, but it turned out he was more interested in making pornography than winning a Palme d'Or, and she took a job working at a perfume counter.

That night ended with him walking her back to her hotel room, where they shared a small but meaningful kiss. It wasn't earth shaking, but it was enough to make them hunger for the next time they would see each other, which for him took two excruciating days too long to happen. They became fond of taking long walks together, holding hands as they stopped to watch a street performance.

Harold had never been intimate with a white woman before, though he'd had many opportunities in his day. The closest he had ever gotten was in high school when his debate team went on a trip to Mobile, Alabama, to compete. He had hit it off with Cynthia Kemp, the daughter of the opposing team's coach. Cynthia was one of those girls who was going to do whatever it took to defy what society expected of her, and they had sneaked off one afternoon during lunch and made out in a janitor's broom closet. He remembered her face smelled like mint toothpaste and cream cheese.

The two had planned to meet up at midnight outside his hotel and get it on down by the lake, but when he told two of his close friends on the team about it, they scolded him.

"Nigga, is you crazy? Have you lost every bit a sense? Don't you know these crackers down here will hang your Black ass to dry like laundry? Ain't your ignorant ass ever heard of Emmett Till?"

Thus ended his relationship with Cynthia Kemp.

On his second weekend with Patrice, they took a romantic trip on the train, where they visited Claude Monet's garden at Giverny. The two stayed in a bed and breakfast not far from the garden, arriving on a Friday afternoon. They never left their room that entire Saturday, so smitten they were with the warmth of their mingled skin.

This vibrant infatuation went on for some time, the three-month stretches apart when he returned to the States seeming like an eternity to both. It took a little over two years for Harold to be up front with Patrice about his life back in the United States, and even then, he didn't tell all. She knew he was married, but she was under the impression he was unhappy in the marriage and would soon be ending it. She was also led to believe that he had only one child. He had craftily created this false narrative for his own selfish reasons, and both of his partners were kept in the dark about one another. By the time Patrice learned the entire truth—that he was the father of six children back in the States—it was much too late for regrets. She had already given birth to one of his children, a boy, and a second was on the way.

Countless times, she threatened to leave him for good, and on a few occasions, she did walk out the door. But she always returned. He was consistently apologetic. He showered her with gifts and affection. He was never physically abusive, never put her down with words. She loved him completely, and she believed he loved her back with an unwavering force. He simply could not stop lying.

Harold went on for years being a father and a husband in two relationships across two continents (though only legally a husband in one), until finally time caught up with him and Patrice's patience ran out. When he relinquished his duties at the Paris bureau to his long-term assistant, he promised her that he would still get to Paris twice a year at the very least and that nothing had to change drastically between them.

By this point, Patrice had stopped believing in Harold and was, in fact, repulsed by him. She called him a liar, a lecher, a con artist, and "a cock-sucking Don Juan impersonator." She now believed every word out of his mouth to be false and misleading, designed to obscure.

One day, without letting him know, she moved the children to a new location in Strasbourg, where she had obtained a position as a teacher at a small school. Harold would not hear from her or see any of them for several years. One sunny November afternoon, while waiting for a limousine to take him to a golfing date with colleagues in Upstate New York, he would receive a letter addressed to his office from his *ma gentille fille*. The letter was written by his daughter, telling him her mother, his lover, was dying of skin cancer and that she had only months to live.

He would not make it back in time for her funeral.

It came to be that the curious incident of the bawling in the elevator would forever remain a mystery. Harold would never fully regain use of his speech or mental faculties after that afternoon. The remainder of his days would be spent slumped over in a wheelchair, propped up on pillows in front of a large-screen television, watching some classic movie or talk show, being cared for by Camille and various attendants at their home in Connecticut. *Bessie* magazine would later do a very profound and touching piece on their longtime editor, written by Kassandra herself (the article would make zero mention of his family in France), and a large scholarship for aspiring Black journalists was set up in his name at Howard University.

At the time of his stroke, both Michel and Dahlia were in their thirties, living together in an apartment Harold had purchased for them in the Meatpacking District of Manhattan. In hushed tones, the Paynes all surreptitiously referred to the light-skinned children as *le duo français*.

Michel and Dahlia

The small recording studio in East Harlem was not an ideal place to be on an August afternoon. The temperature outdoors reached 106 degrees, and the air inside the cramped room felt like that of an active microwave. This was primarily due to so many people packing themselves into the dense space like so many ants in an ant farm. All the spectators were youthful, dressed in the fashionable street choices of the season, all or most high on some substance or another. There were nine Black girls (two Jamaican), four Puerto Rican girls, four Italian girls, three Turkish girls, two dark-skinned girls (Ethiopian, someone had said), two Israeli girls, and one Japanese girl. There were also six Black guys (one Haitian), three Dominican guys, two Puerto Rican guys, one Korean guy, and one Tongan guy. All were drinking various bottled drinks, mingling together behind a glass window that looked into a dark studio.

In that studio, with large headphones attached to his oft-made-fun-of oversized ears, stood the man who was the center of their attention. To many of the people in attendance, history was being made tonight. The first breakthrough French Black rapper in the States was about to lay down the final track on what was sure to be a debut album that would take the hip-hop world by storm. Sucre Noir (a.k.a. Black Sugar) stood in front of a suspended microphone in his blue jeans, white tank top, and silk black button-down shirt opened all the way. On his nearly bald head sat a black stocking cap clenched tight around his scalp. He was bopping to a rhythm only he could hear. His eyes were closed, and he mumbled as if in a trance of his own devising. His light-brown skin gleamed, a mix of sweat and baby oil.

A crude voice boomed over the speakers in the room. The accent was unmistakably New York 'hood.

"You 'bout ready to take care o' this shit?"

"Sho' nuff," shot back Sucre Noir, lifting his head, opening his sleepy brown eyes, and flashing a peace sign. His accent was a peculiar hybrid to his friends, part forced city streets, part European streets. He knew his accent was popular with certain women, and he milked it like the gimmick it was.

Any rumbling in the studio ceased, and a pregnant calm overtook the space. Crude Voice counted down from three with his fingers, and when he was done, a fast, almost violent and deafening beat filled the room, part recorded drum, part haunting piano riff. In unison, all the bodies behind the window began to bounce and sway in a display of unchoreographed symmetry. Sucre Noir bopped and waved as he lifted his chin to the microphone. Without warning, he coughed and waved off the beat. The room went silent as he sauntered over to a corner stool where a bottle of water sat in a bucket of ice. He downed the bottle in one swig and went back to the microphone.

He didn't notice the lone side door to his right open and the entrance of a young woman so strikingly beautiful she filled the room with color. She darted in and, without taking notice of him, ran into the crowded room behind the window, slamming the door shut after her. The young woman was the same exact skin tone as the rapper and shared with him other similar features: a muscular face with high cheekbones, a thin nose, pale brown eyes, the comical ears, and that complexion—beige, like mildly burnt butter. She wore what resembled a waitress uniform—short black skirt and white button-down blouse with a skinny black tie. She was lithe, on the thin side. Her shiny, thicket-like hair was pulled back tightly into two pigtails that dangled on each side, framing her soft, incandescent face.

People in the room acknowledged her with a nod, and she mechanically returned a few of them, clearly uninterested in the scene. She avoided eye contact with any one person and instead turned her full attention to the rapper in the window. Unlike the others, she didn't move and sway to the beat when the music started up again. She stared at him, arms crossed over her chest, with an intense, hawkish focus.

Sucre Noir swayed and shimmied again, and this time, when he put his weight into the microphone, he was clearly poised to strike. The words leaped from him in a loose yet steady flow. His tone was fierce, hypnotic, and confident.

> They call me Black Sugar
> but I'm tart like year-old lemon
>
> got more rhymes than a terrorist got Yemen
>
> rippin' through New York like my name was Speed Racer
> drinkin' hefeweizen cold with a Stoli chaser.
>
> Tellin' you I was born in Paris,
> raised in the streets
>
> bustin' major vocabulary
> other rappers seem effete
> crushin' competition with incomparable beats
> niggas bow to me like they was washin' Jesus's feet.

They tell me these are the hard days
my sins is greater than the deadliest seven
people fall around me like the towers on 9/11
rappin' seems to be my only ticket to heaven
I just hope that a nigga's at the gate.

The beat went on for a few seconds and then stopped. The room of spectators clapped, and Crude Voice boomed over the speakers. "That was tight, nigga. Let's take ten and come back for the seconds."

Sucre Noir nodded and flashed the peace sign once more. He removed his headphones and closed his eyes. He murmured a chant under his breath, kissed his gold chain, and then looked up to the window. He pointed a long finger at a group of women and unleashed a sly, charismatic grin. The women all squealed and yelped as he walked over to the door and opened it. In a second, his group of people was on him, slapping his hands, his back, his shoulders, complimenting him in numerous languages with various means both verbal and physical. He held court and engaged in brief conversations with everyone he could until he caught the eye of the young woman, the one so different from the rest.

Feeling fortunate to have made contact, she lifted her arm and pointed at her wrist where a watch might have been but wasn't. She jerked her head to the left and made several detailed signals using some secret sign language. He sighed, answered her back in the same sign language, and returned to speaking with his friends. The young woman walked out of the noisy room.

Dahlia watched as Michel—Sucre Noir—took in the adulation of his crew. She then opened a large, thick door and walked out onto a bare terrace that overlooked a park across the street. In the park below, several children—some in blue uniforms, some in yellow—were engaged in a game of soccer. She pulled a light fan with a colorful Chinese pattern out of her purse and cooled her sweaty face. The effort was futile, the humidity so overpowering.

Minutes later, Michel opened the door and walked out onto the terrace. He went straight to her, lighting a cigarette and not looking at her. He instead took in the soccer game below.

"I don't have much time to fuck around, Dahlia."

"Get over yourself, Michel." Her accent was like his, minus the street affectation.

"What did I tell you?"

"What?"

"What did I tell you about my name?"

"You didn't *tell* me anything. You *asked* me."

"Yes, I have asked you repeatedly to refer to me as Sucre Noir."

"Save it for your groupies."

"I thought it was a simple request."

Dahlia smirked, shook her head, and picked up the pace of her fanning. She stared at him, hoping he would return her gaze but knowing he wouldn't. She knew he didn't have the strength to match her attention. It had been this way between them for most of their lives, since that time when they were children and she checkmated him in nine moves in front of a small band of onlookers in the Jardin du Luxembourg.

"It is fucking amazing what happens to people," she said, turning her back to him.

The two stood in silence for a few moments. Below, the blue team celebrated a goal. Finally, Michel turned toward her.

"What is it that you want, Dahlia?" he barked out.

"What do you think?" she shot back. "Your girlfriend is walking—"

"She is *not* my girlfriend. I have told you."

"Then what is she, Michel? Why the fuck have you invited her to come live in our home if she isn't your girlfriend? Why have you done such a stupid thing? Please, tell me. All this discomfort, this inconvenience, for what? A fuck buddy?"

Michel threw his half-smoked cigarette against the wall. "I don't have to answer to you, Dahlia! When will you understand this?"

"Selfishness! This is the story of your life, Michel! Selfishness! You are worse than our father."

Michel clenched the edge of the terrace. He murmured something unclear, closing his eyes as he did.

"Do you know what she's doing right now, Michel? Do you? When I left the apartment, she was on the phone, crying in hysterics to her mother. And do you know what she was telling her? She was telling her that she was going to kill herself. That she was going to kill herself and your baby. That in that way, she would show you a thing or two. She was maniacal!"

He spoke in a slow and calm tone. "Natalie is an extreme personality. She is overdramatic. She kind of reminds me of you, really. Threatens to kill herself every couple of weeks."

"And that is okay with you, eh? You feel it isn't a problem that the mother of your child speaks of cutting open her wrists and throwing herself off bridges regularly? Ah, what do you care? You are never home anyway. You have your posse and your underaged *putes* and your so-called *handlers*. What do you care? It is I who must concern myself with the shit you leave behind. *Fils de pute . . .*"

Every insult dripped from her mouth like so much acid. Each left scars on his soul. Michel curled up the left side of his mouth in a frustrated snarl and turned to face her, his finger pointed directly at her nose.

"You're pushing me, Dahlia. I'm warning you."

With fascinating speed, she grabbed at his finger and yanked it away. He lunged for her shoulder and pulled her down. She got up quickly and kicked him hard in his left thigh. He launched at her throat, but she slapped his face with such ferocity it caused him to fall to her side. He knelt there for seconds, slapping the ground.

"*Je m'en fous!* Grow up, you fucking child!" she spat at him, and walked to the opposite end of the terrace.

His shoulders slumped, and his entire body seemed to shrink. Five minutes ago, he was the grandest of peacocks, now a wounded pigeon. He rose slowly, massaging his leg.

"What would you have me do? I can't turn back time, Dahlia. I wish I could. I wish I could have told her—forced her—to get an abortion. But it's too late. I can't. What would you have me do?"

"I would have you act like a man, Michel . . ."

He buried his head in his hands and clenched his smooth skull. His eyes narrowed, and he mumbled to himself, his breath erratic, on the verge of something approaching an anxiety attack. Dahlia took his face in her hands and pulled him close. At first, he resisted, but his resolve was no match for hers. He burrowed his face into her warm, sweaty neck and held her. He could not look her in the eyes. Below, the yellow team celebrated a goal, though less exuberantly than the opposition.

"Michel, you always used to say you never wanted to be like our father, and I always admired you for this. But please, look at yourself now. Look in the mirror. You're not who I once hoped you would be."

"I've always been a disappointment to you. Always. Ever since we arrived in this country, you've distanced yourself from me."

Dahlia stood there, gently rocking him. "You know this isn't true."

Michel wiped his nose and abruptly pulled away from her. He walked over to the edge of the terrace and looked down at the game in the park while lighting another cigarette. Dahlia watched him as he pulled himself back together, tucking and pulling at his clothing, removing the stocking cap, and palming his head. She could not help but feel for him.

"I thought you needed to know this Michel, because I won't be around to babysit Nicole anymore. I am going to Los Angeles tomorrow. I don't know when I will return."

"Los Angeles?" He turned to her, his brows raised. "Why?"

"Devon called me. He is moving. He could use help."

"He's moving again? Jesus, this guy."

"Apparently he got a promotion or something. All I know is I could use a break. This city . . ."

"So you leave tomorrow?"

"Nine a.m. flight out of Kennedy. I didn't get a return ticket. Devon says he can cover it."

"Really?"

"That's what he said."

"You know he's back in the game, right?" Michel watched her closely. If she heard his last statement, she did not show it. He nodded to himself and looked down. After several drags on his cigarette, he tossed it to the ground and mashed it out. "Ah, what do you care? Devon can make all the mistakes in the world. Devon is the brother you've always wanted, isn't he?"

"I don't have time for this, Michel."

"Fine. What should I do about Nicole?"

"I think you should send her back home. At a time like this, she needs to be around people who love her. You obviously do not."

"Send her home? Her parents detest her. They accused her of being a nigger lover to her face. She shamed them long before she ever met me."

"I don't know what you do then, Michel. She is not my problem. It might amaze you to know that I have problems of my own. My life doesn't revolve around your drama. I can only tell you she is a most unstable girl. You have to give this serious consideration. Listen to me. Do you know she stole Tante Marie's necklace? The one she gave me for my sixteenth birthday?"

"Really? How do you know this?"

"I know. I am not an idiot. I am telling you she is your problem alone now, and you have to do something. Soon."

In an instant, she was in front of him again. With surprising alacrity, she reached out to him and kissed both of his cheeks, then his mouth, holding him close afterward.

"I love you, Michel. You are my heart. But you kill me often. You kill me more than this city does."

At that moment, one of Michel's homeboys opened the door to the terrace. He shrank immediately at the sight of them, realizing he was intruding on a tender moment.

"Yo, Sucre, sorry. They about ready to start again."

Dahlia didn't look at the young man at all, only into her brother's eyes. She stroked his cheek. His gaze was fixed on her as well.

"I'll be in touch," she said. She turned and walked past the young man, who now held the door open for her. She stopped and turned back to her brother. "And by the way, using 9/11 in your rap so soon after is rude and tasteless. I would suggest you change that lyric."

The elevator door opened. Dahlia rushed out and smacked head-on into an old lady and her vivacious poodle, both of whom were waiting to enter. The dog yelped at her.

"Merde!" she said as she darted past them and ran down the dimly lit hallway.

"Look where you're going. You trying to kill somebody?" the old lady snapped.

Dahlia stopped at apartment E, put her key in, removed the ties from her hair—her hair draping around her neck—unlocked the door, and dashed into the apartment. Music was coming from a stereo, Nat King Cole or Johnny Mathis, she couldn't tell which. She headed for the living room, a large sunlit space where Gus Tran sat on a wooden stool. An easel stood before him with a blank canvas set atop it. He smoked a cigarette with the gentle arm stroke of a ballet dancer.

"I am so sorry," she said, putting her bag down and removing her headphones.

Gus was a dark-featured man in his midfifties and had a serious face, tough and slightly defeated, like an over-the-hill boxer's mug. He wore circular gold-rimmed glasses. His long black hair, with a thin white streak on the left going all the way down, was pulled back in a tight ponytail. Once, during a very brief time in her childhood when her parents seemed happy together, Dahlia and Michel had taken a trip with them to a small island in Australia. It was her mother's birthday weekend, and the first night there they had eaten at an outdoor restaurant and watched the most beautiful sunset Dahlia had ever seen. Gus's skin reminded Dahlia of the texture of that sunset. It was the first thing that attracted her to him.

He sighed as he exhaled a thin stream of smoke.

"That seems to be your favorite phrase lately."

"I have a lot to get done before—"

He swiftly raised an outstretched palm to her. "I don't need explanations! If you would be so kind as to get to your spot. The usual?"

"Please," she said, a little saddened. "I'm sorry, I forgot. My personal life is of no importance to you."

Gus rose and slowly walked out of the room, his gait that of a man who never went anywhere quickly. With methodic deftness, Dahlia stripped down until she was completely nude, folding her clothes neatly and putting them in a pile on a counter on the shelf. She squeezed and pulled at her tiny pert breasts as if that added something extra to them. She went over and checked her body and hair in a closet mirror before heading over to the plush green couch positioned under a window directly across from the easel.

She sat down and posed, one leg crossed over the other, her wiry arms dangling on either side of her. She glanced around the room, proud of the fact that she was in the home of an art lover. Numerous paintings, an even mix of impressionist, abstract, and surrealist, filled the walls. Some leaned against a chair or a table leg, waiting to be hung. Many were paintings of women, some nudes, some not. Most of the works were Gus Tran originals.

He returned with a small glass of red wine and handed it to her.

"The child's communion," he said. Their eyes did not leave each other as she took a deep sip and handed the glass to him. He took a similar-sized sip, mockingly, and handed the glass back to her. He returned to his stool. "Don't ever say your personal life is of no importance to me. It affects everything we do in here. And we both know I'm in love with you."

"Love has such a peculiar way of showing itself nowadays."

"Love looks the same as it has always looked. It is the lover who changes."

He moved a couple of paint tubes around his easel and hummed along to the song "Chances Are." She frowned at him.

"Has your lover changed, Mr. Tran?"

"Like a chameleon. Find the sun, please."

She slid back some and turned her body so she was tilted to the window. A new sheen of sunlight blessed her already bright complexion. She stared at the apartment directly across the street, at a skinny, topless man splayed on a couch, watching television.

"Your neighbor is dying."

"What makes you say that?"

"I saw him down at the corner bodega after I left here last week. He was with his boyfriend, cute Peruvian guy. They were discussing his latest chemo treatments and how he thinks he should stop them and live out these remaining months with dignity. It was sad to hear them discuss it in line buying Pringles and Colt 45."

"You would prefer they were buying brie and champagne?"

"Don't do that."

"Do what?"

"Twist what I say to sound trivial. Superficial."

"That's your insecurity talking, lover, not me. You have a new bruise."

"Meet the new bruise, same as the old bruise." She waited for a reaction that didn't come. "I'm going to miss you."

"I already miss you. Started last week."

"Sometimes I forget that you actually can be beautiful at times."

"I never forget that you're beautiful all of the times."

"I'm letting my bush grow out. Do you mind?"

"It is your bush to do with as you please. May I ask you something? Do you think you will take a new lover in Los Angeles?"

"Come on, Tran, you know me. I don't plan such things."

"Ah yes, Little Miss Impulsive."

"Don't make fun. Impulse drove me into your arms."

"Money drove you into my arms, Dahlia."

"You cheapen me. Maybe I should leave."

They both turned and looked at the hallway, the only exit out of the room. They grinned at each other, and he lit another cigarette and sketched with a pencil while she returned to the view from the window. Out of the corner of her eye, she watched his arm move gingerly across the sketch pad.

She adored this part of him. She recalled the first time she saw him on the C train. She was returning home from a workout and wore sweaty leggings and a hoodie, eating a slice of pizza. He sat next to her and joked about how if she was going to eat on the train, she had to share with everyone. He was older, sure, but not in a grandfatherly way, and he seemed fearless. She responded that pizza was one of those rare foods never meant to be shared, and when he heard her accent, he gave her shit about how the French had been a thorn in his country's side for as long as he could remember. He told her that she owed him at least some crust. She told him that she had no history of Vietnam other than the occasional American film. He had snorted something about propaganda, and she noticed that sometimes the lumbering of a subway through the tunnel was like a heartbeat.

"A man came into my restaurant the other day," she went on. "A fairly handsome man, I would say. He looked like that actor, the one white women love from the '60s and '70s. He was in *Bonnie and Clyde*."

"Redford, I think. Robert Redford. No, that's the Butch Cassidy guy."

"Whoever. Anyway, he ordered a chicken-salad sandwich and asked me to hold the chicken. I think he thought it was funny. Instead of a tip, he left me a poem with his name and phone number at the end."

He put down his pencil and waited for the ending.

"Classy. Was the poem any good?"

"It was simply dreadful. Rhymed *beauty* with *cutie*. *Bloody* with *putty*."

"Why did he have to bring blood into it?"

"Who knows?" she replied. "I doubt he had any idea how bad it was."

"Well, I can't say I blame him for being inspired by you."

"Inspiration indeed. He liked my ass."

"Such a crass young woman. Who taught you to speak this way?"

"American TV."

"Can't argue there."

"My, my, Gus Tran not arguing with me. That's a first!"

She saw him snicker, and it made her feel pride that she could bring out the humor in him.

"Oh, Dahlia. You play a dangerous game. Will you call your Robert Redford?"

"Please. I've already got my Robert Redford. His name is Gus Tran."

"Perhaps you should finish college first; then we can talk marriage."

"Is that an ultimatum?"

"Just promise me one thing—when you do leave me, it will be for another brown man. Don't ever leave me for a white guy. Or if you do, don't tell me."

"What makes you think I want to leave you at all, ever? You are always preparing yourself, aren't you, for my inevitable exit?"

"I would be a fool if I wasn't."

She got up from her position and went out of the room with her wineglass. She returned moments later with a full glass.

"It's no way to fall in love, Tran. No way at all. I wonder what he did for a living, my Robert Redford."

"You see, you *are* curious. It is as I suspected. Just be careful is all I ask you. Be very careful of these American men with their love of war movies, their flags on their lawns, pinned to their jackets. Their blatant whitewashing of all their sins. There is a depravity to them. An unwillingness to accept responsibility for the pain they have inflicted on so many. Denial is their ally. They wallow in the shadow of evil as they teach their children that Christopher Columbus was a genuine hero, Thomas Jefferson was a genuine hero, just as they are. Be careful, Dahlia. They twist the truth and weaponize it. They give it nicknames like Fat Man and Little Boy. They hide deception in blankets and present it as a gift for you. You won't see them coming in the light of day."

She watched him closely, studied his face as meticulously as she had ever studied any other. A familiar warmth grew inside of her. She sat on the windowsill and leaned back.

"Who was it, Tran? Who was it that hurt you so? Sometimes I want to kill her with my bare hands."

"*Sacrebleu*, a little dramatic, don't you think? Did you cut your hair?"

"I did. I love that you noticed."

"Okay. Now is the time that I ask you to stay still for the next several minutes. Can you?"

"Not yet. Not yet. I think my pallor could use a little more luster, don't you?"

And with this statement, she lifted her left leg up ever so lightly and balanced it against the windowsill. He looked at her and sighed. As the voice of Nat King Cole crept through the room, he put his tools down and walked over to her. He knelt before her lap and kissed her belly with the delicacy of a masseuse. She rolled her eyes up and took in the sun over the rooftop. She could smell the cigarette smoke in his hair as his mouth moved downward. She ran her fingers through his mane as a pleasure seized her like a fever.

"That day, that Sunday, that summer . . ."

The Mills of the Gods

On the morning that Devon learned he would be going to jail for at least six to eight years (three and a half with good behavior), he was awakened by the piercing sound of a car alarm going off fifteen stories below his bedroom window.

It was around six forty-five in the morning. Devon stared up at the ceiling, shook his head, and hoped the noise would stop soon. After five minutes, when the siren continued to wail (high pitch, low pitch, high pitch, low pitch, whirring noise), he dragged his legs to the side of his bed, transferred into his wheelchair, and rolled out into the living room, over to his balcony to get a look at the street. There had been several car break-ins in the neighborhood recently, and he wanted to see if there was anything out of the ordinary going on.

The sun had just started its ascent, giving the Los Angeles sky a peach-colored tint. He looked down at the vacant street below, and he couldn't tell which car blared away. From this height, they all looked like metallic gumballs on a life-sized board game. He looked to his left and saw Nadia standing on her balcony. She wore her normal morning uniform—a high-quality white silk robe tied loosely in front. She smoked a cigarette, also checking out the street below. Although Devon had known her for more than a year now, there were still moments when her natural unapologetic beauty caught him off guard. Once, back home in Connecticut, he had taken a painting class, and he some-times felt shame from the perverse joy he took out of painting the nude models who changed on a weekly basis. The class helped him develop a keen respect for the human body and all its thorns. Seeing Nadia like this now made him wish he had continued painting.

"I think it's the red BMW," she said to him while pointing down. Only a trace of her Eastern European accent remained. As such, she sounded like a mediocre actor might sound, trying their best during a production of a Chekhov play. "It looks like maybe the window is broken."

"The world is becoming a dangerous place again."

"As if it ever stopped. How long have you been asleep? I didn't see you come in."

"Not long enough. You have coffee on?"

"I do. I bring you."

Nadia walked back into her apartment, and Devon took in a deep breath of caustic air. He had liked so much about California when he first arrived all those years ago—the climate, the women, the beaches, the trees—but the air was something he could never get over. It sat on his chest like a heavy cat. He coughed, and it felt as if he were choking on cotton candy. He was mostly through his fit when Nadia emerged, her robe now closed and tied tightly around her. She leaned over the cement partition separating their balconies and handed him a cup of coffee with extra cream in a sky-blue handmade ceramic mug, his favorite. This had become their routine, like that of an old married couple who had done this very thing a hundred times before. Devon appreciated this familiarity, and for a moment, a sadness took a hold of him that he found often took place with Nadia, one he struggled to understand.

"I tell you all the time—now would be a good time for you to stop smoking weed," she said, taking a seat at her tiny end table.

"But I don't smoke weed. It's a bad idea to abuse your own product."

"This is a stupid rule, Devon. It is really stupid rule."

"Yeah well, a society without rules . . ."

He took a sip of his coffee and cleared his throat. Nadia's coffee was always rich and hit the spot. He looked out across the neighborhood. It was quiet now. The windows of all the skyscrapers were dark and empty, and the streets were relatively free of traffic. It was his favorite time of day. He told himself he should try to wake up this early more often. This was Los Angeles at its finest, when the city was just being reborn. It held a postcard-like quality. If he closed his eyes, he could pretend he hadn't made so many costly mistakes.

"Late night?" he asked.

"No later than usual, you know. One of my best clients, he open a new restaurant in Brentwood. He has to show me off. He tell me maybe I can become hostess there."

He nodded and looked at her. She stared off into the landscape. Despite her translucent beauty, there was a stony hardness to her features best noticed from his current angle. Early in their friendship, over the course of several nights in which each had shared too much wine and vodka on these balconies, Devon had learned a great deal about Nadia. It did not take him long to realize how different they were, despite appearances. Devon was the privileged one. He had grown up with great material wealth and rarely wanted for anything. Nadia, on the other hand, came from hard-core poverty. She described to him a bitter childhood. Her parents had fled from a financially disastrous situation in their country before she was born, and they settled in East Los Angeles. He couldn't recall if it was Bosnia or Serbia or Croatia— something with an -*ia* at the end. She grew up hearing her parents tell stories that detailed the travails they experienced in their home country. The long lines for food, the absence of running water on a regular basis. How they survived on mainly cold soups and breads for most of their years. When they reached the States, her father was lucky to get a job as a janitor at a local mall. Her mother was lucky to get a job as part of the maid service at a luxury hotel in Calabasas. She and her siblings wore secondhand thrift-store clothing straight up through middle school. She was nothing like him.

For this reason, he respected her more than he did most people in his life.

He watched as she raised a cigarette to her mouth in a robotic manner and inhaled, her gaze fixed on a place he could not see, would probably never be able to see. He thought to say something but chose not to. He figured the place she was in was better than here on this balcony, and he didn't want to disrupt it. One thing he knew for certain about her—she had an appreciation for silences.

Nadia was a call girl, though she preferred the term *escort*. And not just any escort. As her unique gifts warranted, she was a high-end courtesan, often in demand. There were times Devon didn't see her for weeks, when she had been shipped to "work from the Vegas office," as she put it. Once, on a balmy July 4 evening after they had downed a bottle and a half of cognac, she let slip a few of those on her client list. They included B-list celebrities, a state senator, and one renowned ex-professional basketball great who now coached at a high school in the area. One time, he had seen her on television, at the red-carpet ceremony of one of those shamelessly phony awards shows, on the arm of a popular musician. He imagined if she owned one, her black book could be worth a fortune someday.

"I have question for you, Devon."

He hadn't expected her to speak so soon, and he stopped mid-sip to address her. "Sure thing, princess, shoot."

"What does it mean this saying: Don't throw out the baby with the bathwater? Someone say this to me last night, and I have no idea what he is talking about."

Devon gave her a look that asked what kind of question that was before they both looked down at the street. The car alarm had just stopped.

"Well . . . it's not a phrase I hear often, I'll be honest with you. But if I remember, I think it has something to do with judgment, with being careful about your judgment."

"Judgment?"

"Yeah, judgment. Like, don't be too quick to make big decisions, you know? Or don't be too hasty in how you judge a situation. Honestly, I don't know, princess. But I promise you I'll look it up later and get back to you."

"It sounds stupid, this baby with the bathwater."

"We say a lot of stupid shit in this country. I wouldn't be too concerned."

On the morning that Devon learned he would be going to jail for at least six to eight years (three and a half with good behavior), he was in his car and on the freeway by ten.

He couldn't eat anything, so troubled he was by his first appointment of the day. Last night, Des Oak, his boss and main supplier, had called him from a pay phone to say they needed to meet right away the next morning. Des had chosen a spot that Devon knew all too well: the basketball bleachers at Venice Beach, where they could have a sensitive conversation without the threat of being recorded. The game had heated up a good deal in the last year or so, and Desmond Colson, originally from Oakland and now one of the highest-ranking drug dealers in East Los Angeles, was not about to get caught by these police out here.

"Hay-ell no, these coppers taking my shit!"

With the traffic at a crawl, close to a standstill, Devon popped a piece of cinnamon gum in his mouth but quickly found he couldn't enjoy it. He could barely produce enough saliva, and thus the flavor was wasted on him. At times like these—and these had come along more frequently lately—Devon wondered how he had ever let things get this far.

He had moved out to Los Angeles to escape his family on the East Coast. Sure, he had some scattered, unfocused interest in filmmaking, but what he had wanted most of all was to get away from the drama of the Paynes. The guilt associated with some of the bad choices he had made in his youth. Los Angeles was supposed to be his refuge, a place where he could rehabilitate his poor image. Things hadn't exactly gone as he had planned.

He pulled off the freeway at the first Venice Beach exit and looked for a disabled parking spot. It would be a daunting task at this time of day, as all those spots were already taken by fake-ass disabled drivers. He'd watched them park so many times, hang their disabled placards, and walk out of their cars without so much as a limp all the time. He didn't know their stories, but it was infuriating reality that made his life harder. Maybe at some point in their life they had stubbed their toe and some bullshit doctor had written them up a prescription for a placard. The thought of the phoniness of it all made his blood pressure rise and simmer.

How had it all come to this? His mentor, Jeremy Fiske, a paraplegic he had met in the hospital, white dude who had been paralyzed after diving into a pool, had become the talk of their small town. He had written a screenplay, a science fiction tale about dueling street gangs in the twenty-fifth century during a nuclear holocaust, and it had been made into a summer blockbuster. Jeremy became a multimillionaire overnight. Fiske had told him that anyone could write a screenplay, that it didn't take a genius. He watched with envy as Fiske moved to Los Angeles, and a year later, in an ironic twist, got so high on coke that he drowned in his Bel Air swimming pool. Still, the seed had been planted in him.

Devon wrote the beginning of a screenplay, a romantic comedy about a high-school football player and the cheerleader he falls for, and he moved to Los Angeles to shop it around. He applied to UCLA. The plan was to get a degree in cinematography, film history, film production management, whatever, and become a player in the Hollywood engine. In his fantasies, he would become one of the few high-powered Black auteurs in the industry. He would win his first Oscar by the time he was twenty-five. At the podium, he would thank his wife, their two children, and end by thanking Sidney Poitier for being such a powerful role model.

But none of it had turned out that way. To Devon's surprise, some semblance of talent was expected to get accepted into film school. He had only written forty-seven pages of *Love Blitz* and showed it to a few people he respected, and he realized that nobody was going to confuse him with Spike Lee anytime soon. He quickly came to know rejection on a very intimate level.

Then he met Des Oak and his crew one afternoon at a barbershop in Carson. It was like he had known Des forever. With Des's East Coast charm and moxie, Devon had hit it off well with him, and before he knew it, he had been invited to a barbecue, then a house party, then a recording session with a rapper Des was backing. Over the course of a few weeks, the two became tight as first cousins. Des appreciated the fact that Devon was in college (he had enrolled in a night class at UCLA), and together they hatched a plan to distribute marijuana, coke, special K, heroin—whatever the student body craved. Des, being a major player on the scene for some time, had already had a special in with the staff there. He needed a cool, charming, intelligent campus presence to make his pitch. Devon fit the bill perfectly for many reasons, but mostly because no one would suspect a quadriplegic student from an upper-class East Coast family of being a dealer, much less a highly competent one. And for a good while, it worked out extremely well for all involved.

Until it didn't.

Devon spotted Des in his usual location—middle row of the bleachers, surrounded by three hazardous-looking guys that made up his muscle. Devon rolled around the left side of the court, where a five-on-five game between locals raged. He was met by Des's first line of muscle, Nat K, a Jamaican with large sunglasses and a head of unruly dreads like a scarecrow's. Nat always had a blunt in his mouth, usually unlit. When they hugged, Devon smelled the ganja in his hair.

"Ya playa," Nat K said. "Tis a good day to be alive, no?"

"Feel that. No doubt."

Next up, he hugged Italian Felix, a slightly obese, light-skinned bald guy with a frame like a classic wrestler. His mother had been born in Northern Italy, and his father was born in South Central LA. When he first came on board, they all called Felix "Ravioli and Ribs," but it became too much to utter after a while, and they settled on Italian Felix. The fact that the dude could speak fluent Italian made him an exotic, often entertaining presence.

And then there was Des, the ex-linebacker for the University of Southern California, a potential NFL career derailed by genetically inferior hamstrings. Despite his limp, he walked with grace. Des carried himself like a seasoned politician. He always wore black slacks and a white button-down shirt, as if he had to go into the office at any minute. After they pounded fists and embraced, Devon pulled into a spot under the bleachers that provided a great view of the beach action. Des pulled up a chair beside him and flipped it backward before he sat. The muscle flanked them like sprouting trees. Devon watched a volleyball game of young women—college students, he imagined—taking place several yards away. A sense of foreboding caused him to avoid eye contact with Des. Des sighed before he spoke, confirming his suspicion. Devon looked up at the sun beaming down on them like a searchlight.

"Here's da thing, cuz. You know the heat been turned up for some time now. We been feeling it in stops and starts for over a year. Fucking Fidel, man. That nigga is a relentless bitch."

Devon shook his head and stared at his sneakers. He recalled the first time they had all met Detective Aguilar, a smooth-talking, charismatic man who looked like he could have played the lead role in any telenovela. A little over a year ago, Detective Aguilar, wearing an expensive tailored suit, proudly displaying his badge around his neck on a gold chain, had walked up to the entire crew on Des's own porch and shook hands with him while they enjoyed beer and weed. Aguilar introduced himself as the new sheriff in town, told them all he had been transferred there from his regular beat in Miami Beach, where he had amassed a stellar reputation for pursuing and collaring local drug dealers. He referred to himself as the hired help, and after he lit up a formidably sized Cuban cigar, he assured them that it was his goal to take half of them down within a year's time. Eleven months later, his numbers were below his projection, but he had been effective. Tweedy Zee was in prison. Marshmallow was in prison. Detroit Nick was in prison. Junior Colombia had mysteriously gone missing. Devon thought he might be next on the list.

"So I been talking with Armstrong," Des continued. "He saying they building a major case based on the lab records off the Strand bust, you know?"

"Yeah, I saw that coming. That was a big catch for them, man. I told you then. So what's Armstrong's advice? Pack it in for a bit?"

"Shit, ain't no packing it in, dawg. If anything, now is the time to go more strong. This shit done intensified civil strife, you know?"

"Yeah. They still holding Shakespeare, right? He gonna go down or what?"

"Nah. I can't have Shakespeare going down, dawg. He my top earner, and I'm a need that soldier in the fight. We about to storm the beach at Normandy, you know what I'm sayin'?"

Devon nodded and looked past him to the walkway along the beach, where a homeless man pushed his shopping cart full of what appeared to be everything he owned in the world. The man looked withered, Black and sweaty. His hairstyle was half-afro, half-cornrows.

Devon wondered who had cared about the man enough to perform the time-consuming task and then stopped. He wore headphones and danced to the music in his ears. Despite the man's circumstances, Devon envied him.

"We gonna need someone to go down in Shakespeare's place, Dev. Someone strong, someone dependable. Someone who could do the time and not be a little snitchy bitch about it, you feelin' me?"

Devon nodded. He had known this was coming, as obvious as a bad plot in a soap opera. He moved to speak up, but an impotency took hold of him, and all he could manage was to spit over his shoulder. He knew this was no democracy. That was clear from the first week he had met Des, when he watched two members of the crew kill a rival drug dealer, Spice Boy, while he begged for his life on his knees in the vacant parking lot of an IHOP. The die had already been cast. Life as he knew it was about to change. But it was okay. He had been through this before. He knew a thing or two about transitions.

"Armstrong says with your background, your clean record, your family history, you could probably get six to eight, but be out of there easily in three and a half with good behavior. Shit, by the time you back on the scene, them Lakers might even be good again."

"Well," Devon replied, "let's hope it don't take *that* long."

"That's my dawg."

They hugged again, a deep prideful embrace. Devon smelled the powerful cologne Des had always worn, a cedarwood and vanilla mix. It reminded Devon of his father. The homeless man passed them slowly, and Devon heard the man merrily singing a song.

"They tried to tell us, we're too young . . ."

Devon drove into the sunlight and stopped his car about a mile down the beach. He killed the engine and sat there with the radio playing an old R&B favorites station. His mind whirled with so much of what he and Des had discussed. It was as if while they talked, a small balloon in his chest filled with ice-cold water, and it kept filling up during their conversation and continued to do so after they had parted ways.

Now, with Devon at a distance and able to digest all he'd heard, the balloon burst open. Devon had never had a panic attack, but he knew well what they looked and sounded like. Margeaux had had a few in her day, and the details lingered in his memory. He recalled once in New York, he and Alexis having to rush to an emergency room in Greenwich Village with Margeaux after she argued with a bike messenger and was struck in the face. He remembered wondering if she was going to die right there in the back seat of the taxi, so difficult was her ability to breathe consistently. He learned later she had such attacks once every few years, and they were often triggered by violence.

Now, with his breaths caught up in a bottleneck in his throat, he remembered the techniques he saw Margeaux employ. He stared straight ahead at the ocean and focused on one spot where the sun hung bright like a tangerine in a pool of blue. He tried to listen to the rhythmic flow of his heartbeat, and he repeated one of his favorite quotes over and over in his mind:

"You came here empty handed, and you will leave empty handed. What is yours today belonged to someone else yesterday and will belong to someone else again tomorrow."

Juana had shared that quote with him a little over five years ago when she made her surprise return to Los Angeles. It made perfect sense to him that he should reflect on her now. Everything about this moment was connected to his beautiful and troublesome relationship with the woman he still thought of as his mentor. He went over it all—her strength, her composure, the power and force of her influence. He felt his breath returning to him. He grew supremely confident with the knowledge that he was not going to die—not today anyway. His mind journeyed back to where so much of his current life was formed.

After he left UCLA, ego shattered beyond repair, he languished in a state of pathos and self-recrimination. What a fool he had been to believe that he, a crippled Black man with minimal education or world experience, could possibly make films that spoke to and educated society at large. What an abject fool he saw himself as, and yet it enraged him to see that a few of his classmates had found some success. Many of them he found had less of a voice than he did, but they were on the path.

Jedediah Springer had signed a two-movie deal with a major studio after his short film debuted.

Antoine Pressley had started assistant directing and mentoring with a renowned Oscar-winning documentarian after the debut of his short film.

Worst of all, the student he suspected was a white supremacist, Neil Falcone, had been granted a three-year scholarship with one of the most prestigious film and television companies known in the industry.

Devon had considered himself just plain unlucky. He moved back into Shane's mother's guest room, got a job as an assistant manager at a Kinko's in Eagle Rock, and did nightly hits of weed and cocaine with Shane and his girlfriend, Xenobia, a yoga instructor.

One early afternoon, Devon was eating a sandwich on the patio when Shane came out postshower, a concerned look on his face. Shane told him he needed to tell him something, and he advised him he might want to stop eating. Devon listened as Shane relayed he'd noticed over the past several weeks that there were copious amounts of blood in his bowel movements. At first, Shane thought it was related to a constipation issue, but he had recently started to doubt that. He asked Devon to contact Roxanne for any advice she might have for him.

But Devon and Roxanne had not spoken for two years, not since a dinner in honor of James's wake, and Roxanne had confronted him by the pool.

"I'm just curious . . . do you feel anything?" she'd said. "Like, remorse, regret, anything?"

He had looked her in the eyes. "I feel like sometimes in life the bad things you do have a way of catching up with you. You know what I mean?"

Now Roxanne was completing her residency at a respected hospital in the Pacific Northwest. From what Devon knew, she was relatively happy there, might even be engaged. When he called her, she was short with him, almost businesslike. Truth was, he was grateful she had even spoken to him.

"So honestly, Devon, that could be a number of things. It could run the gamut from hemorrhoids to colon cancer. I would advise Shane to go see his doctor right away. If it is colon cancer, as with most cancers, early treatment is key to a healthy recovery and survival. Don't let him dillydally on this. Hang up and call his doctor."

Shane took her advice to heart and did just that. His doctor, Paul Mukherjee, after performing a stool test and a biopsy, confirmed what Roxanne had suspected—Shane was in the early stages of colorectal cancer. Surprising for someone of his age, but not unheard of.

Over the next few months, Shane underwent several uncomfortable medical procedures, and he worried constantly that at some point chemotherapy would be next. The very idea of losing his waist-long beautiful blond hair was simply unfathomable. Devon and Xenobia did their best to assure him that should it come to that, they would find him the best wigs that money could buy, even if they had to travel to another country to get them. Humor was their preferred method of dealing with the frightening situation, and they stuck by each other throughout the entire process.

Fortunately for Shane, the treatments proved to be successful, and he was declared cancer-free at the end of the year. Dr. Mukherjee made it clear Shane needed to always be present, always aware of the fact that his cancer was in remission. There was no cure-all that would eradicate it forever. He would need to monitor himself.

He was a survivor, yet again.

When the new year began, Devon saw a few unexpected changes in his best friend. While in the hospital, Shane had been referred by his oncologist to a support group of people who all struggled with various types of cancer. The group gathered weekly at a meeting room at his local hospital, and over donuts, sandwiches, and coffee, they shared the unique experience of living daily with a disease that was, as the facilitator put it, "trying to kill you every day."

At his third session, Shane met a breast-cancer survivor named Leanna Woodson. Leanna wasn't really Shane's type physically. She was rather plain looking and in her early forties, but she spoke with great reverence and passion about her respect and appreciation for her Lord and Savior, Jesus Christ. Over time, the emotion behind her words had a profound effect on Shane.

Devon watched as Shane progressed relatively quickly from a pot-smoking druggie who attended strip clubs twice a week after work to a Sunday churchgoer who rose at 8:00 a.m. daily and read a section of the Bible over his morning coffee. He did away with several things he considered a vice in his life (including Xenobia), and spent much of his spare time trying to do "the Lord's work." He became involved with Leanna's daughter, Beatrice, a portly girl from Arkansas in her midtwenties, and they started a Bible youth group Beatrice led weekly at a small community center in Palmdale.

Devon was happy Shane found something he felt grounded him and made him stronger, but Shane's new lifestyle put a great strain on their friendship. Devon resented being on the receiving end of sermons and lectures, which popped up just about anywhere, be it at the breakfast table, the gas station, or the local taco joint. He felt he was always being talked *at* in these moments, not talked *to*, and as these instances grew in regularity, his patience waned.

Shane's mother also found it all a bit disconcerting. One night after work, she and Devon found themselves in the same local bar. They shared shots.

"I didn't want to go home," she said, amused. "Little Billy Graham Jr. over there has a tendency to drive me crazy lately."

"I hear you on that. I swear, I miss the guy who came home smelling like weed and lap dances."

"Yeah, I fear we've lost that guy for good. Which is a shame, really. He used to be the most fun kid you ever saw. What happened to him, Devon?"

"I wish I knew so I could avoid it at all costs."

"I'm actually hoping that he marries this fat church chick of his and moves to Texas with her or wherever these ministries thrive. It would be nice to have the house back to its hedonistic ways."

They toasted. However, much to their chagrin, no such marriage took place. Instead, Beatrice moved in with them, at which point the house became a bit too crowded with sanctimony for Devon's liking. He couldn't smoke a joint in the backyard without hearing it from either of the couple. Late one night, Beatrice caught him watching porn on cable and launched into him.

"You know that taking in this type of sexual deviance is a sin, right?"

"I'm sorry, I missed the reference to porn in the Bible."

"It's sinful to look at a woman, other than one's wife, with lust in one's heart. Job said so himself."

"Yeah well, Job probably never had access to *Late Night with Suzy and Samantha*."

"It's unhealthy, Devon. I'm trying to help you."

"You wanna help me? I could use another Heineken."

"Matthew said, 'The eyes are the lamp of the body. If your eyes are healthy, your whole body will be full of light. If your eyes are unhealthy, your whole body will be full of darkness.'"

"It's just two women going down on one another, Bea. Goodness gracious. It's sex. Sex is healthy. Don't you and Shane have sex? Y'all ain't married. What does the Bible say about that?"

"Shane and I have a loving, committed relationship in the eyes of our Lord and Savior, and if he does not like our behavior, he will judge us when the time is right."

By the fall, with all the money he'd saved living at the Tollefson house rent-free, Devon decided it was time for a change. He got himself a studio apartment in Inglewood. He still met with Shane for the occasional lunch or dinner about once a month or so, but he usually regretted going, as Shane rarely ever went anywhere without Beatrice.

Through a friend in the film department at the University of Southern California, Devon got a side job three nights a week reading and reviewing hundreds of film and television scripts that were submitted to a growing film production company in North Hollywood called Bay Bridge Films. The company had recently signed on to represent several B-list actors, and his job was determining whether any of the scripts were good fits for these clients. He hated the work, but it paid decent money. He read some of the worst writing he had ever seen in his life, and he could not believe that somewhere out there people who considered themselves artists were actually writing some of the shit he took home.

He couldn't fathom how someone could sit down at a typewriter or a computer and type out *Robot Romance* or *Moochers in Minneapolis* or *The Austin Alien Sex Laundry*. The latter was a screenplay about two aliens from Saturn, men who had the ability to shape-shift to resemble any human they wanted—these two chose bodybuilders. When their spaceship crash-lands in a backyard in Austin, Texas, they decide to pitch a tent in the backyard and work on repairing their ship. Of course it is the backyard of a sorority house, and many hijinks ensue as the aliens help one girl's mother run a local laundromat. When he gave that script a two out of ten rating and threw it atop the "reject" pile, which outweighed the "consider" pile by about fifty to one, his supervisor, an executive in project development, called him a week later to rip him a new one, yelling over the phone, "How could you pass on *Austin Sex Laundry* so callously? Jimbo Specter read it over the weekend and fell in love with it. He thinks it could be his launching pad into films and wants us to start production meetings on it. The thing has Specter's physical humor written all over it. Watch what you're reviewing, Payne. If this one had slipped through our fingers to New Line or something, that coulda been your ass!"

It never got any better. Once, over Valentine's Day weekend, he was called into the office along with about fifteen other readers. They sat in a large conference room at a table with about a hundred scripts on top of it. They were told that this was to be a marathon reading session and they couldn't leave until they had found an appropriate project for Natalie Cella, one of their biggest clients and a rising star after the back-to-back successes of *Prima Donna* and *Prima Donna 2: Back to Kansas*. All sixteen readers were fed a steady diet of pizza and canned soda and spent about thirty-six hours poring over some of the purest drivel Devon thought he had ever beheld. He called Alexis early the second morning, telling her his eyes were bleeding.

In the end, each writer had to select at least two scripts for the company to consider, and Devon selected *Camp Xanadu*, a story about a young college graduate who runs a roller-skating camp for teenagers, and *The Last Mile*, an uber-sappy drama about a single mother and marathon runner who is told she has six months to live after doctors discover she has an inoperable brain tumor (the catch is, in the last act, they realize they mixed up her CAT scan with someone else's in the lab, but she learns to truly appreciate life!). After the entire process was over, several of the readers decided to meet up at an all-night diner a few blocks away. Many funny stories were shared, many drinks were downed, and Devon wound up going home with one of them, a Russian woman named Yulia, a former film major who managed a bike shop in Studio City.

One April afternoon, Shane called him during his lunch break at Kinko's.

"What's up, preacher man?"

"Hey, hey, good to hear your voice, brother. It's been a while."

"Yeah, you know how it is. Hustling. What's up?"

"Well, I know this is short notice, but I wanted to see if you were free tonight for a drink at the Roosevelt. I have some exciting news to share."

Devon knew what the news was—Shane and Beatrice were engaged. He accepted the invitation, not because he was excited about the assumed announcement, but because he liked the atmosphere at the Roosevelt Hotel. Shane ended saying, "Seven sharp, don't be late! You ain't gonna wanna miss this!"

Devon arrived at six thirty and settled into a nice spot at the end of the bar. He ordered a Scotch and soda and took in the scene. The bar was filled with fine-looking people, many of them who he knew to be in the entertainment industry in one way or another. He picked up his knapsack and took out a copy of *The Karaoke Killer*, a script about a serial killer who frequented karaoke bars. He was a third of the way through and figured he could finish while he waited. Just as he flipped open the script, he heard a familiar voice.

"Hey, sailor, come here often?"

His heart jolted, and he whipped his face up from the script, anxious to see the source of the voice. Juana's figure was as close to a heavenly vision as he could imagine. It had been a little more than five years, but she was even more beautiful than he remembered her.

They hugged for an extended length of time, neither wanting to let go. Her hair still smelled like strawberries, and he was instantly at ease. They pulled back and took each other in. Both had grown and developed good upper-body strength since the last time they were together. Juana's hair was thicker, shinier, longer. She wore designer jeans and a satin blouse. Life had been good to her, healthwise. She squeezed his shoulder, admiring the tone.

"You looking good, *hermano*. Shane wasn't lying, you don't look a day older."

"I could say the same for you, *chica*. That Salt Lake City air must be amazing."

"Ah yes, Salt Lake City." She smiled at the reference. "We have so much catching up to do."

They got a table and spent the next several hours rehashing one another's lives. Devon listened attentively. He was extremely curious to learn just what happened with the person she went back to Salt Lake City to settle a score with. In classic Juana fashion, she held back nothing.

"The dude who shot me was a gangbanger named Anthony Ball. We called him Small Ball 'cause he didn't have any game. He had these gold teeth. Everybody knew him. He wasn't welcome at any of my homeboys' events, but he showed up with a tiny crew. I saw him pull the gun out from my booth. I was just switching out albums when it all went down."

The drug dealer who hosted the party had always planned to retaliate but was unsure just how he wanted to go about it. When Juana showed up back in town, she reached out to him right away and let him know that she needed to call in a favor. The host, upon hearing the favor she was calling in, did not hesitate to act. Within two days, Small Ball was kidnapped coming out of a local mall while carrying a car stereo. His body would be found days later by the tracks of a no-longer-active railway stop. Ball had been shot a total of seven times, one for each injured victim at the party.

"How did that feel?" Devon leaned in, fascinated by her manner. "To know that you were responsible for taking another person's life?"

"You want my honest answer?"

"You know I do."

"I did a lot of reflecting on it in the days after, and it's possible that in the future, somewhere down the line, I might feel differently, have some regrets. But in this moment, I'm cool with it. It feels a lot like justice."

She hung around SLC for about another two months before moving on to a new rehabilitation facility in Atlanta, where she spent three months. "I kept my nose clean there. None of those Silver Mountain hijinks." The social worker helped her get her own apartment in a complex for seniors and people with disabilities. She stayed in Atlanta for about a year and a half, where she became involved with a guy who would eventually get her back into the line of work she felt most suited for—drug trafficking.

The guy, Marco, was a bartender at a popular night club, and he also ran drugs at the club and in two strip joints. Marco heard of an opportunity through his supplier that he believed Juana would be a great fit for: a high-level Jamaican drug dealer was using a few strippers to smuggle drugs to Jamaica, Puerto Rico, and Canada by packing them on their bodies in sensitive locations and boarding planes. It occurred to Marco there were numerous places that a woman in a wheelchair could pack drugs on her person where airport security would never think to look. It took only four successful trips to Jamaica and Bermuda before it became apparent to the higher-ups they could move a lot more product through Juana. Soon enough, she was making more money a month than she could ever see in years of disability payments.

Juana was relocated to Miami, where she spent years moving all types of contraband through various international locations. Only once did she have a close call, in an airport in Frankfurt when a drug-sniffing dog sniffed her a little too closely, but she was able to charm the officials there, telling them she had recently started smoking marijuana in Amsterdam, mainly for medicinal purposes.

Devon was intrigued by it all and was surprised to hear that there was even more. Juana had, as of a month ago, been relocated to Los Angeles, where she would start her most successful and financially rewarding runs of all, moving drugs to and from several cities in Mexico. She had just purchased a two-story house in Manhattan Beach and, having ditched Marco a while back in Miami, was living alone again and feeling a little lonely. Shane had told her all about Devon's recent trials and tribulations, and Juana came prepared to pounce.

"So listen, *hermano*, I'm sure Inglewood is simply lovely, but I gotta tell you, I could really use a man like you around the house. Someone to cook, clean, pay the bills, make me laugh. I've missed you like you can't know."

At first, Devon thought she was joking, but a scrutiny of her eyes revealed she was quite serious. She put a strong hand on his shoulder.

"There's not too many people I can truly call family, *hermano*."

He moved out of his apartment at the end of the month. Though Juana's place was nowhere near as large as the Tollefson house, it was still impressively spacious. They had a pool, a yard, and huge dining- and living-room areas and were within walking distance of the beach. They developed a routine of dining out by the pool at night after Devon returned from work. Juana would order from one of many local takeout options, and Devon would pick it up on his way home.

Occasionally, Shane and Beatrice joined them, but Juana found it a struggle to enjoy time with the couple, as she found their proselytizing tiresome.

"I can't believe what happens to some people," she said to Devon one late Sunday afternoon. Shane and Beatrice had joined them for brunch and then left to run a church service.

"I can only imagine that Shane was looking for something, needed something in his life after that whole cancer scare. And I suppose these people filled that need. That's what I have to imagine."

"I get that, but don't try to push that shit on me because you think you are saved or absolved of all your sins or whatever. I mean, I'll be honest with you, I've been doing some reading. When I was in Miami, I met this dude who was into the Bhagavad Gita."

"The what?"

"The Bhagavad Gita. You never heard of it?"

"It sounds like something you get after eating really bad shellfish."

"College boy over here, never heard of Bhagavad Gita. It's like the Hindu Bible. I don't really know how to describe it, but it's got a lot of wisdom in it. I read the whole thing in a month. That shit is like seven hundred pages. It's like a dialogue about life, death, our purpose, and the nature of existence. It's deep and spiritual, but not judgy like a lot of that Catholic bullshit. It reminds me constantly that we are here for a very brief time, but we will live forever. This is just a body, and someday that will leave us. But the soul will always carry on."

"Seven hundred pages, huh?"

"Yeah, if you ever want to check it out, I always keep it by my bedstand."

"Is there a movie version?"

Juana was normally gone for a week, sometimes two, and Devon, though he missed her, also appreciated having the whole house to himself. Every now and then, he would invite Yulia over, and they would have dinner and watch a movie, and she would spend the night. Twice over the summer, Alexis, Dahlia, and Michel came out to visit. He loved watching them enjoy all the amenities of the house, and he was proud to see how well Juana got along with all of them. He and Juana did agree it best to keep her real profession a secret, and they told his siblings she was a traveling saleswoman. Possibly the greatest benefit of this living arrangement was Juana did not charge him any rent to stay there. She just asked that he maintain the house in good condition and handle all the bills while she was gone. This allowed him to quit his agonizing second gig reading scripts and work four full-time shifts at Kinko's, Sunday through Wednesday.

One afternoon in early October, Juana came in the front door with two well-built, well-dressed men, one an Italian, the other a Black man with a West Indian accent. She introduced them to Devon as Nicolo and Jean-Pierre, two work associates. He thought they came straight out of Central Casting for a buddy-cop film, so slick and polished they looked. They sat by the pool and drank beers with Devon and Juana. Days later, Devon realized their presence was more of a job interview than any genuine conversation. Juana had suggested to them they give Devon a look to see if he could perform a similar role to hers. He learned he passed the interview when, later that week, they called and asked him to meet them at a popular sushi restaurant in Brentwood.

"They're gonna make you an offer you can't refuse," Juana joked.

And that was how Devon found himself back in the business of the drug trade. As with Juana, he would store goods on his person and primarily in select spots on his wheelchair. Devon had never owned a passport, but he applied for one and was able to travel to Canada, Mexico, Germany, and occasionally Japan. Together, he and Juana made so much money that they moved out of Manhattan Beach and into a home in Bel Air, where they each occupied their own wing of the home.

Everything went well for them, and it seemed there would be no end to their success.

But as Devon would learn time and time again, nothing lasts forever.

One early morning on a Tuesday in New York City, two planes crashed into the Twin Towers. The days of casual airport security came to an end, and Devon and Juana had to transition to new roles. Devon moved to transporting contraband locally up and down the I-5 corridor, which included Oregon and Washington. Periodically, he would travel to Mexico, where he could still access certain cities without too much trouble. Juana, however, shocked him by choosing a completely different route. She asked him to meet her at the Roosevelt Hotel for drinks.

"Listen," she said, sipping on a mojito. "I have to tell you something, and it's going to completely fuck your brain."

He took a shot of his bourbon and chased it with a beer. He couldn't imagine what she could possibly say that would be that alarming.

"What, are you pregnant?" he blurted out. She had been seeing a Honduran guy recently.

"Pregnant? Get outta here. I ain't trying to bring no kid into this fucking world. No." She brought down her tone substantially, which Devon knew meant she was about to say something meaningful. "So I've done something that I maybe shouldn't have done, but I can't help myself. I was warned about this three, maybe four years ago and was punished back then. Clearly, I didn't learn my lesson."

Devon leaned in close. Tension took a hold at the top of his neck and made its way slowly down his spine. He listened with great interest as Juana told him a tale that involved her skimming money off the top of many of her runs—a thousand here, two thousand there. It all added up to several hundred thousand over the years.

The first time she had been caught, her boss back then, a Mexican in Chicago, had some men break her right arm and kill her dog, a pit bull named Apollo. She had to use an electric wheelchair for months while her arm healed. She was warned that if it ever happened again, she wouldn't have to worry about ever needing a wheelchair again.

But as she said, she was hardheaded.

She could not help but follow her lesser demons. A close associate gave her a heads-up that her new boss, who was also Nicolo's boss, a hardened Jamaican, had reason to believe she was skimming again. She was not about to wait around to find out if he could confirm it or not.

"After I leave here, I'm heading to the airport. I'm boarding a plane, and you will most likely never see me again."

Devon felt a lump in his throat the size and texture of charcoal.

"I wish I could tell you where I was going, but I wouldn't put you in that position. Just know it will have lots of sun, trees, and beaches. They are going to ask you where I am, and you have to tell them you have no idea. You just tell them that I just up and disappeared, which is the truth. They won't hurt you, trust me. Nicolo adores you. Jean-Pierre adores you. More importantly, Duarte has tremendous respect for you. Your work ethic speaks for itself. They would never hurt you to spite me. That's not how these guys operate. They want me. And they most likely will never stop looking for me. Just know that wherever I am, I am going to be fine. And know that I love you like I have loved very few men in my day. I left my copy of the Bhagavad Gita by your bed in case you ever want to do a little reading. I think it will speak to you and some of the things you've gone through in life. I want you to listen to me now and know if there is one thing I've learned it is this—believe in yourself." Devon scoffed, but her face was grave. "I'm serious, *hermano*. *Believe in yourself.* Know yourself. Because there are not a lot of people out there who are going to give you the benefit of the doubt. Know yourself and believe in yourself. It makes all the difference."

That was the last time Devon ever saw Juana. On occasion, he'd receive a postcard in the mail, postmarked from Los Angeles with a photo of a generic tropical island under the words "Greetings from Paradise." The signature always read:

Love, Your Silver Mountain Sis

Juana was right. They did come to him looking for her, and when he told them he did not know where she was, they eventually left him alone. As time went on, he would bounce around from job to job, boss to boss. In time, he would find the Bel Air place too big, not to mention too expensive for his salary. He moved to an apartment in Westwood. Not a day went by when a small part of him didn't wish that he could have joined Juana that night and boarded that plane for a tropical island somewhere.

But it wasn't meant to be. As Roxanne had once said—he still had more music to face.

The afternoon that Devon learned he would be going to jail for at least six to eight years (three and a half with good behavior), he realized he needed to talk to someone he trusted, someone he respected. He needed the comforting, supportive voice of someone outside the game. Normally that would have been Alexis, but he required a physical presence. He knew he'd find Claudia Solis on campus either in her office or at the library. After a quick stop by her empty office, he headed halfway across campus to the film department library. There, he found her reading from a large book and jotting down notes.

Professor Claudia Solis was short, like, dwarf short. That pleased Devon very much because he had never particularly cared for tall women. He found them to be terribly difficult to relate to, both physically and emotionally out of reach. It was one of the reasons why he had liked Claudia right away. She was accessible. He had never met anyone like her in his life. She was half-Cuban, half-Nigerian, and her skin was the hue of ripe coffee beans. She had a thick mane of silver-and-black hair that she always wore back in a tight ponytail. Coupled with her nerdy bifocals, her look conveyed a certain geekiness that both appealed to and intrigued Devon. A year earlier, he had taken her summer class, open to the general public, on "The Theme of Revenge and Poetry in American Cinema." He had left the ten-week course feeling changed in ways he could not immediately articulate, but he would write in his review of the course,

> I feel like this class opened my mind to so much of the darkness and the light that we see in everyday life that we are conditioned to walk by without truly observing. Professor Solis took me on a weekly journey that reminded me how valuable film can be in holding a mirror to society's beauty and flaws. I am a film fan for life!

He sought her out after classes to discuss various concepts and themes she had introduced. Often, she would invite him to join her for *cafecitos* at a spot she liked in downtown Westwood. He had been shocked when he first learned that she was the mother of seven grown children. One of them, her youngest daughter, had been tragically taken from her by a crazed gunman at an abortion clinic four years ago. The grief had proved too hard on her marriage, and she and her husband parted ways shortly thereafter. It was this aspect of her that Devon most related to. They were something like siblings in suffering, their physical appearances causing them both to always be alone in a crowd. He had the impression she appreciated his company, and perhaps saw a kindred spirit in him as well.

"Hey, if it isn't the boy wonder!" she said as he rolled over and gave her a hug.

He couldn't remember why she called him the boy wonder, but she had been doing it for as long as he had known her, and he loved it.

"Professor Solis. Hard at work on your next thesis?"

"Actually, no. I'm just preparing for freshman film noir. You know the drill—*The Big Sleep, The Postman Always Rings Twice, Mildred Pierce.*"

"Ugh, that Joan Crawford. What a piece of work."

"She had her moments. How is your writing going? Am I ever gonna see that finished screenplay?"

"Not likely, Professor. Not anytime soon."

"Qué lástima."

She told him she could use some fresh air. The two of them left her things behind and strolled out of the library, eventually finding seats in a nearby courtyard. They sat in silence for a bit, taking in the loveliness of the day around them. Devon was glad he had come to her. There was a clock ticking for him now. Des had told him to show up at Armstrong's office next Monday, ready to turn himself in. This gave Devon five more days to appreciate the outside world.

"So, what brings you by, young fella?"

"What? I have to have a reason to visit my favorite professor?"

"No, I didn't say that. But it's been, what? Two months now? I think you visited last right before spring break."

"Yeah, that may be. I guess I've just been thinking." He watched as a dog wandered around their vicinity, a labradoodle or some such. He saw no owner nearby, and that disturbed him a little. "Remember in one of your earlier lectures about revenge, how as an example you showed us that scene from *Godfather Two*?"

"Ah, the return to Sicily, yes? Great scene."

"Yeah, it's funny, you know I've watched that scene several times, and I've reread that essay on Iago that you wrote, 'The Iago Complex.' It's weird. Like, why are some of us so focused on revenge? Why does it matter to some of us so much?"

"That, my friend, is a good question. It's interesting you should bring this up. I was just reading this great article on these mothers in Rwanda. These strong African mothers who had their sons taken from them, murdered, sometimes brutally, by other men, and really so many of them were just kids, you know. It was kids killing kids. And how, once all the bloodshed was over, as part of the healing process, some of these women found themselves raising as their own sons the very same boys who had *killed* their sons. A lot of these boys were left orphaned and in need of a mother, and these women were able to put their anger and rage aside and actually welcome these murderers into their lives with open arms. It might just be the greatest act of forgiveness I've ever heard of."

"But those women, they must have needed to do that to heal, right?"

"That's what I assume."

"Maybe the way some people need to forgive to heal, maybe some people need revenge to heal, you know? Is that possible?"

"It is. Let me ask you this—where do you stand on the death penalty?"

Devon looked over at her, and he felt a wave of déjà vu overcome him. He had had this very same conversation with his older sister Roxanne once over Christmas dinner. Just then the owner of the labradoodle appeared holding a chain leash in her hand and reading a magazine article. She was an attractive white student wearing what looked like a geisha's outfit. It was a peculiar sight.

"The death penalty? I'm for it, I think. I'm pretty sure I am. I don't really see why someone should be allowed to get away with taking another life. I know that if someone killed my kid—" He bit his lower lip and cursed himself under his breath. His cheeks stung with shame, and he was relieved to feel her hand rubbing the back of his neck, comforting him.

"It's okay. I am not so fragile, Devon."

"I know, it's just . . . I'm so stupid sometimes. I'm sorry, Professor."

"You are too sensitive. So, you are for the death penalty, yes?"

"Yes, I am. There are some deeds that should not go unpunished, right? I mean, Robert De Niro at the end of *Godfather Two* feels pretty satisfied once he offs that fat old fuck, doesn't he? And he should. I know I would."

"Well, I imagine he does. Or so he thinks he does. But the reality is, it hasn't changed his situation. He is still a son who grew up without his mother. Without his brother. There is still a void in him that will never be filled. That scum who took my Caroline—I cursed him for the first two years she was gone. But it was not constructive. I did not grow from this anger. In fact, it mostly held me back. I feel much stronger now. I have no weight to uphold. Her killer does not get to take two lives in the process. He does not get to wield such power."

Devon looked over at the labradoodle and the owner again. Geisha girl was down on one knee now, talking to her dog while tickling it behind the ear. She seemed to be having an intense conversation with the animal. He felt terribly awkward, like he was intruding on an intimate moment.

"But why do you ask me these things, Devon? Is there someone for whom you seek revenge? Someone you want to give a Sicilian necktie?"

"I was hurt once, deceived by two people very close to me. It was more than ten years ago, and still, to this day, I can't let it go. Even though one of them has already passed on. I want . . ." His tongue froze as his lips attempted to go on without him. It took him a few seconds to finally speak up. "I want revenge against God, Professor Solis. I want revenge against that bullshitter who abandoned every one of us, even his only son, left us all to languish here in this terribly imperfect place. I want to see him suffer like so many of us do."

If his words stunned or offended her at all, her face revealed nothing. She simply smiled the toothless, sad smile of sympathy. She gently squeezed his shoulder.

"Well, I can assure you of this, my friend—you are in good company."

The early evening that Devon learned he would be going to jail for at least six to eight years (three and a half with good behavior), he drove back home. He was in a restless frame of mind. As much as he enjoyed time spent with Claudia, this visit had left him dissatisfied, hungry for more. And he knew just why that was. He had not shared with Claudia what he had truly come to share. He had wanted to impart to her his own story of revenge. He had wanted her to know what a horribly small, wretched human being life had turned him into.

He had wanted to tell her about James. About a phone call with Gina in which she did everything but get down on her hands and knees and plead with him to get a bone-marrow test that might, just might, save her husband's, his brother's life. His response to her had been cold, much cruder than his response to his mother.

"Thank you, but I'll pass. James is gonna get what he has coming to him now. He's going to learn what I've known all these years: what it feels like to lose everything."

He hadn't shared that story with Claudia for a simple reason—he chickened out. He was afraid to see the look in her eyes that would surely convey her utter disappointment in him. Her almost certain judgment would open a wound he had sealed shut long ago. His adoration for Claudia meant she had the power to make him bleed, and Devon had bled enough. While sitting in standstill freeway traffic, he recalled the first time he'd rolled into Claudia's classroom that brisk summer morning. The room had smelled like lemon disinfectant, and written on the chalkboard he saw:

The Mills of the Gods Grind Slowly, but They Grind Exceeding Fine

He realized he had to tell someone. It was just too much to keep inside, and who knew just when or if he would ever have the opportunity again? He would tell Nadia. She would be disappointed too, but she wouldn't judge him, wouldn't detest him. They had shared too much, been to each other's dark spaces. She wouldn't absolve him, but she wouldn't make him want to crawl into his own skin and die either. He would also explain to her what was about to take place in his life and why she would not see him any longer for a few years. That conversation might be harder.

While stopping for drive-through takeout, a thought hit him. Soon, all these little freedoms, something as simple as picking up shitty fast food, would be a thing of the past. He would be on a prison schedule, eating prison food three meals a day. No iced lattes or Frappuccinos, no so-called Happy Meals, no burrito supremes with extra guacamole, no cheesecake or tiramisu to finish it all off, no night caps. This reality depressed him, and he drove off, no longer having the heart to wait in the drive-through line.

He went to knock on Nadia's door but stopped when he heard loud voices coming from inside. Nadia was arguing with a man, both speaking in her native tongue. He listened for a few minutes, just enough to get the sense that she wasn't in danger, and then opened the door to his own apartment.

The walls glowed a fiery orange as his apartment caught the beautiful sunset so endemic to Los Angeles. He poured himself a glass of wine, put on Miles Davis's *Sketches of Spain*, and rolled out onto his balcony. Below, rush-hour traffic made the streets look metallic and grimy. The image of the stockpiled vehicles made him angry.

When did we decide we needed so many cars? he thought.

During a visit to Manhattan many years ago with Margeaux, she had told him in overly morbid fashion while they shared a slice of pizza,

"Between the US, China, and India, the earth is assured a miserable and painful death. Right now, we have the earth in a concentration camp, and we are slowly walking it to the gas chambers."

Classic Margeaux, he thought, *always the dramatic one.* Still, her words gave him chills. He made a mental note to write her a letter soon, before he left for prison.

He wondered what he would do with his car while he was inside, when a male figure appeared on Nadia's balcony. The man lit up a cigarette and looked out at the sky and then down below. His body language conveyed a simmering rage, as if he was in danger of being consumed by it. He was young, with long black hair. He wore black leather pants and a chic light-blue button-down. He could have easily been the lead singer of a rock band, but Devon knew him, had seen him in pictures in Nadia's apartment. He was her brother, the one who lived in Chicago. For some reason, Devon believed he was a pharmacist or something like that. The picture of her family on her kitchen refrigerator featured all of them at a ceremony, the brother in a white lab coat, wearing a graduation cap. It reminded Devon of another family portrait taken long ago.

Soon Nadia walked out to join him. She wore a tiny tight white skirt and a pink tank top. It was obvious she had been crying, and her hair was disheveled. She said something to her brother, and Devon could tell by her tone she was pleading with him. She reached out to touch his face, but he slapped her hand away, threw his cigarette off the balcony, and said something vile and dismissive to her, again in their tongue. And then he was gone from the balcony, and Devon heard the front door to her apartment slam shut.

Nadia watched the spot where he had once been. She was frozen in her own pain. She began shaking and wrapped her arms around her waist as if attempting to hold her intestines in. She slunk to the floor of the balcony.

The charm of the family portrait is that it has a magnificent ability to convey perfection. There is nothing quite like it.

It had been a while since he had thought of Kassandra.

"Nadia?"

She appeared startled from her dark dream and looked over to him. She wiped her eyes.

"Oh, Devon."

He wanted to go to her and hold her, but the partition dividing their balconies was too high. He moved as close as he could.

"You okay, princess? That was your brother, right?"

"Some brother. Some fucking brother!" She spit as she spoke. Devon had never seen her so distraught. "My sister, she tell him what I do to make money. She tells me it is for my own good. Fuck her! And fuck him! You know what he call me? He call me two-ruble whore. He say I bring such a shame to the family he can barely stand to look at me. He say my . . ." She struggled to get the next words out, choked with emotion. "He say what I have between my legs is a dirty sewer filled with the filth of a thousand men. This is what my brother say to me. And then he say he is going to tell my father everything."

Devon watched her, not knowing what he might possibly say to her. She wept with uncontrollable bursts that shook her body. Devon felt helpless.

The cruelty of brothers. What a piece of work was man.

Nadia turned to him. Her mascara had run down her cheeks like ink bleeding from her eyes. "I cannot tolerate that, Devon. I can live with many things, but not the shame of my papa."

"Surely, he didn't mean it, Nadia. Surely, he was just being cruel."

"He has always been cruel, Nikoly. He has always been superior. He does not understand the weight of struggle. He was always the protected one."

Devon watched as she stood up and turned to go back inside. He reached for her.

"Nadia, you will get through this. In the morning, we'll go to the Golden Egg. My treat. We'll talk this out over some omelets, pancakes, some fresh-brewed Guatemalan coffee. We can even have bacon."

Nadia looked at him, a look he had never seen from her before, in the condescending way a wise old grandmother looks at a baby child who has fallen and cannot get up on their own.

"My friend," she said. "I am not worthy of bacon."

And then she was gone, back inside her apartment. Seconds later, Devon heard the familiar sound of her shower running. He remained there on the balcony for a few more hours, finishing his bottle of wine and listening to music as the sky changed from an amber glow to a heavy black curtain. He changed the CDs. Sade to Stevie Wonder, finally falling asleep to Nat King Cole. It had gotten chilly on the balcony, and he pulled his hoodie up tight around his face. He dreamed of his childhood dog, Petey, named after the dog on *The Little Rascals*. In the dream, Devon had a chicken leg and made Petey play dead before he gave it to him. He would point his finger in the shape of a gun and shoot him down. Petey played along every time. What was dignity in the face of a fried chicken leg?

Devon awoke to the sound of Nadia's balcony door opening. She walked out in an opulent white robe, glowing as if she had been swimming in the moon. Devon barely had the time to register her presence when all at once she lifted herself up and like the most beautiful of birds launched herself off the balcony. The sheer grace and fluidity of her movement made her as magnificent as any dove.

It took Devon several seconds to realize what had just transpired. The sound of a car window shattering woke him from his stupor, and he held his hand to his neck to feel his pulse. A car alarm pierced the air once more—but different from before. For an instant, he thought he might be dreaming, prayed to be dreaming, despite not being a believer. There would be no breakfast at the Golden Egg in the morning. There would be no one to share his story with now. He would never have another conversation with this woman whom he had grown to love, come to appreciate so much in his daily life. No more chance meetings at the mailbox. No more elevator rides, bopping to pop Muzak from the '80s. It had all come to a jarring halt. The pungent sadness of family disappointment had claimed yet another soul. Tears rushed to fill his eyes at the thought of how terrible things could be. And would be.

He knew that he didn't want to go to prison, not even for three and a half years with good behavior.

He had made mistakes, yes, but now was not the time to suffer for them. No, suffering could always come later. Now, there was unfinished business. His mind went immediately to Gina. The last time he had seen her had been at his brother's funeral. It hadn't been pleasant. He had been sitting outside the church, waiting for Alexis to bring the car around so they could head over to the wake together. Gina had suddenly walked up beside him, holding a sleeping baby in her arms. He was stunned by the image of the two of them, but did his best not to show it.

"I'm gonna skip the wake," Gina told him bitterly. "I just wanted to say to you, may God have mercy on your soul."

"May he have mercy on your soul as well, Gina. Though I have bad news for you. In case you haven't noticed, there is no God."

"I wonder how you sleep at night."

"How did you sleep all those nights beside my brother?"

She stared at him, her eyes hard and feral. He got the sense that if she didn't have a child in her arms, she might strangle him then and there. He was grateful for the child.

"I won't allow anger to control my heart, Devon. I'm not going where you've gone."

"Good, good for you. It's not a place for everyone."

He'd watched as she walked away out of sight, gently holding her child's head. He remembered the way his hands shook as he realized his parents had been at the foot of the church door, watching the entire scene.

The sound of a far-off siren getting closer and closer brought him back to the present. He wondered what Nadia could have said to those she loved and who she thought loved her to possibly alter this horrible fate. Or maybe, just maybe, he thought, there was nothing one could do once the damage had been done. Maybe unfinished business should stay unfinished.

At the very least, he had to try.

Seeing Mr. Curry Off

To Alexis's surprise, the Van Wyck Expressway was not terribly busy on this Thursday night, understandable as it was the most popular night for Americans to stay home and watch television. Still, she hadn't expected the trip to go this smoothly. She would be at John F. Kennedy Airport in less than ten minutes. That put her back to Mr. Curry's apartment by nine thirty at the latest, in the bathtub by ten. This all pleased her immensely, but she didn't smile. She didn't want Mr. Curry to think that she was happy to see him go, even though deep down she was ecstatic.

Daniel Curry, in his midsixties, with a full, impressive head of silver hair and stunning silver-blue eyes, sat beside Alexis in the passenger seat, wearing his customary brown corduroy pants, white cotton button-down shirt, and olive-green cashmere vest. He jotted down notes on a yellow steno pad. Periodically, he looked up and his mouth moved as if he were reciting a speech in his head, and then he went back to writing. The local classical music station played in the car, a violin concerto by Vivaldi, and a light rain tickled the window.

The two of them had sat in silence the whole ride, but Alexis knew it was too good to be true. Eventually, he would have to say something. He could not help himself. She knew him better than she knew almost anyone.

"I trust you won't forget my dry cleaning tomorrow." His was the slightest of New England accents.

"I would never allow such a crime to occur," Alexis replied, allowing a smile.

"I'm well aware you think me just a silly old curmudgeon, but you must trust me on this one, Lexy. If you don't come pick up your cleaning within a week's time, those damned Chinese retain the right to give your clothing away to the Salvation Army, and they will do so without a second's hesitation. I've seen them do it. I used to have this recurring nightmare that I would see my Uncle Taylor's beloved cardigan on some homeless character in Times Square."

Alexis knew he had never had such a dream, but in the year and a half she had been working as the very personal assistant to Daniel Curry, revered off-Broadway playwright and theater society "bad boy," she had come to appreciate his dramatic ways. Truth be told, she was even quite fond of them. His demeanor gave him an edge and a melody that she needed in her life at this time. He was rarely dull, that much was certain, and unlike the other five assistants he had blazed through in two years, Alexis had somehow managed to unlock the secret door. She had discovered the right balance of patience, sacrifice, and fortitude that it took to deal with him on a daily basis.

Most important was she never took anything personally, even when he was screaming at the top of his lungs during one of his famous tantrums (it was rumored that he had once thrown a typewriter through his bedroom window, sending shattered glass everywhere and nearly killing a pedestrian some seventeen stories down below who was walking his dog on West End Avenue). In return for discovering how to put up with him, she had received his unwavering respect and affection.

It was an unspoken truism that their relationship had grown to the point where he found it impossible to live without her. Some days, he would call her at four in the morning, fretting that he had run out of creamer for his coffee and needed some "right at that instant" if he were to finish writing the day's scene. In these moments, she would magically appear at his door some twenty minutes later, half-and-half and lightly buttered cinnamon-raisin bagel from his favorite coffee shop in a brown paper bag in hand.

Anyone who knew him well could see that Alexis had become a necessary presence in his life. Alexis loved the power that she had inherited, and she was careful never to abuse it. Like any good companion, she took great pleasure in simply knowing it was there at her disposal.

Kassandra had gotten her this job. She had been one of Daniel Curry's most trusted friends and confidants for over a decade, and when he found himself in need of a new assistant, he asked her if she knew of anyone at her magazine who might want a change of scenery. Kassandra knew Alexis was frothing at the mouth to leave her job as an assistant to a hedge-fund millionaire, and she gave Curry her sister's number with a warning: "She'll be the smartest assistant you've ever had, and she doesn't suffer fools. Treat her with respect."

To Alexis, she gave one piece of advice after learning she received the job offer: "This man is a psychoanalyst's wet dream. He will push you and push you and push you because his need for unconditional love is so intense and he has to *know* that you will come back tomorrow. He needs to *know* that he can bash you and beat you to a metaphorical pulp and that you will still show up the next morning. Fucked up? Yes. It is the only way he knows to develop trust. But if you can show him that you can *endure*, the rewards will be great. You have to take my word on this, kiddo."

And rewards there were. Trips to award banquets, shopping sprees to buy him new suits where she was always gifted a new dress or blouse, the occasional sojourn out of state where he held numerous workshops, even a trip to Paris where she toured the city on her own for three days straight while Curry led a seminar, "The Memory Play and Its Place in the Modern Theater," at a university.

And then of course there was the sweetest fringe benefit of all—his apartment. She loved the classic four-bedroom penthouse with the cozy patio overlooking the Upper West Side of Manhattan. It had become her little pied-à-terre whenever Curry was away, and now, she would have it all to herself for three weeks. Three weeks! Just the thought of it warmed her like Sunday oatmeal. She could barely contain her excitement as she pulled the car up to the British Airways drop-off section of the terminal, braking too abruptly and causing the tires to screech.

"A little overzealous, are we?" he asked, turning to her.

His was a simple, handsome face. There was a lush sadness in his deep eyes, bluer than any August noon sky, that often affected her. If tomorrow he was stricken with a paralyzing disease, she would drop everything and care for him until his last day.

She smiled as she opened the door, leaving the car running.

"I just don't want you to miss your full-body pat down, lovey."

As was the norm, Curry waited until she had come around to his side and opened the door. He emerged with a long beige coat folded over his arm, which he put on while Alexis fetched his bags.

"Oh, Lexy, I do wish you were joining me on this one."

"Ah, but you decided it would be best to have the 'solitude of being an American in London.'" The last bit her best Daniel Curry impersonation.

"Yes, well, that all sounds good in October when one is first thinking about the trip and making plans and what have you, but this is June now, and June is no time to be alone in Covent Garden. I could buy you a ticket right now. We'll get you a week's worth of clothing at Harrods first thing in the morning."

"I don't have my passport on me, lovey," she said, handing him his black leather computer bag.

"Yes, that would present a problem, wouldn't it? I wonder if we could find some dainty young thing who looks like you here and pay her off to give you her passport."

Alexis laughed at him, loving when he was silly like this. She knew that he genuinely needed her, feared life without her.

"I thought you had a young lady friend there in London."

He narrowed his eyes at her, a soft intimidation as he wrapped his cashmere scarf around his neck. "First of all, she's in Liverpool, not London. And second, don't you go sharing that bit of information with anyone now, you understand, Miss Lexy? There's been quite enough gossip swirling around me lately, don't you think?"

"I think it's been wonderful," she replied as she placed a small suitcase by his side. "Nothing like a little scandal to keep New York's favorite playwright fresh."

"Hmmmm. Methinks you have been spending way too much time with that dreadful sister of yours. She had the audacity to send me a case of wine last weekend, a half-hearted attempt to make up for standing me up at the opera over Easter."

Alexis stood before him and adjusted his scarf and collar to her liking. It was possible that anyone looking at the two of them in this moment easily assumed they were lovers or even a married couple.

"Truth be told," he went on, "I'm not really interested in Mallory in that way. I believe every man and woman have their time and place, and ours, sadly, has long passed."

"Can't you even leave the door open for the possibility?"

"Possibility, my dearest ducky, is for you young people. When you get to my level of wisdom, all you have is pale certainty. No, it won't do. Do you know why people eventually stop marrying? Stop seeking companionship altogether? Hmmmm, do you?"

"Because they grow cranky?"

"No. If only it were that simple. It is because of trust. Trust, my dear, is like a fine piece of silver. It erodes over time and loses its luster. What was once precious and unique begins to rust and all at once becomes plain and tawdry, a thing to be ashamed of. Losing the ability to trust takes its toll on you. It is the heart rusting. If I wish you one thing in life, it is that you may never lose the ability to trust."

"Surely you know that silver doesn't really rust. It oxidizes."

"Sounds like a great title for a play—*The Oxidization of Alexis*."

"Mr. Curry, for someone with so much love in his heart, you can say the melancholiest things."

He deftly placed his gray top hat on his head, his signature fashion statement.

"One person's austerity is another's prosperity. Nibble on that while you drink my best Scotch tonight, why don't you?"

With that, he turned to his right, and stepped in line with all the other folks entering the terminal. But he wasn't really a part of them. He was distinct like that one section of a dream that doesn't quite fit in with the rest of it. The one that makes you wonder from where in your subconscious it sprang. She watched his hat disappear through the electric doors, and a familiar feeling surged in her stomach, and tears welled in her eyes. She recognized once more the affection she had for him.

She was passing the Queensboro Bridge when her cell phone went off. Normally, she wouldn't have moved to answer it, but she expected a call from Kassandra, and when she saw her sister's name appear on the screen, she snatched it up.

"Hey there. The silver eagle has taken flight."

"Lucky you," replied Kassandra. "Let the liberation celebration begin. We still on for Saturday?"

"Yeah. I was thinking maybe we could catch the matinee of *King Lear* at the Public. It's supposed to be a great production."

"That's with the Black Lear, right?"

"Yeah, and a Puerto Rican Cordelia and an Asian Goneril and—"

"Yeah, yeah, I get it. You know, if it's a nice day, I think I'd just as soon take a walk in the park or something."

"Ooh, a walk in the park. *Très romantique.*"

"I could use the workout too. Things are looking good on the parenthood front. Gonna have to get my body ready."

"Oh yeah, how's all that working out anyway? You think she'll follow through? What was she, from Indiana or something?"

"Kansas. And she'll be great. There has been a complication, but I'll tell you all about it on Saturday."

"Great. Looking forward to it. Speaking of complications, have you heard about Devon?"

"Nothing recent? He started prison Monday, no?"

Alexis lit a cigarette at the red light and opened both her window and the passenger window. The cool air hit her like a brisk wave.

"He never showed up for his sentencing."

"What do you mean he never showed up for his sentencing?"

"He asked them for a seventy-two-hour extension. They, of course, said no. He was dead set on needing to settle one more piece of business before going in. So there's a warrant out for his arrest as we speak."

"Get out of here! What could he possibly need to do that was so important he puts his entire sentence at risk?"

"It's simple. He went to go see Gina."

"Gina? Are you sure?"

"I'm positive. He called me from a phone booth in Atlanta two days ago. He drove across country for this. He thinks it's important that he say some things to her in person."

There was a long silence as both considered what that reunion would be like.

"Would love to be a fly on *that* wall," Kassandra said.

"Tell me about it."

"Well, if anyone is gonna get the whole story, it's gonna be you."

"Fucking Gina, the gift that never stops giving."

There was another long silence between the two of them that creeped into all the empty spaces of the car like the smoke from Alexis's cigarette. A soft rain splattered against the windshield. Somewhere nearby, a cat screeched at a raccoon.

"Deadlines, kiddo. Let's talk on Saturday."

"See ya then."

Alexis closed her phone and placed it deep in her pocket.

Hector, the young Dominican doorman, stood perched at his pedestal, watching the Yankee game on a small television set. When Alexis entered carrying two shopping bags, he moved from behind his counter and smiled at her with a full set of healthy teeth. His hair was slicked back, and his complexion was impeccably smooth, a wolf in uniform.

"Some help with those, madam?" he asked, approaching her.

"No, thank you, sir. I believe this *chica* can manage."

"I know that. Still, it's nice to have a man around for certain things, ain't it?"

She looked into his grinning face, aware of their game. "Certain things, sure. This ain't one of them."

"Well, if you think of something, you call down and let me know, okay?"

He winked at her, and in return, she batted her eyes, playing the role of the damsel in distress. Once, over Thanksgiving break, she had taken Hector up on such an offer, and they had had a good time. But not tonight. Tonight, she was very much looking forward to being alone.

"I'll keep that in mind, *señor*. But don't hold your breath."

She winked at him and walked to the elevator, knowing he was looking at her ass and appreciative of it.

The bathroom was an idyllic scene, like something one might see in an impressionist painting. The walls, a powder blue, glowed in the soft candlelight. Alexis, sitting in the warm bath, felt as though lodged in a womb of sky. Hanging directly over the head of the tub was a large, framed poster of Daniel Curry shaking hands with Lena Horne. The photograph had been taken after a concert, and Curry beamed like a child who had just received a lifetime shipment of chocolate-chip cookies. He looked straight at the camera, and she (radiant as Lena Horne always seemed to be) looked at him as if trying to remember just where they had met before. A live Nina Simone recording played on the stereo in the neighboring room.

Alexis turned on the faucet and let more hot water bleed into the bath. She returned to the small end table on the left side of the tub, where there sat a full glass of red wine, toe-nail clippers, a string of dental floss, a toothbrush, a half-full tube of toothpaste, a lit cigarette, an old fountain pen, and a half-written two-page letter. After taking a hit off the cigarette, she opened the letter and reread the first paragraph.

"Jesus," she muttered. She put down the letter, reached over, and turned off the water. She felt overwhelmed by the heat, and raised her face to the ceiling, breathing deeply for fresh air. She went back to the letter and opened it. She grinned, amused by her own wit.

Dearest Devon,

I have just dropped my "old man" off at the airport and am now preparing myself mentally for three weeks of kicking back and chilling. Sure, there will be the occasional assignment from abroad—a run to print off seven hundred copies of this, or a trip to New Jersey for this new wicker chair or that new oak bookshelf—but for the most part, I will have the next three weeks off. I'm wondering what the hell I should do with myself. Maybe I should go back to that thesis on Paul Robeson? Ah, who am I kidding. That thing is never getting finished. You and I, we really aren't the types who complete things, are we?

Speaking of, you'll be happy to know that I have officially completed one thing—my seedy relationship with Andrew Mashburn. You know, he had the nerve to ask me if I would ever consider signing a prenup if and when he ever decided I was good enough to leave Becky for and settle down with. I simply replied to him that I highly doubted that he had enough balls to ever leave Becky (his cash cow) and that I had recently come to the realization that I had been a fool—that I had fallen for a ghost with fine clothing and great salsa skills, but that he was not the man I would ever even remotely want to spend the rest of my life with. I mean, really, what the hell did he and I even have in common, eh? I ask myself, why did I ever lose my head over this architect/ex–international dance competitor? Why? Was the sex that great? Well, it was pretty damned fabulous, I have to say, especially early on with all of those weekend trips to his place in Maine and all, but really—what did I see there? I will tell you I've thought long and hard about this, and I think I now know what it was I saw. He shared a story with me once about his mother who was dying of some form of inoperable cancer and how he basically dropped everything and moved back to Seattle to take care of her for months. How he was forced to take a leave of absence from work to basically become his mother's live-in nurse. He and his sister trading shifts every week and all.

And here's the kicker. When he told me the story, he had tears in his eyes. They overflowed like Mom's little hanging plants would whenever I watered them. And his voice would quiver just a little, just enough, and I think his story reminded me of how I used to take care of you when you first got out of the hospital. That first year that you came home from Silver Mountain, and you would get this infection or that infection, or you had to wear that horrid brace all those months, or that time you had that *mysterious fever for two weeks straight. Anyway, I think it struck a chord with me—no, it reminded me—that not many men are able to really, truly care for someone else. I remember how it seemed like Dad could barely come into your room to see you. And how James couldn't really be bothered with many of your needs. How it seemed to be beneath him in some way. I remember how they both had this attitude like "he-made-his-bed-so-let-him-lie-in-it," and it sickened me to no end.*

Well, suddenly, Andrew Mashburn, wiping his mother's ass and feeding her oatmeal and tea in the morning, became the most sensitive, caring man I had ever seen. And it placed a soft halo around him for the first few months of our affair. I guess I neglected to remember that he was also cheating on a pregnant wife who already had one kid with Down syndrome and that he was a real asshole to any type of person serving him, whether it be a waiter or a taxi driver or the guy at the falafel stand. Jesus, what a jerk he was. The mind is a powerful, complex beast, Devon. Never forget that. It can achieve things beyond our imagination, and yet it can also break us down to the core. It's a thin line between achievement and self-destruction. But I don't have to tell you that.

Oh, and one last note on sex. You will be happy to know that I could have been making the beast with two backs tonight with my old man's very cute, disarmingly charismatic doorman, but instead, I chose to spend the evening in the warmth of the bathtub writing to you. Can you feel the loyalty seeping through these pages? I have addressed my letter to the prison address you gave me last week, but now, in light of your phone call, I have to wonder if you will even show up for your sentencing.

You know, a small part of me wouldn't blame you if you pulled a Juana, drove to the border, hopped a ferry boat to Canada, caught a plane to some tiny apartment in Saint Thomas, changed your name to Henry Maddox . . .

This was where the writing stopped. She put the pages down, put her finger to her chin, took a sip from her wineglass, then reached over and released more hot water into the tub. Suddenly, there was a noise filling the space like the old classic phone rings. It was the phone used by the doorman to call upstairs to tenants. She shook her head and turned off the hot water.

"Not tonight, *hermano*," she said. She grabbed the fountain pen off the end table, picked up the letter, and, after some meditation, continued writing.

Of course, I would miss you for the rest of my life. There would be a hole in my soul, never to be refilled. But I want what is best for you. What you believe is best for you. Always have, always . . .

She stopped cold as the thud of footsteps on the apartment floor reverberated; they were the reticent, uncertain kind. The first thing she thought of was Hector. But why would he come up to the apartment? That wasn't really his style. No, he would never do such a thing. He would want her to come to him. No, he had called to let her know someone was on the way up. But who would be visiting at this time of night? The bathroom door was wide open as to let the music in, and she heard the footsteps coming closer to her. She braced herself, and a friction slivered through her as she waited. Horrible headlines from the *New York Post* streaked through her mind with the black capitalized terms *Bludgeoned, Butchered, Murdered* hovering over the story. Then came a male voice, young and insecure.

"Hello? Dad? You back here?"

She exhaled and loosened her grip on the fountain pen.

"Hello? This is his assistant, Alexis."

A small, angular face with oval-rimmed glasses and a slight goatee poked into the bathroom and, immediately aware of the intrusion, bashfully retreated.

"I'm sorry, so sorry," he said. She felt his nervous presence outside the bathroom door.

"It's okay. It's Horatio, right?"

"Right. Yeah. I'm really sorry."

"I'll be out in a minute, Horatio. Your dad's actually out of the country. Just left tonight. I'll be out in a minute."

"Thank you. I'm so sorry."

"Not a problem. Feel free to grab a drink or something."

She rose, dropped the letter and pen on the end table, and leaned over to the toilet, where her bathrobe sat. This was the son, the one Curry rarely ever spoke of. There was a tension between them, that much she knew. Wasn't he away at a school in Spain somewhere? She recalled a picture on Curry's end table by his bed. It was a picture of himself and two children, one his daughter, Elizabeth, the high school language arts teacher in the Bronx. The other was the younger, Horatio. Elizabeth was the one he bragged about to no end. "She could have done anything with her life," he'd said, "but what does she choose to do? She chooses to go to one of the worst neighborhoods in the city to teach underrepresented Black and Puerto Rican kids. To deliver them a foreign world. She brings *Hamlet* and *Moby Dick* to kids who could literally give two shits about such things. Isn't that phenomenal?"

But Curry never talked about Horatio. In fact, there were several pictures of Elizabeth scattered throughout the house, but there was just the one with Horatio in it. There had been a falling out of some kind, though she couldn't recall what it involved.

Wait. Isn't he gay or some other Curry horror?

Her bathrobe tied firmly around her waist, she grabbed her wineglass and left the warm lilac-scented bathroom.

If Alexis had any concerns for her safety, they left her when she reached the kitchen and saw Horatio standing by the window, eating from a box of low-sodium crackers he'd pulled down from the cabinet. The lights were off, but there was sufficient natural light from the window, and it cast the room in a pale yet dark silhouette. She could see by his outline that he was skinny to the point of frailty. His nibbling, his mannerisms, his twitching reminded her of a frightened hamster. His demeanor held a certain rickety quality, a settled-in meekness. All at once, she felt sympathy for Horatio Curry. She wanted to embrace him, but thought it would be terribly awkward, and so she did not.

"Can I get you anything? Tea? Soda?" she asked, opening the refrigerator, casting a white triangle of light across half his body. The light seemed to stab at him, and he winced. "Sorry," she said, and closed the door quickly. There was serenity in the darkness.

"How about a glass of that wine you have there?" he responded. His voice had a soft, nasally manner about it that fit him.

"Hey, are you old enough?"

"In most countries," he said with a forced grin.

She concluded his smile was not his best feature. She walked out to the guest bedroom and grabbed the open bottle of merlot sitting near her discarded jeans. She quickly checked her cell phone, saw no calls had come in, and walked back out to the kitchen. When she got there, Horatio was seated at the table, his legs crossed at the ankles. He had turned on the dim light above the sink and was thumbing through a copy of *Vanity Fair* that had been sitting on the table. He rose to meet her, an empty wineglass already in his outstretched hand.

"Thank you so much. I'm really sorry if I interrupted anything."

"No problem. I was just unwinding. Busy work week and all."

She poured his glass half-full and placed the bottle down on the counter. She watched him as he delicately raised the glass to his nostrils, closing his eyes and raising his eyebrows as he did. It was a pure Daniel Curry gesture, and it warmed her to observe it.

"Um, did you expect to see your dad?"

He opened his eyes and turned his full face to her. She couldn't quite tell what color his eyes were.

"I had hoped to, yes. I emailed him a couple of times from Vienna to let him know I would be in the city for a while. When he didn't respond, I figured I'd surprise him. I took his lack of response as him not minding if I just popped in for a visit. I should have assumed he'd be off somewhere."

"Vienna? Not Spain? I thought you were studying in Spain."

"Oh, I quit that program last fall. Things weren't really going well for me there. Madrid is too social a place for me. I wrote Dad and Elizabeth about it. He doesn't talk about me very much, does he?"

Alexis gave him a slight nod and then took a sip from her glass. A silence lingered for a minute. Alexis tested her knowledge of geography, trying diligently to visualize a map of Europe. *How far are Vienna and Spain from each other?*

"I've heard nice things about Vienna. Are you living there?"

"For the time being, yes. I'm thinking I'll have to come back to the States soon, though. Europe is expensive for an American with no job. Was it Alexis?"

"Yes. Your dad calls me Lexy."

"He has a nickname for you? Nice. He only does that with people he likes. And that number is not many. Do you know what a friend of mine asked me last week? He said, 'Horatio. What kind of parent names their kid Horatio?' I didn't have an answer for him. Tell me, what do you make of that, Lexy?"

The tone of his question dug at her, as if he had already decided that she was too close to his father.

"Oh, I don't think it's such a bad name. I think it has a certain royal quality about it. And wasn't there a famous writer named Horatio?"

"Yes, there was. And he was also Hamlet's best friend. They were probably lovers."

"Funny. I always thought of Hamlet as a virgin."

"Well, he definitely never fucked Ophelia, I can tell you that much."

"Oh, I beg to differ there. No woman could possibly go that insane over someone she didn't know *intimately*."

Horatio's cell phone let out a chime; he had received a text message. Alexis wanted him to check it, but he ignored it.

"Don't worry," he said. "I won't stick around here long. I've got friends in the East Village who are expecting me."

For reasons she couldn't fully explain, she felt a sense of relief.

"Hey, no worries. There's lots of room here as you know."

"Yes, thank you. That's kind of you, but I really just wanted a break."

Alexis knew in short time she was not fond of the young Curry heir. There was a slightly privileged arrogance to him that hit her like the aroma of cheap cologne.

"A break? From what are you breaking, may I ask?"

He smiled at her, a sort of wry, cunning smile. Alexis tilted her head toward him as if to ask, "Well?"

"Oh, some things are better left unsaid, Lexy," he responded, tipping his wineglass to her and taking a sip.

"Come now, you can't get a girl all curious and just leave her hanging like that."

She pulled a pack of cigarettes and a lighter from her bathrobe pocket. She offered him the pack. From the breast pocket of his jacket, he produced his own pack, a European brand unfamiliar to her.

"I think I see why my father likes you so much."

"What makes you think he likes me?" She stopped him from lighting up. "We have to go out on the patio. Your father is adamant about cigarettes in the house."

"Right."

They took their wineglasses and headed out of the kitchen.

The rain had ceased minutes ago, and the night air was clean and smelled like freshly sliced cucumber. On the patio sat many comfortable chairs, a large grill so clean it appeared to have never been used, and a large wooden picnic table. A half-moon hung in the starless sky, and somewhere, a neighbor skillfully practiced the violin. Alexis thought maybe Tchaikovsky.

Horatio stood at the end of the penthouse, looking out across the city. Occasionally, he glanced back at the patio as if taking it all in for the first time. Alexis sat on the edge of the picnic table just a few feet away from him, smoking with one hand, brushing her hair with the other. Her wineglass sat dangerously on the edge of the table, sparkling in the moonlight like the North Star. She took a sip from it and placed it back in its perilous position. She was wearing a pair of pink bunny-rabbit slippers. One of the ears of the left slipper had frayed, the result of an overexcited dog she had once cared for.

"Look at all the windows," Horatio said. His voice had an adolescent quality, full of wonder. "Each one with its own story to tell. There is so much life in this city."

"That's one way to look at it," Alexis replied. She was focused on a scene in a neighbor's window a few floors below. A heavyset man loomed over a much smaller, sitting man. The heavyset man was cutting the smaller man's hair with scissors while they both looked into a mirror. Either her eyesight was failing her or the heavyset man was wearing a green tutu.

"Did you grow up here?" he asked.

"No. Northwest Connecticut."

"Hmm. I grew up here. At first, we lived in Crown Heights, a two-bedroom walk-up. All this came along later. Me, Elizabeth, Kevin, we had no idea just how good we had things once we got here. We thought everyone in this city must live like us."

Alexis stopped looking at the two men in the window and turned to him, confused.

"Kevin?" she asked.

His back was to her, he continued to drink it all in, but his tone changed ever so slightly.

"The old man doesn't ever talk about Kevin, does he?"

She looked at him more intently, wishing he would face her. It seemed a personal affront to her that she didn't know *everything* there was to know about Daniel Curry. She thought she was *the* expert on him by now. She put the hairbrush down and moved slightly in his direction.

"No, he doesn't. Is he younger, older?"

"He *was* the youngest of us all. But he wasn't meant for this earth. That's what Mother used to say anyway. He must have been too beautiful for this earth. Sometimes I used to wish *I* were too beautiful for this earth too."

She stood up straight now, mashed her cigarette out in the black ceramic ashtray placed there just for her by Daniel last spring. She grabbed her wineglass and stood beside him.

"What do you mean? Did . . . did your brother die?"

"He did. Horrible accident." He turned his full body in her direction. She could see his eyes were a severe blue, like cough medicine. Again, she was reminded of his father.

"Just horrible. Elizabeth was bathing him, in that same bathtub I found you in just now. Don't let it get to you. He was still a baby, you see, and she did so enjoy him. My mother, God bless her, let Elizabeth bathe him once in a while. Always under supervision . . . except the one time she wasn't there. She was at the pharmacy . . . said she'd only be a few moments. I remember it so well because I was in the kitchen, playing with a new paint set I'd been given. I was painting my own rendition of Van Gogh's *The Old Tower in the Fields*, and I asked her to bring me back a chocolate-chip cookie from the bakery next door.

Anyway, Elizabeth gets a phone call from our Uncle Peter. He wants to talk to her right away about bringing her to Africa with him on a business trip, and she gets all excited. I had handed her the phone. It never occurred to me that she would leave Kevin there in the bathtub while she went to talk to him. And it never occurred to me to check on Kevin while she did. No one ever thinks of such things until . . ."

He stopped and wiped his mouth with an open palm. Alexis couldn't tell if he was removing a piece of lint that had gotten lodged in his goatee or perhaps just giving himself a moment to recuperate.

"And then after she hung up with Uncle Peter, she looked at me, and I looked at her . . . it was odd. We didn't say anything to each other, but it was like we were both asking each other something . . . with our eyes. We both knew that something wasn't quite right. And just then, Mother came walking into the apartment, carrying my cookie in one hand and her prescription in the other, and the first thing she asked was, 'Where's Kevin?' And then we all noticed there was that silence. That silence that says too much. Fortunate are those who never know such a silence."

Alexis watched him closely, knowing all too well just what that silence felt like. She clutched her wineglass tight like a dagger, threatening to shatter it.

He turned away from her again and looked up to the moon. "When you were a kid, did you believe in heaven?"

"I suppose. Don't we all at first?"

"I suppose we do. Heaven—what a crazy idea. My mother deserved a medal, a fucking Purple Heart for dealing with that man. After Kevin, he treated her like she was his bedpan. And she took it all. And Elizabeth—with Elizabeth, he took extra measures to assure she would never, ever feel one ounce of guilt for what he deemed a horrible, horrible accident. He pampered her and threw gifts and treats at her . . . as if every new bike, every new dress, every set of new encyclopedias was going to eventually crush the memory of that baby floating facedown in a bathtub full of water . . ."

His cell phone went off again, another text message. This time he did look at it. He pressed a few buttons and put it back in his pocket.

"But how did I get off on this morbid trip? I'm in New York City, the city that never weeps. What did you put in my drink, Lexy? May I call you Lexy?"

"Why not? Coming from a Curry male, it sounds natural."

"Oh please, not that label. Please, don't call me a Curry male. I want nothing of that stigma."

She looked at him, taken by a feeling that surprised her. There was vitriol in her throat. She wanted him to stop berating his father, yet at the same time, she was intrigued by this new perspective he brought to the table. She wanted more, but she didn't want it to hurt. She thought of something Devon once said to her: "If you can swallow the poison of the street, it makes you stronger."

"It's odd," she said, turning away from him and going back to the table where the half bottle of wine sat. She refilled her glass. "Hearing you talk about him this way. I know he can be difficult, very difficult . . ."

"My friend, you don't know the half of it. That man, who has somehow managed to be so affable, so generous with so many others in his life, that man drove my mother to the edge of a dark cliff . . . and then he pushed her off it just because he couldn't manage to deal with his own grief. He needed to take it out on someone."

"But I don't understand. Your mother seems fine. She lives in a gorgeous house out in Montauk. I've talked to her on the phone once or twice. I write her a check every—"

"My mother is so hopped up on antidepressants every day of her life that she barely knows what day of the week it is."

The sound of his voice rose substantially, and though he wasn't necessarily yelling, the overall tenor surprised them both. They stood there, each on their own islands, taking in the unrelenting orchestra of the sounds of the city mixing with the violin. Alexis saw the men in the window. Green-tutu barber and smaller, older gentleman had been joined by two women, bleach blonds in cowgirl outfits. Their breasts were terribly oversized, and Alexis felt sympathy for them, having heard of the back pain that came with such "gifts."

This is one fucking amazing city.

Horatio mumbled something under his breath, and she asked him to repeat it.

"I said, 'Whom the gods would destroy, they first make mad.'"

Alexis nodded. She was uncomfortable. A coldness took hold of her that had nothing to do with the temperature, and she drained the rest of her glass. Fifteen minutes later, after she had walked Horatio downstairs and seen him off into a cab heading downtown, she went back up to the apartment and immediately looked up the phrase in a book of famous quotes on Daniel Curry's desk. She wouldn't find it there, and she made a note to look it up online later. She returned to the bathroom and stared at the bathtub in a whole new light, where her letter to Devon lay soaking in the middle of the tub.

For Hannah,
Dancing with Angels Now

"I'll have you know this is the last of the butter pecan that I'm taking out tonight. If anyone wanted to have a cup before bed, now would be the time to behave."

Gina looked up into her daughter's face and waited. Jamila, twelve years old going on forty-two, glanced up from the sketch pad she had been doodling on and returned her mother's bland gaze from her stool on the other side of the empty bar. It was as if Jamila wanted her to know that they had played this game long enough and she didn't really have time for it anymore. Gina wondered to herself why it had to be this way. Nothing about Jamila had ever been easy. Nothing. She thought Jamila probably felt the same way about her.

"Listen, Mom," the child said, a palpable tone of condescension in her voice. "If you don't believe I deserve a scoop of ice cream, then that choice is yours and yours alone. I happen to believe five pages is enough."

"Not when the assignment called for fifteen, Jay. I'm telling you right now, this is unacceptable."

"Well, I guess we will just have to agree to disagree on this one."

"How about we agree that I beat that ass if you don't do it?"

"Violence will get you nowhere, Mom. Use your imagination."

Gina turned away from her daughter and cleared a series of half-empty wineglasses from the bar. The number of times she had fantasized about driving Jamila to the train station, putting her on the train, and walking away from her forever as the train took off, she assumed, wasn't healthy. But it was reality. She looked around, relieved she would not have a busy night ahead of her. Normally, the popular soul-food joint she inherited from her aunt would be brimming with customers at this point in the evening, but there was some important sporting event taking place on television tonight—a decisive game seven or something—and most people had stayed in. She would close early.

She pulled out a rag and wiped down the bar. The rag bumped up against a book sitting next to Jamila's cup of hot cocoa.

"Start getting your shit together. I'm closing soon."

Jamila looked up from her sketch pad. She had been working on a portrait of the three older Black women who sat at a table twenty feet away against the far wall. These three women were the only real sign of liveliness. A Hispanic couple sat by the open door, and a lone, well-dressed gentleman in his early fifties, the only white person in the place, sat on the far end of the bar, reading the *Wall Street Journal*. Soft, soulless jazz music played over the speakers. When she was done loading the dishes into the dishwasher, Gina removed her apron and folded it. She still had a stellar figure, a benefit of teaching yoga two nights a week at a spa on the coast.

Brooklyn, the twenty-two-year-old bartender, emerged from the kitchen, carrying a tray with two cups of white tea and a Mexican coffee, and went straight to the table of three women. Brooklyn had long, fine dreads, bleached blond and tied in a ponytail that went all the way down to her bottom. She wore nonprescription glasses. She and the ladies laughed as Gina grabbed the silverware setting from in front of Jamila.

"One way or another, you are reading those ten pages, young lady."

"Jesus H. Christ!" Jamila slammed the sketch pad down on the bar and snatched up the book, a well-worn copy of *Bury My Heart at Wounded Knee*. She opened the book. "You happy now?"

Gina struggled to hide her elation in seeing her daughter react in the same dramatic fashion that she had often reacted with to her own father. She bit her lip to suppress a smile.

"I'm gonna go in the office and set up tomorrow's menu. When I get back, you and I are going to have us a nice little talk about what respect looks like. 'Cause this attitude of yours? It ain't gonna cut it. I can tell you that right now."

Gina snatched the cup of hot cocoa, spilling some of it onto her black turtleneck. She cursed under her breath as Jamila let out a tiny giggle. She shot a cold stare at her daughter and briskly disappeared through the curtains leading into the kitchen. Brooklyn came behind the bar and began her regular routine of closing out the cash register. She shook her head at Jamila.

"You know, little girl, one day you gonna push yo mama a little too far. I've seen smarter girls than you get put up for adoption."

"Yeah? And I've seen smarter girls than you flipping burgers and serving coffee at Burger Haven. What's your point, or don't you have one, Brooklyn?"

Brooklyn looked at the younger girl as if trying to decide which would be the least messy way to murder her. "You think it's cute, don't you? Being a little bitch?"

Jamila laughed, slightly amused and a little offended. "Really, Brooklyn? You want to have this conversation now?"

Neither had the chance to press the issue any further. Just then, a figure rolled into the restaurant in a wheelchair. He moved much faster than either thought anyone in a wheelchair should be moving.

Jamila had not seen her uncle since she had sat on the other side of the church from him nearly a decade ago. And yet, there was something ever so familiar about this man who rolled straight up to the bar. Devon wore a black suit jacket with black slacks and a salmon-pink button-down shirt. A loosened black tie hung lazily around his open collar, and shiny diamond earrings spotted both of his earlobes.

Brooklyn smiled, instantly drawn to him. "Good evening to you, sir," she said as he parked himself two seats down from Jamila, who couldn't help staring at him.

"Good evening to you, madam."

"Just so you know, we're doing last call."

"Then I'm just in time. Rum and Coke, please. Man, I just had the funniest experience," he said, addressing them both.

"Funny experiences are good," replied Brooklyn. "Do share."

"Well," he started, then stopped himself. He placed a finger on his chin in a reflective manner.

During the pause, Brooklyn placed a glass of water before him.

"I guess in retrospect it's not really all that funny, but I'll be damned, this old lady didn't just call me 'colored.'"

"Get out!"

"No, straight up. She had to be a survivor of the *Titanic* or something. I was across the street, looking at this restaurant, and she was coming out of the bookstore, and she saw me and said to her husband, 'Honey, go see if that colored boy needs any change.' That *colored* boy! Can you imagine?"

"Old folks have some funny ways."

"Old habits die hard," chimed in Jamila with a bright smile, proud of herself for the contribution.

"Well said, kiddo," he responded. "Well said."

Jamila's face scrunched up, and she watched him curiously. There was something about the way he called her "kiddo."

"Do I know you?" she asked, leaning in to get a closer look.

Devon avoided her gaze, grinning slightly. "You might not know me, but I definitely know you. Whatcha reading?" She turned the book so that he could see the cover. "*Bury My Heart at Wounded Knee*. Sounds deep."

"It's not too deep for me."

Brooklyn placed his drink before him. "I made it a double. You look like a man who likes it strong."

"You are a good judge of character, sister," he said, tipping his glass to her and taking a sip. "What's your name?"

"Brooklyn."

"Well, Brooklyn, I want to thank you. This is most likely the last great drink I will have for the next four to five years."

"Oh really? You going somewhere?"

"I am," he said. "I am."

"You gonna be a priest?" Jamila added.

"I should be so lucky, kiddo."

"Why do you call me kiddo?"

"I'm sorry. You prefer Jammy? Or Mila?"

Jamila tilted her head to the right, an even more curious expression on her face. Out of the corner of her eye, she looked at Brooklyn, whose face held the same bewilderment. Devon sipped his drink and smiled at them.

"It's a funny thing, you see—" he started, but at that exact moment, Gina reappeared from behind the curtain, wearing glasses, carrying a calculator and a thick financial log in her hands.

She was just about to address Brooklyn when she saw Devon sitting at the bar. She stood in front of the curtain, coldly still, and stared at him. Brooklyn watched Gina and sensed the unease instantly. She turned back to Devon, who calmly returned Gina's stare. Brooklyn got the impression he had been waiting for this moment for a long time.

Jamila felt the tension as well. She looked impatiently back and forth between her mother and the peculiar, somewhat familiar man in the wheelchair, waiting for one of them to break the moment and say something, anything. She would have to wait quite a bit longer, as her mother seemed to be struggling to come to grips with whom she was seeing, what he stirred up within her.

When Gina broke the silence, her voice quivered and splintered. "Devon . . . what are you . . . what are you doing here?"

He finished off his rum and Coke and slowly brought the glass down. He stared into it for a few seconds before he looked up.

"I'm fine, Gina. It's good to see you too. The years treated you well. You look fantastic."

Gina watched him, her lips moving but not speaking. She slowly removed her glasses and placed them down beside her along with the calculator and the log. When she turned back to him, she was more composed, centered.

"Brooklyn, I need you to do me a favor."

Brooklyn turned to her, waiting nervously.

"Yeah, boss?"

"Brooklyn," she said, never looking at her, focusing solely on Devon. "I need you to call the police."

Devon smirked and shook his head. Brooklyn looked at him, then quickly back at Gina.

"The . . . the police?"

"You don't have to do that, Brooklyn. I just left my mom's place this morning, Gina. I assured her I was turning myself in to the authorities tomorrow. It was never my intention to be a fugitive from the law. I just needed a little extra time."

"You saw your mother?"

"I did. Shocked the hell out of her. It was like she had seen a Black ghost."

He looked over at Jamila, who was at a loss for words for the first time in her entire young life. She stared at him.

"I'm sorry, kiddo. I didn't mean to play games with you."

"You . . . you're Uncle Devon."

"Brooklyn, I need you to take Jamila home now. I'll handle closing."

The three of them looked at each other, all waiting for the others to do something first.

"Mom, I don't wanna go home . . ."

"Jamila!" She said her child's name with such ferocity that nearly everyone in the place turned. She caught herself and eased up. "Jamila, I need you to *not* argue with me this one time, okay? Just listen when I tell you—I need you to go home with Brooklyn."

Jamila looked back at Devon. He smiled and winked at her, which made her even more confused.

"No need to worry, beautiful. Your mother and I, we have a bit of catching up to do. There are things your mother wants to say to me that no child should hear."

"I don't need you to explain anything to my daughter. Brooklyn, take her now . . . please."

Brooklyn moved quickly. She grabbed her purse from behind the counter and came around to the front of the bar where Jamila sat.

"Get your things together," she told the child while stealing a glance at Devon.

"It was a pleasure meeting you, Brooklyn," he said to her. "Next time, I can only hope it will be under better circumstances."

He smiled at her and his niece. Before he could react, Jamila ran over to him and clutched him in a moving embrace. He felt the warmth of her tears smudging his neck.

"Jamila!" Gina snapped.

But it was too late. For a few drawn-out seconds, time froze over and all the horrible past tensions in Devon's life dissolved. For him, there was only a young girl clinging to a man she barely knew, but a man who wanted so desperately for this girl to love him like a father. It broke him. A wave moved up through his chest and flooded his eyes. When she pulled away from him, the family portrait broke in its frame, and she ran out of the restaurant. Brooklyn charged after her, keys jingling in her hands.

Devon collected himself, at least physically. He straightened out his jacket and shirt. The embrace was harder on him than he could have ever imagined. In one simple act, the young girl he dreamed could be his own daughter had wiped away his entire veneer of arrogance. For a moment, he was a stranger to himself. He rubbed his palms together and checked his watch.

Gina looked at him long and hard, uncertain of where she should go next. She surveyed the room. The Hispanic couple had just left, and the white man who had been reading the newspaper was now walking into the bathroom. The three women sat talking happily among themselves. Gina clenched her fists and made a move to speak. That was when she realized there was a hot lump in her throat.

"It's funny the way life works out, huh?" Devon asked.

"I don't—I don't think anything is funny. Nothing about *this life* has turned out funny for me. What are you doing here, Devon?"

And now the tears came for her. She defiantly wiped her face and nose, angry with herself.

"That's a good question. I've been thinking about you lately. I think of you often."

She went over to the table that the Hispanic couple had occupied and began clearing it.

"I don't have anything to say to you, Devon. Everything I had to say to you I said at James's funeral."

"I wasn't very kind to you back then."

"You don't say."

Gina brought the dishes back behind the bar. She went to throw them in the dish bin but missed by an inch. They went crashing to the ground. The three ladies at the table all looked over briefly. Gina stared at the leftovers and the shattered dishes. When she looked back over at him, it was with familiar hateful eyes.

"You have five minutes, Dev. Then I call the police."

"I swear that isn't necessary."

"Your mother tells me you were smuggling drugs into and out of Mexico and Canada. Is that true?"

"I'm sure my mother wouldn't say it if I wasn't."

"What, did you just give up on your film career? I thought you were gonna make the Black *Citizen Kane*."

"I don't know who was more ruthless, drug czars or studio heads. Let me be clear—I made some bad choices." He checked his watch and was suddenly anxious. The Gina he remembered was not the type to make a threat and not carry it out. Part of him thought about getting out of there, driving straight to the airport, leaving his car in long-term parking, and going straight to the Los Angeles courthouse to turn himself in. But he couldn't bring himself to leave. He had come this far. He needed this minute in time. He watched her pick up the dishes. "I was cruel to you at the funeral."

"No shit, Devon. I'm not interested in going down memory lane with you."

"No, no, you wouldn't be. That would mean you might have to look at yourself a little bit and see your own part in all of that mess."

She picked up a half of a wineglass from the stem. She studied the jagged edges. With the right thrust of the wrist, she could pierce a jugular with it. It wouldn't be the first time Devon had evoked that type of rage within her. But almost immediately after, she thought of Jamila. Truth be told, the kid would probably be just fine without either parent; she was that stubborn and independent. But Gina had an obligation to her, and that caused her to gently place the stem in the garbage.

"You have three minutes."

"You were right. I've been angry, Gina. I've been angry most of my adult life. I've never known just what to do with that anger."

"Moving drugs up and down the border, that give you a place to put that anger?"

"You act as if you've never made a bad choice yourself. I would argue with that."

"James is dead, Devon, okay? You got your revenge. Karma worked out just as you said it would. What more do you want? What do you need now?"

"This wasn't revenge, Gina. It wasn't. I took no pleasure in knowing James was dying."

"Really? 'Cause that's not what you said to me. It isn't what you told your family. I believe your exact words were 'karma is a real bitch, ain't it?'"

"I was a different person back then. I was wallowing in anger and self-pity."

They both sat there for a moment as the last grain of sunlight left the room and darkness began to take its rightful place in the sky. The table of three ladies erupted in laughter. The white man left the bathroom, put a tip down under his drink, and walked out.

"You know, it's funny, I was watching Jamila earlier today, I was watching from across the street, through the window. I watched her for almost an hour, and it occurred to me, just as it always does whenever I'm looking into the face of a beautiful Black child, that this kid . . . this kid could have been ours. Yours and mine. If you and James hadn't lied and cheated and behaved like you were the only two people in the world that mattered, I could have known the type of happiness that the two of you knew for so long. I could have felt that way. But it's okay, really. I'm actually over all of that now, and I just came to set the record straight. To let you know—I forgive both of you."

Gina turned her full body to him now. She could not help but crack a tiny, off-kilter smile as she tried to see his face through the white heat that filled her line of vision.

"What did you say to me? *You forgive us? You* forgive *us.* Is that really what just came out of your mouth? *You* forgive *us?* Who the fuck is seeking your forgiveness?"

He held up his empty glass. "I don't suppose I could get a refill?"

She walked over to a cordless phone on the wall and picked it up. They watched each other as she dialed and then spoke calmly. "Yes, this is Gina Payne over at the Soul Station. I'm okay, thank you, how are you? Good, good. Hey, can you send Deputy Platt over here for a moment. I've got a disturbance, kind of like that one two weeks ago, and I could use some intervention. Thank you so much, Carrie Ann, you enjoy your Sunday."

Without so much as giving him a glance, she walked over to the dishwasher and loaded it with plates, glasses, and silverware. Devon's face turned slightly paler. It was hard for him to acknowledge, but it was clear that the life he had once lived was ending. Freedom would no longer be a thing he could take for granted.

"Did James ever tell you about our last conversation?"

She went on tidying up behind the bar, her jaw clenched to the point of discomfort.

"It was Christmas Eve, his last. He called me, and I knew he had to be a little bit desperate, because it was like eleven at night my time, so two o'clock in the morning your time. He pleaded with me. Said it was his last appeal to my sense of decency. But I had no decency by then. I told him I wouldn't get tested. Not only would I not get tested, but I wouldn't give him a kidney for all the gold in Fort Knox. I actually said that. When we hung up, I felt this deep, deep pit in my stomach. Like a swamp. A swamp I wanted to drown in. I started to cry. Dahlia was visiting me at the time, and she held me. She held me and she took me out for Chinese food. And throughout the entire meal, I couldn't stop crying. And I couldn't explain why. I didn't know why."

"You actually believe you were somehow the victim in all of this, don't you?"

"At first, yes. I'll admit that. It took me years to realize that wasn't true. We all know there was only one true victim in this entire fucked-up scenario. And that was Hannah Baldwin.

"You know I stopped by the Baldwin house last night? Remember how we used to all play croquet on their lawn every July 4? That great barbecue chicken her dad used to make? And Hannah would always have some new cheerleading moves to show us." There was a far-off look on Devon's face now. He had to shake his head to return to the present. "Anyway, her sister was there. Remember the real quiet one, Celeste? Well, she's like a born-again Christian or some shit like that. She was surprised to see me, as you can imagine. And I told her that I wasn't really sure why I was there, but that I just needed to apologize to them one more time, to the whole family. Celeste lives there alone now. Her parents moved to Boca Raton. Anyway, she told me I had nothing to apologize for. That I just needed to make my peace with the Lord, all that bullshit. She even hugged me. Then she took me to the cemetery. We went this morning. She took me to Hannah's tombstone. There was a fresh wreath sitting on it. The words on it said, 'For Hannah, dancing with angels now.' She deserved better. We all deserved better."

Gina had been watching him for some time, hands on the bar, looking and listening. The jazz CD had ended, and the only sound was the whirring of the dishwasher. When she moved, she went back behind the curtains. She came out with a broom and a dustpan and cleaned up the shattered glass. Devon looked at her and checked his watch. He glanced at the entrance a couple of times.

"Listen, Gina, I'm on the first flight out of here in the morning. I'm heading straight for the police station. I'm ready to pay my debt. I know, I *know* that I've got a lot of growing to do. I just hope it's not too late for me."

She looked at him long and hard. Then a police car pulled up outside. She went into her purse, pulled out a cigarette and a lighter, and walked out the front door. Devon looked at her. She and the deputy, an avuncular white guy, hugged and shared pleasantries while she smoked. He checked his watch again and started to wonder how it would all work out. Would he be arrested here and then extradited to Los Angeles? He did not want to spend the night in a prison here in small-town Maine. He wondered if it was a mistake coming to see Gina, but that thought subsided quickly. He knew, regardless of the outcome, it had been the right thing to do.

His eye caught something on the floor, below where Jamila had once sat. It was a sketch pad. He went over to it and picked it up. He looked at the sketch she had been making of the three ladies. He flipped through the book and landed on a sketch, drawn in pencil, of Gina. Above it were words written in a child's penmanship, "Portrait of Mom." Below it, written in the same hand, were two questions:

How much is family worth?

What is the color of family?

He blinked as he pondered the questions. He looked up, concerned again about time. To his great relief, he saw Gina pat the deputy on the shoulder before the man got back in his squad car and drove off. He watched her put out her cigarette and reenter the restaurant. She went behind the bar and poured herself a glass of whiskey. She walked over to him and handed him the bottle.

"You can take that with you. I have to finish up and get back home to Jamila."

He clutched the neck of the bottle. "Thank you, Gina. Thank you."

He watched her disappear into the back. Jazz music filled the place again, and he watched the three ladies gathering themselves to leave. He unscrewed the whiskey top, took a quick swig, drew a deep breath, and tucked the bottle between his knees. He rolled out of the front door and into the mild evening air. He told himself to remember exactly what this felt like. To be alive in the warmth of the night. To look up at the full moon and have options. He realized now, this was a gift. All of it was.

"I came here empty handed," he said out loud to a vacant sidewalk. He looked to his left, looked to his right, and chose to go straight in the direction of the moon.

Acknowledgments

First and foremost, all appreciation and respect to the woman who believed in me from the very beginning, my agent, Priya Doraswamy.

So much gratitude to the Little A team headed by my wonderfully supportive editor Laura van der Veer and the tenacious editor John Vercher. I always felt safe and respected with you folks.

Special shout-out to the late J. D. Salinger, whose *Nine Stories* once inspired my high-school self to someday want to tell my own story about a large and quirky Black family.

And of course, Lorrie Moore. Just because.

About the Author

Jerry McGill is a writer and artist. He is the author of *Bed Stuy: A Love Story* and the memoir *Dear Marcus: A Letter to the Man Who Shot Me*. After receiving a BA in English literature from Fordham University in the Bronx and a master's degree in education from Pacific University in Oregon, Jerry went on to teach high school and travel the world mentoring disabled children. He lives in Portland, Oregon.